P9-BVF-953

DISCARD

101783884

LEXINGTON PUBLIC LIBRARY

LEXINGTON, KENTUCKY

EAGLE CREEK BRANCH

DO NOT REMOVE CARD FROM POCKET

CHARGE FOR LOST OR DAMAGED CARD

A World Too Wide

by the same author

Paths of Fortune

SUSAN MOORE

A World Too Wide

St. Martin's Press
New York

3884a
ABE-5258

A WORLD TOO WIDE. Copyright © 1989 by Susan Moore. All rights reserved.
Printed in the United States of America. No part of this book may be used or
reproduced in any manner whatsoever without written permission except in
the case of brief quotations embodied in critical articles or reviews. For
information, address St. Martin's Press, 175 Fifth Avenue, New York, N.Y.
10010.

Library of Congress Cataloging-in-Publication Data

Moore, Susan.
    A world too wide / Susan Moore.
        p.   cm.
    ISBN 0-312-03454-7
    I. title.
  PR6063.0644W67   1989
  823'.914—dc20
                                        89-10344
                                            CIP

First published in Great Britain by Fontana Paperbacks. Printed and bound
by William Collins Sons & Co., Ltd.

First U.S. Edition

10 9 8 7 6 5 4 3 2 1

CHAPTER ONE

Liverpool, 1812

Tom's first memories were important ones. Especially to the people in them.

One winter morning his parents took him down to the dock. He knew today was different, from the moment they set out behind the man with the barrow carrying Papa's luggage. For one thing, it wasn't Mama but Mary, the young woman who was his nurserymaid, who held his hand among the crowds, stooping to talk to him as they went.

Mama, her arm through Papa's, walked on ahead. She had less to say than usual, and all the way there she looked at no one but Papa.

Sometimes Tom's parents would speak to each other as if no one else in the world could make themselves seen or heard. When this happened, as it had a lot in recent days, he found it a little frightening.

But today Tom, silent with interest at the busy place where the great ships lay, was happy enough. He didn't even mind that when Papa spoke to him he did so in the voice he used whenever Tom had hurt himself.

At length, though, he sensed the feelings of the grown-ups this morning and began to squirm about in Mary's grasp.

'Look – look!' she said, to turn his attention elsewhere. 'See the cow fly!'

Tom stood still, and his face took on a blank look of absorption. Nearby was the ship on which his father was about to sail. The *Cassiopeia* was bound for Halifax, Nova Scotia, with two hundred garrison

5

troops held back from the desperate campaign in western Spain against Napoleon. From there she was to carry His Majesty's mails to Boston. Right now she was taking on milk for the voyage, in the form of a Shorthorn cow hoisted in a sling.

'And look at this!' said Mary, holding out his little paw for him by the wrist. 'You can feel it without touching.' Tom stared at his hand, its fingers splayed, as he felt the chill from a wall of ice blocks. The ice was being handled up on to the ship by a chain of men, working rhythmically.

His fat little legs with their turned-in feet began to ache as Mary walked him about, trying to interest him in other things besides his parents. There was a pedlar selling wedding rings at fivepence each, and a dog barking alongside a cart loaded with crates of live poultry. An ensign in a new scarlet uniform was being embarrassed by the farewells of his mother, who was wearing a hat like a frilled coal-scuttle.

Some of what Tom's parents were saying caught his attention anyway. For years the word 'Mississippi' would mean nothing to him so much as the sight of a soldier's wife being cussed by the people behind her as she paused with one foot still on the quay and a fortune-teller reading her hand. And for a while, the names of his relatives in America would only call up a memory of the Royal Lancashires marching to board the *Cassiopeia*. They came tramping down through the town behind a colonel on horseback with their band playing a country dance.

The time came for Tom's parents to part. Sophy Fraser watched James, her husband, bending to pick up their little son so that he could reassure him as he took his leave. To his wife, James Fraser was restrained – in the eyes of any stranger, indeed, merely courteous. Their real embrace of farewell had been some time earlier, before leaving home.

Soon the tall ship, like a wooden village set afloat, was being towed into the estuary. It left behind a mass of smaller vessels that rode with their bowsprits gently tilting at the windows of the waterfront houses. In midstream the *Cassiopeia* ceased to move, while the full tide turned all about her in the sharp January sun. A huzzah broke from the figures crowding her deck, and a moment later the canvas of her mainsails was loosened. While she stood motionless her sails hung like dewlaps; then, as she went about, dark against a streak of brightness on the estuary, they filled, and she began to strain towards the ruffled open sea.

Groups of people who'd come to see her embark began dissolving into the quayside crowds. 'Let's walk on beside her,' murmured Sophy, ' – shall we, Tom?' turning aside to the child to pick him up.

By the time they passed the end of the Strand the ship had ceased to tower above all the others about her and was one distant vessel among many. She was carrying all the canvas she had as she set forth into the Irish Sea. It was four hundred miles from Liverpool to her rendezvous with the convoy escorting her across the Atlantic, and there were not many days to lose in joining it. Each time she tacked, slowly in and out of the wind, her sails gleamed white, then darkened as she changed course. Every few minutes she became almost invisible as her mass of canvas turned edgeways on towards the watchers ashore. Soon she looked no more substantial than a windblown leaf held upright by the violence of the blast.

Sophy shushed the child in her arms, whose eyes and nose were running from the cold, and went on gazing out to sea. Was she sorry that she'd hidden her fears from her husband? In any case, what could she have said? The hazards were obvious, setting forth into the North Atlantic at this time of year to spend nearly the rest of winter pitching about in a vessel whose

7

'tween decks were sheathed in ice. Her sister Kate had written her that even on a ship carrying despatches, and without attack from the French, she and her husband had been at sea fifty-three days without a landfall. To voyage down the coast to their home on the James River had taken almost as long again.

Tom wriggled, and stared at his mother's face as she looked out to windward. 'Want to go home.'

'Soon, dearest. When we've seen Papa go.'

'Papa gone home?'

'No, dear Tom.'

'Why?'

'Because he's gone to visit your aunt and uncle Lee.'

'Why?'

'To build your uncle a new kind of ship.'

'Why?'

'To help your uncle's business.'

Tom was not old enough to ask 'What's business?' Instead, he fell to kicking a boot to and fro beneath his little-boy's petticoats and fingering a new tooth. It was both dull and strange to see his mother so quiet.

Mary was likewise watching for the last glimpse of the ship. 'He – Mr Fraser – he couldn't have sent his plans out secretly, then?' In opposing Bonaparte by means of blockade, the government had forbidden the export of patents even to neutral countries.

The ship was now hull down beneath an indistinct horizon. Sophy said, 'I think James could only smuggle that much information if it was in his head.' The war with France had brought Sophy's husband ample work of a routine kind. In Ireland, whence they'd recently returned, he'd travelled widely, extending a naval dockyard and supervising construction of coastal fortifications. But after nineteen years of war, not even the Admiralty was prepared to venture capital on the trials and delays of a new invention.

'Is it so new, though?' Sophy had asked him, one

8

evening in their lodgings. 'Even I've seen a steam boat – several times.'

Fraser had paused in what he was doing before answering her. He'd been at an improvised worktable, making a model ship. Eventually it would serve as a toy for young Tom. Meanwhile he was rigging it to test an idea he'd had for an improved block-and-tackle system. 'I know you have – but no one, yet, has patented an engine whose centre of gravity would be low enough within the hull to rival a ship under sail.' His eyes dwelt on a detail of the model in his hand, so that he spoke with a lingering frown of concentration. 'And if they had, there'd be no use for it until it was fit to leave the inland waterways and put to sea.'

'But there are such boats at sea.' Sophy, too, rested her eyes on the beautiful little ship as, pausing about her household work, she leaned against his chair. She was a finely wrought woman of twenty-one whose colouring was so fair that in some lights her complexion and hair seemed silvery.

Fraser had already hinted at his plan of going to America. He avoided his wife's look as he answered her. He too was fair and slight, and for a man still short of twenty-five he was unusually serious in his manner. People who knew him only slightly tended to think him something of a young stick.

'Those sort of vessels are only used for coastal traffic. There's not one of them that couldn't be taken by a poorly manned frigate.' And, since he found her apt at following such things, he briefly described the perils of trying to operate a steam boiler on anything as corrosive as sea water.

'And that's why it's for use inland? This boat you're determined to build?'

Even as she emphasized the word 'determined', Sophy felt ashamed. After all, she had no intention of persuading her husband, with inadequate capital, to

9

perfect his design for use merely on the Thames or the Somerset Avon. With the aid of her brother-in-law's fortune, Fraser could build one of the Mississippi's first vessels to voyage upriver as well as down. In Britain the Admiralty might declare itself bled dry of funding. But no one thought to ask if Joseph Lee lacked a few spare tens of thousands of dollars. His timber business extended west of the Appalachian mountains, and brought him an income that many a European principality might envy. For him, with Fraser's help, money might clamour to beget money. If steam power could be used to ship mahogany more swiftly down to New Orleans, it was clear enough that the same vessels could also be sent upriver, to carry to the wealthy of comfortless Cincinnati and St Louis everything they desired in the way of pianofortes or French wines.

Scarcely for a moment could Sophy have thought to oppose her husband's ambition. As she stood in the cold at the seaward end of the waterfront, it seemed that Fate had been bound to carry her here, to watch without complaint as his ship passed from sight. On a day as hazy as this, water and sky blurred so that the horizon could only be seen as the point where the packet boat began to vanish. After the hull was gone, her spread of sail was still visible, a misshapen speck of whiteness suspended in vacancy. In little more than the beat of a gull's wing the mainsails disappeared too; then the topsails.

Still Sophy looked on. She remembered the day her husband had first mentioned his scheme. On their return from Ireland they had been posting down to London, where Fraser had been commissioned to build a cannon-foundry in the marshes across the river from Westminster. They were a day's journey from town, at a village in Northamptonshire where they had stopped to dine while their horses were baited and watered. All around, the autumn evening was so quiet you could hear a ploughman a mile away as he whistled to his team to halt. It was while walking out to their chaise that Sophy noticed her husband staring at something utterly unexpected.

Beyond the elm-shadowed highway a pasture ran up to a low skyline. There, moving alone and soundless through the Midlands countryside, was a giant wheel. It stood as high as a room, and instead of turning it glided.

Sophy glanced at her husband, expecting him to propose that they walk up the field to examine it. Instead he hustled them all – Sophy, little Tom, and Mary – into the chaise and told the postboy to make haste.

Half a mile on, the road turned a corner round the end of a hedgerow partly grubbed up, and passed over a new hump-backed bridge. Here, on Fraser's orders, the chaise was stopped. Sophy, guessing his purpose, forebore to ask why; and for several minutes they sat in silence, their horses drooping their heads and twitching off the odd fly. Below, a canal wound out of sight among dimming hedgerows in which late birdsong grew fainter, field by field, all the way into Oxfordshire.

At length they glimpsed what they were waiting to see. A draught horse, with a boy astride it, came into view on the towpath. Behind, looking like a tall piece of cheese on a dish, floated the wheel, lashed upright into the hull of a barge. From the inn, a shallow cutting had hidden everything but the wheel itself.

'It looks a little like part of a watermill,' said Sophy.

Yes, Fraser told her, but in such a case it would have been made for local use, instead of being carried down the main Birmingham–London trunk route. He said, clearly thinking about something else, 'This must be travelling some distance, to be going by water at such an hour.'

The canal followed a contour line, indifferent to any other feature of the landscape, so that the nearest waterside buildings were some miles away. As the barge edged under the bridge he went on looking in the direction whence it had come. 'Let's wait a few minutes more.'

The carriage, standing behind the parapet, was little more than a silhouette against the evening sky when, from the same direction, the apparition repeated itself. This time the horse carried a man who lay backwards along its rump, fast asleep.

'They would have left Birmingham this morning, right enough,' Fraser said, ordering the postboy to drive on.

'*Two* big wheels. A boat, worked by steam engine?' Sophy asked.

'Aye, one of those,' Fraser said. 'To judge from those other parts.'

'From whose works?' A girlhood spent partly in genteel destitution had made Sophy anxious to reassure herself that she understood how their bread was won and buttered. When her father, a not very able lawyer, had died suddenly, he had surprised his family by proving bankrupt. For Sophy's sister Kate and George, their younger brother, the upshot had been humiliation and uncertainty. But for Sophy there had been also bewilderment, as she realized only by degrees that she could no longer go frivolously dressed and be ignorant of household economy. There'd been a time when, beleaguered with her timid mother in the remote Wiltshire village of Cannings Fitzpayne, it had seemed that her life had ended before it could ever begin.

'Probably it comes from one of the foundries near Dudley, in the Black Country.' The road followed the canal for some way; and the chaise, a plume of dust blowing away from beneath its wheels, overtook the barge. Fraser let the window down to take another look. 'From the look of some of those sections, they're transporting an entire iron hull.'

Sophy, craning forward, tried in vain to understand for herself what it was they saw. She realized nonetheless what must be meant by certain drawings in his office when, next morning at their inn near Buckingham, she awoke from a lurid dream. A metal creature like the insides of a giant clock had scuttled down a foreshore smoking a bolt-upright cheroot, climbed into a tin cockleshell, and see-sawed itself out to sea.

From the coast of Lancashire, meanwhile, where the little town of Liverpool ran itself out in a wilderness of unfinished streets, not even the tallest masthead of the *Cassiopeia* was still in sight. Sophy looked some moments longer at the rim of the sky, sought in vain for something hopeful to say, and turned away.

But by the time they'd reached their lodgings in Castle Street, Tom found his mother acting as cheerfully towards him as he could wish. Mary, too, was anxious to smile at him, even as she grumbled that spoiling him so would do him no good. If he wished, he was to have nothing for supper but port-wine pudding, his favourite; and he could stay up as late as he liked, till no doubt near to tears of longing for his bed. And tomorrow they would go out to where the red-and-blue rocking horse, the clockwork singing bird and the toy hussars in formation were displayed for sale, and have every one plucked out from the very shop window.

Had Tom been old enough to make comparisons, he would have thought today had been good. But as he slept, breathing soft and sweet with his thumb lapsed out of his mouth, Sophy, with a bolster to stop the

13

draught where her husband would have lain, saw the day break before she finally cried herself to sleep.

While the ship carrying Tom's father was being pitched about in the wild North Atlantic like a clapper in a bell, and while Sophy laboured to hide her sense of loss, a young woman from her recent past, by name Charity Michaelmas, was watching her child too acquire early memories.

Little Georgiana Michaelmas did not live with her mother, but visited each day. She, a housekeeper, a scullery boy, a maid and a succession of nurserymaids had their own house next door. Georgiana's home was on the edge of London, in countrified Knightsbridge. Like Mama's, it was new, with new furniture, new shrubs in the garden, and freshly planted lawns surrounded by a wall high enough to seclude a convent. The nurserymaids came and went fast; Charity was formidably strict with them. The child was too young to think it unusual that her mother, not yet twenty, spoke to her servants as though she carried the experience of a lifetime. Or that on every day of the week but their special one together Charity wore evening dress in the forenoon.

It was on one of these special days that a stranger appeared in Mama's house: a man. Since it was the Sabbath, other folk might wear their best clothes. But for Charity, this was when she dressed informally, in a plain muslin housedress, with her mass of dark hair restrained beneath a frilled cap.

Such apparel made her look younger than did the shimmering robes she usually wore. But her visitor, coming in unannounced, seemed not to approve. As she stood up to greet him in the pretty, overfurnished sitting room, he looked her over with a show of surprise.

Georgiana, playing on the floor, paused and stared

14

up at him. Her face was empty of everything but curiosity. The man, youngish and well-dressed, glanced down at her. His expression said, I see that child. But I shouldn't have had to.

Charity, perceiving this, had already rung for Georgiana's nurserymaid. Even though it was her business to please him, she made no move to offer her visitor a seat.

'Did you not expect me?'

Taking care how she answered, Charity said, 'Of course. How else are you to maintain this establishment? I know – '

'You know what?' he said, frowning with incomprehension. He had evidently decided in advance not to understand anything she might say. 'What are you talking about?'

'I know,' Charity went on, standing as if to attention, 'that you cannot always send a message here ahead of you.'

'So I was expected?' He was challenging her to contradict him. Sitting on the carpet, at her mother's feet, Georgiana saw the man as two shiny toecaps, with every oiled stitch as clean as new. She looked up at Mama, expecting words of reassurance at the sight of a stranger.

Charity reached again to pick up the bell. As she did so, her personal maid hurried into the room in response to her original summons.

'See that Makepeace is found,' Charity said, 'and takes her charge,' indicating Georgiana, 'home via the kitchen.' She was trying not to sound urgent.

The maid was not used to hearing the child described in such an offhand way; usually Georgiana was 'angel' and 'little princess'. Nonetheless she too tried to look as if nothing was wrong. Not wanting to offend the gentleman by uttering childish endearments in his presence, she scooped up Georgiana without a word

15

and scurried off to where the little girl could be kept quiet and out of sight.

Alone with him Charity felt less at a disadvantage – if not everything a mistress should be, at least less of a mother.

He said again, 'So I was expected?'

She'd never seen him like this. But she knew better than to look him in the eye. 'Since today is Sunday I dare say you couldn't conveniently send a servant on your behalf.' It was as close as she dared go towards reminding him of their arrangement. Only on week-days was she supposed to be ready, night or day, for his arrival.

'I don't know for what reason you tell me how my own household should be ordered.' He looked at her hard. Charity, hands folded before her, stared unflinching at a corner of the ceiling. He said again, 'You expected me, then?'

She hadn't. But she knew he wanted her to say she had. 'No,' she ventured.

His stare was incredulous. '"No"?' A casual onlooker could never have guessed that he was the one in the wrong.

'I mean yes, Buckland.'

It was how she usually addressed him. Yet she knew it would anger him.

He leaned towards her. '"*Yes*"?'

'Yes, sir. I did expect you.'

'So I am right in thinking you consider yourself fully prepared to receive me?'

'You are.'

'I beg your pardon?'

'You are right. And I am fully prepared.'

'In God's name, how?' pointedly looking her over.

'The child is being taken back to her lodging immediately, sir.' This was the first time Georgiana's exist-ence had ever been mentioned by either of them. It

16

had been nothing to Buckland that his money kept not only the mother but her child by another man; he liked to boast how much his mistresses cost. But, by hints, Charity had been put in no doubt. To acknowledge the existence of her little girl would be in the poorest taste. One did not keep a woman of pleasure in order to be reminded of infant prattle and soiled baby clothes.

He snorted with impatience, it being beneath his dignity to do more.

'And in every other way,' Charity continued, 'I am ready to receive you.'

'Looking as you do!' with a gesture of disgust.

'I have always agreed to dress as you wish.'

Her compliance infuriated him. She had known it would be like this the day that he tired of her. And she had been here, after all, for over two years.

He glared at her as if daring her to say more.

She added, 'I am still ready to do whatever you would like. At any time.'

In the tone of one making a final effort to be just, he said, 'I came to this house today at a moment's notice. It was entirely on impulse that I subjected my family to my absence, and my servants to the inconvenience of Sunday travel. Do you understand that?'

She looked solemn, as required. 'Yes, sir.'

'Don't "sir" me, damn you. I haven't kept you here so that you could learn to cringe like a half-trained parlourmaid.' It was a reference to her own humble past – what he thought he knew of it.

'Of course not, Buckland. You and I both know that.'

'And don't be familiar.'

Charity sighed. She could ignore his hatred – rather, his bad conscience at dismissing her – no longer. But she still had to brace herself before finally agreeing to quarrel. After all, where would she go?

She said, 'If I were – at some future time – to be

displaced in your affections, should you like me to return my gowns?'

'To do what?'

She corrected herself. 'To return the gowns.' That much did he own her. 'There are several that have not yet been seen in company.'

He looked at her with a show of disbelief. 'Did I dress *you* in another woman's cast-offs? Or perhaps, seeing where I found you, you could never have known the difference.' To meet a better class of customer, she had added to her earnings from prostitution by working in Drury Lane as dresser to a successful actress.

'Of course not.' She congratulated herself on the success of what had been a deliberate ploy. It was something to know she would be leaving with some changes of clothing.

'And for what reason,' he said, 'do you speak as though it was *I* who had given *you* dissatisfaction?'

'None, truly. I say no such thing.'

'Do you indeed?' He hesitated, looking flushed, in the hope that she would say something more provoking. After all the compliments he had paid, he needed courage now to hate her.

She held his gaze and said nothing. He came closer and said in a low voice, 'You bore me. Do you understand that? You're either subservient and mousey or you're too much above your station. And when you don't present yourself before me looking like a drab, you're too flash to be endured. You're a slut.'

'So you do wish to put an end to our acquaintance-ship?'

He looked at her as if the thought had just occurred to him. In a voice both angered and grave he said, 'Since that seems to be your object, I shan't hinder you. I'm damned if I shall.'

*   *   *

18

Despite Charity's orders, Georgiana was not taken straight home. The servants were too anxious for their own prospects not to eavesdrop; and while Buckland was still in the house all four of them loitered in the kitchen, ready to look busy if need be.

The drift, if not every word, of his conversation with Charity could be heard from across the passage. Only when the front door had slammed behind him did Georgiana's nursemaid pick her up and hurry to the tall gate that led to the garden next door.

Georgiana didn't see her mother until that evening, when she was brought to bid Mama goodnight. Usually it was Mama who came to see her, but tonight Charity was busy. Seated at the escritoire in her gilded and silk-hung bedroom, she was composing a letter. She wrote laboriously, with the care of someone who has learned to read and write comparatively late in life. The wardrobe doors and several trunks stood open and the maid who looked after Charity's clothes and dressed her hair was hurrying to and fro cradling expensive embroideries and sheaves of tissue paper. Both women wore a look of purpose.

Charity took Georgiana on to her lap and embraced her. The child stared at the unfamiliar room and its splendours. 'Daly,' she said, pointing at the maid. 'Daly – pretty.'

'Yes, dearest,' Charity said. 'Daly is packing a pretty dress.' She kissed the little girl absently, her mind still on her letters. While there was so much to do, she must not let resentment of Buckland take control of her. And after all, this had been a safe place to start raising a child: no risk here of any customer refusing payment because he couldn't have the daughter as well as the mother

How much would Georgiana remember? Musing in her rumpled boudoir, her cheek against the child's head, Charity was glad of the things she knew

19

Georgiana would not be able to recall. For many weeks after giving birth, alone in an attic near Spitalfield, Charity had been frail and ashen-faced from loss of blood. After she'd paid for three days' lodging she'd also been penniless. But she soon found there was plenty of work for people who wanted it. During her first months in London she had serviced more men than it would take to people a small town. Only when she had recovered her health and her looks could she graduate to an expensive brothel in the West End and thence, via employment backstage in the theatre, to a single keeper.

At first, Georgiana had had to be carried with her everywhere. Charity could still remember one encounter, in an alley near Middle Temple Lane. She'd taken on two customers, turn and turn about. Throughout, little Georgiana, six weeks old, had lain ignored in the ragged old basket Charity used as a cradle, and given each man an enchanting toothless smile.

To think that Georgiana's father – poor young fool – had hoped, by means of reconciliation, to cancel such times. No wonder Charity had later dismissed his approaches.

Little Georgiana was taken away to bed; her favourite doll, whose loss was feared by everyone, was tucked up with her; and Charity, still at her writing desk beside the big canopied bed, was busy on behalf of them both.

Living in seclusion as she had done recently, she could not hope for another employer to come seeking her. She must look for work on her own initiative.

It was not that she hadn't mated with other men during her time as Buckland's mistress. He'd never cared to have her leave the house, and she knew no one she might have received there. But during his own visits he'd often brought company. Charity, clad only in satin slippers or a string of pearls, had sometimes been worked as hard here, in her daintily appointed Middlesex villa, as when she and Georgiana had been housed with twenty other people in a cellar near Covent Garden. Brandy glass in hand, Buckland and a select party of male acquaintances would sit or stand around the bed to watch each other take turns on her.

Afterwards, 'Tell me, my dear fellow,' he would ask, 'was that not one of the finer experiences of its kind? Would you not say I'd made a good choice?' And he would indicate Charity who, still naked as instructed beforehand, would be sitting before her mirror to have her hair dressed again. 'A thousand guineas a year I pay for her — not counting extras, mind, such as the music master . . . An Aphrodite among women, is she not? . . . Was she not good there with you? Do give me your honest opinion . . .'

So, who was there? Perhaps young Pettifer, who'd refused a place with his father's stockjobbing firm in order to become an architect. He might be one of her best prospects, if his allowance was adequate. She hadn't much liked coupling with him before wit- nesses; he didn't take it indifferently enough. All the more reason why he might be useful. How proud he had looked, at having just completed a public act of shame like a man.

The other good candidate was Milsome. He was an amateur scholar of independent means, who had sev- eral times shown interest in Charity's belated edu- cation. His wife, with whom he lived happily enough, had a formidable reputation as a bluestocking. But her accomplishments, being no longer new to him, could not impress as much as Charity's attempts to write correct grammar or sing a line of harmony in tune.

She wrote first to young Pettifer.

My dear Pettifer,

Oh! My heart is broken – yet that is not why I entreat you. Save me! Oh, save me and my child!

My heart is broken – my dear Buckland loved me once, God knows. And though his way of showing it lacked delicacy, yet I was not ashamed to accept his love, and treasure it as the best thing he had to give.

But now he repents! And though I am only a poor creature, yet – oh, in this you must believe me – I can still hold up my head with the noblest and purest women in the land. For am I not a mother? Does not my heart ache with the tender hopes and fears of every mother, from the highest to she who has sinned worse than the Magdalen herself?

And now – what is to become of me? Help me! Oh, help me to protect the innocence of my child. For myself I care nothing – but for my daughter's happiness and purity of mind I am prepared without a single blush, may God forgive me, to offer my body – nay, my very soul. If you would but save me! Not in the name of our desires, but for your own conscience's sake!

I can write no more – already I am shamed by what I say. Fear not for me. If you cannot rescue me and my child, I can yet steel myself to suffer what I must . . .

For her second letter, to the bookish Milsome, she was careful that her spelling should not be too good. Better that what she wrote should hint at improvements yet to be made. By him, of course.

Today Buckland was heer and surprized me by saying menny things in anger, witch he nevver did befor and menny things that I say wer cruwel, too.

Now in al the times that we declared our luv wun for another I was humbeled by his wisdom in

22

so menny things of witch I, an ignorant girl, new nothing. So that, from admiration for a man of intellekt, as I thort him, I wood do any thing he desired. If my mynd was too por, sed I, then let me serve the hyer good in whatever way I can.

I mean, my dear Milsome, with my body.

You may think me a verry grate fool but I say it still. Werever I see a way to those matters of scholarship and hi cultur that I as a barefoot cuntry girl never dreemed of, then I will folow that way, cost my pryde wot it wil.

She was thinking of herself astride Milsome, surrounded by his friends. Silhouetted in the candlelight they had all paid such attention that the only other moving thing had been the smoke of a cigar.

But now wot must I think, since Buckland hates me? I confes to you, tho to no wun else, that tho the maner of his going rung my hart, if he had not gon, then I should hav. I no I must seem ungrateful, but in matters of intellekt and wot people call accomplishments, such as my music, he and my present teechers cood no longer satisfy me.

And for this, you, Milsome, must bere the blame. Without you I might nevver hav nown my ignorance for wot it is.

And now you may think this coldly put. But in truth I trembel to think I might yet be allowed to serve you. I care not which part of me you desire. I am so much in awe, my hope for a share in the superiority of yor mind overcomes me. It is like a flud that breaks into every part of me . . .

'I think at least one of these should do ever so well,' said Daly, who had helped with the spelling of the letter to young Pettifer. 'Which gentleman do you favour, ma'am?'

23

'Whichever one answers first.' Charity tilted a page against the candlelight to see if the ink still shone wet. 'Leave the writing things. It might be prudent if I took copies.'

Georgiana, years after, would chance upon what her mother had written. Artful though both letters were, did not each one more or less tell the truth?

As she prepared for what might be their last night at that house, Charity believed so. Even that stuff about going barefoot was no invention. She leaned her head backwards as Daly drew out her hair to its full length with steady strokes of the brush, and allowed her mind to dwell on that time. It had been before her life as a whore – before her arrival in the capital even, after a journey on which she'd wondered if each small town she passed might not be London. It had been far from here and now felt long ago, when she had lived as a fieldwoman and servant and lain with no one but Georgiana's father, in the Wiltshire village of Cannings Fitzpayne.

CHAPTER TWO

By now, Sophy guessed, her husband must have been in America for some weeks. It was April, and she had taken to walking out each day to see if there was anything from him at the post office. Sure enough, by one afternoon's second post a letter had arrived, despatched only a month earlier from Richmond, Virginia.

Such a packet was too wonderful to keep unopened. It was also too precious to be read in the street. Sophy ran all the way home, arriving with muddied petticoats and a flush of expectation.

Shutting herself in her bedroom, she went to open it by the window, where a cloudful of spring rain was being tossed against a sunlit pane. With the profile of her curly fair head and long nape as still as a cameo, she read, skimming at first, then scrutinizing every word. Here at last, enclosing another letter, from her beloved elder sister Kate, was news of Fraser's safety, in his own hand.

And – since he'd been born in poverty, and grown to manhood before learning to read and write – in his own imperfect spelling. Sophy's face gleamed with pleasure at the sight of his familiar mistakes.

My own dearest Sophia,
God knows with what feelings of saddness I
watched you both as I was carry'd out of your sight
and away from England, thinking who can say
when next we shall meet! Almost I wished you
might be gone from view sooner, so that since we

25

*must be parted, at least I could stop suffering the
dred of that parting . . .*

Alone in the waning afternoon light she read and re-
read all twenty pages, until Mary came tapping at the
door to ask if she should like candles brought. Day by
day he had written to her: across wintry seas where
climbing each wave seemed like a separate journey;
voyaging south from Boston, in a vessel armed against
pirates; and on his arrival in Virginia, to plan yet
further journeying. The next part of his travels would
take him inland by stagecoach to Pittsburgh, to see for
himself conditions on the great rivers for which his
craft was to be designed. He had passed through tremendous dangers and arrived with his hopes for success all the higher.

Yet everything he described – places, people, war-
time perils survived on the high seas – all seemed
phantoms compared to the real subject of his letter.
Whether writing with fingers dead from cold in the
darkness below decks or breakfasting at noon on quail
in aspic in the cool of his brother-in-law's mansion
above the James River, the thing that filled his mind
was that he and she were parted.

'And yet,' he wrote, 'with every mile that seperates
us more, I am more thankful. For onlie think – the
further I travel away from you in space, the closer in
time I come to that day when we shall meet again.'

'Yes – yes,' exclaimed Sophy, smiling as she read,
'that is exactly how it is!'

She grew solemn, though, as she read the last part of
his letter. Not from dismay, but from unlooked-for
hope.

His travels would last longer than he had expected.
But would she, he asked, be prepared to risk the same
journey he had just made, to join him in New York,
and shorten their separation by half a year?

26

He knew it was not a small thing he proposed. Tom would have to be left at home in Mary's care rather than suffer the hardships of such a voyage. His letter also mentioned reports of fighting in the Atlantic between British vessels and ships of the American navy.

Kate's letter touched on the same rumours. But like Fraser she mentioned them only to say that they were unimportant.

> As to talk of war, here it takes three courses, depending on whose views you overhear. Joseph is all cheery cynicism, and says the American army is not to be taken seriously even by its own side, because at present it counts for little more than an old man, a boy, and a lame dog with the vapours. Then there's also talk of national honour – and here you must picture Joseph's sister Euphemia, sharp-faced with disapproval of all foreigners. For her, to fight Britain would be to side with Bonaparte; and, since Bonaparte is even more of a foreigner than King George, it follows that it's he, rather than His Majesty, who is the arch-enemy of freedom, and we should have nothing to do with him. (So far, so fair. But – poor Euphemia! Nineteen is too young to be so angry in all her opinions. I wonder if she'd have been different, had she been pretty.)
>
> My own view is that if America and Britain cannot trade, both sides will suffer. The New England states would leave the Union, to go on making money from Britain on their own. And Britain would starve at last into surrendering to France. Depend upon it, there will be no war.
>
> Besides, if you could only join us! So that we might be together again without the passing of who knows how many years . . .

At all this, so thoughtful was Sophy that only when the pages of both letters slid from her lap did her attention return to the darkening room where she sat. And it was some time before she roused herself to pick them up again.

But however intent she might be, there was not a moment of doubt about what she would do.

It took only a few minutes to admit this to herself. Even before thinking how to break the news to Tom, she had run back downstairs to the parlour and was setting out pen, ink and paper, ready to write to her husband in reply.

She sent a long, long letter – more a diary, full of Tom's sayings and doings. To this she added her joyful acceptance of Fraser's suggestion that she join him, travelling to New York at the same time as he, to meet at a hotel whose address he had enclosed. The whole package, together with a fat letter for Kate, was in the hands of the Liverpool post office by sunrise next morning. Sophy herself was to follow it overseas as soon as she could arrange her passage.

So it was no later than June, on a morning of violent heat, with the inland forests quiet and the highways giving off little whirlwinds of dust, when the ship bearing Sophy's letter went about into the broad mouth of Chesapeake Bay.

But already Kate's prediction of peace was proving wrong. Back in April, as the crew had their last sight of England, sure enough both governments had been trying to agree on the terms of America's neutrality in the war between Britain and France. But as the convoy protecting the ship was watering in the Azores, Spencer Perceval, the British prime minister, had just been shot dead in the House of Commons by a madman. And as it was separating from its escort, ready to enter

American waters, in Congress the faction eager for war with Britain was about to triumph. American proposals for peace had been met by silence from London. In Washington, where news had not yet arrived of the shooting of Perceval, no one realized that the British government had been thrown into chaos.

So on the morning that the Liverpool packet arrived at last, out of a hot sunrise, Chesapeake Bay was thickly clustered down its south-western shore with fighting ships and reconnaissance craft making ready for war. The packet boat left the ocean behind and entered the brilliant, shallow expanse of the bay. As it did so, any observer looking out across the marshes at the mouth of James River could have seen it pass within shouting distance of another ship, setting out to make the same voyage in reverse, three thousand miles back to Britain.

The packet boat, going about into the wind, paused like a dancer on tiptoe, then started to beat back and forth up the bay. The smaller vessel was skimming before the breeze, and seemed at first to run broadside on at the other ship. Then the packet turned once more, to tack across the navigable channel down the bay. Though the two ships passed clear of each other, their wakes intermingled. For a moment the wavelets turned up by the course of the seabound ship could be seen knitted into the trail of the other. Then each white furrow faded, and the waters went as blank as before.

The smaller ship made ready to enter the Atlantic. Unlike the British vessel she was not sailing with an escort. She was not so large, nor so tall in the water. But she was faster, and she was armed. She was a frigate of the American navy, built for speed in dangerous waters, and carrying a declaration of war.

*　*　*

By the time England was just a smudge across the curve of the horizon, Sophy had no fears on her own account. The bad moment had been when she had hugged Tom for the last time. She had had to climb up into the cab with her veil down so he wouldn't catch the shocking sight of Mama in tears.

Aboard the *Odysseus*, on which she sailed, nearly a dozen other passengers were grand enough to have their own cabin. Or, rather, a little damp box like a buried coffin. Once the convoy of which the *Odysseus* was part had put to sea, the worst thing was the boredom of living semi-caged. Whenever the ship made good progress, the decks were almost impassable to any landsman. Their windward side rode some yards higher than the other, like a sailor with a monkey on one shoulder, and the sails streamed water faster than a broken gutter. The spring weather was blustery and chill, and from the fifth week a lookout had been posted in case of icebergs.

Most of the passengers spent their time in the saloon, gossiping, bickering or playing cards. This was the most spacious part of the ship, but it was still so small that to let someone pass you had to stand up.

By day the big window in the stern revealed a following cloud of seabirds. Gulls drifted and wheeled; below them stormy petrels skimmed the billows like airborne fish. At night the ship left a trail of embers, flying through the wet rigging from a stove amidships on the deck. The lantern suspended in the saloon cast shadows that swayed in time to the creaking of the timbers.

Twice the convoy met with a great storm that lasted over a week. During these times the ship's officers were hardly ever seen below, and avoided the passengers, going about their business haggard and intent. Cooped up in their cabins, the passengers sat or lay in darkness, or tried to read by the light of a candle, all

30

the while feeling as though locked inside a bandbox that was being swung about by a distraught giant. Some were stoical, some so noisily seasick that they could be heard by all their neighbours. The woman in the cabin next to Sophy's sniffled for hours at a time, in hopes of being heard by no one in particular and everybody in general.

Below decks, the boom and howl of the sea became confused with the sound of the water they'd shipped, smacking up and down the lower decks amid a wash of old vegetable parings and recently plucked chicken feathers. Day and night were hard to tell apart. If anything the daytime was worse. It was possible, in complete darkness, to believe one might soon watch the sun appear. But by the half-light of noon, with a murky ceiling of cloud just clearing the main topgallant, it seemed they'd never see anything cast a hard shadow again.

At least, being shut up during a storm, you didn't have to see your own feelings on the faces of others. Bored and apprehensive, but glad to be alone, Sophy lay on her narrow bed in darkness. If you lit the candle, the muzziness of its light only showed up how damp the air was below deck. With a travelling cloak about her for warmth, she shut her eyes and tried to imagine that this was merely the motion of a rook's nest, secure in the top of an English elm in a south-westerly spring gale. In fact, on such a mighty sea the *Odysseus* was more like a dead leaf being whirled to the top of a steeple at one moment and, at the next, swooping as low as the graves beneath. It was hard, sliding down each wave, not to believe it was only by one's own will-power that the ship would ride upward again.

But there was not one moment when Sophy was not glad to be there. She was convinced she had chosen right in making this journey. Suspended between a gloomy sky and a grim sea, as the weeks became a month, it seemed far longer since any of them had seen snow, or harvest, or spring. But throughout each tempest Sophy savoured a feeling of inner calm. In going to join Fraser, she was not acting rashly, like some silly girl scurrying after a seducer. Others on board might fear for their future or regret the life they'd left behind. But if she could not be reunited with her husband she was indifferent as to whether she perished in the attempt. For she knew that if anything had made her life solid at bottom, it had been her marriage to him.

Besides, she had faced worse than this on Fraser's account. Staring at the dim silhouette of the bulkhead at her feet, she relived her feelings of panic, that time he'd been arrested for debt. Corruption and mismanagement by his colleagues had briefly left him liable, a few years back, for an impossible sum. To be in danger here, on the high seas, was nothing to her emotions on hearing that her husband looked set to spend half a lifetime in the King's Bench Prison. Yet she had reconciled herself to packing her things and taking the stagecoach up to London to share his misfortune.

Listening to the moans of a neighbouring passenger, who had fallen a few days before and suffered a suspected fracture of the pelvis, she thought how much less terrible, for her, this particular journey was. Then, it had taken all her courage, to travel towards the likelihood of poverty without end. Now, she was on her way to join Fraser in what must surely be his most successful venture so far. She knew he cared little for the profits to be made from his work – though her brother-in-law, in addition to a generous commission, had presented him with shares in his new Mississippi trading company that might well become a fortune in their own right. Whatever Fraser undertook, it was the work itself that obsessed him. One day he would complete some invention that others would see

as the climax of his life. Yet to him even that would be merely a problem to be solved and then forgotten, as the next challenge to his ingenuity seized his attention. With an insight she'd lacked before their marriage, Sophy knew that her husband was no more nor less than a slave to his own talents.

She herself saw his career differently. Certainly she'd grown to respect Fraser's ability – though she valued it for his sake rather than in its own right. Meanwhile the experience, twice in her short life, of being dependent on a bankrupt had made money far more important to her than to Fraser himself. If, by joining him now, she gave him no more than symbolic support, she still thought nothing of going halfway across the world to do so.

Besides, she told herself, listening to the monotonous sounds of pain from the next cabin, the greatest danger was one that would follow her no matter where she went. Better to be abroad, surrounded by her family and their servants, than in lodgings back in England, separated from her husband by thousands of miles. After all, her forthcoming peril was as much his business as hers.

Sophy moved herself carefully, trying not to utter sounds of distress on her own account. There were not many positions now in which she could remain comfortable for even a few minutes. When Fraser had sailed, back in mid-winter, she had hardly suspected anything. Now, it was all too clearly important for her to be reunited with him and with her sister Kate in good time. Whatever anxiety she might have for her own safety, she was far more concerned that no hardship should threaten her child. If a premature birth endangered Sophy herself, so be it. But if she *should* perish, shipboard life offered only a modest chance of survival to such a little scrappy thing as a newborn babe.

33

Watchful for attack by the French, through contrary winds and dead calm the convoy strove not to be scattered. Aboard the *Odysseus* the little group of passengers continued by turns hopeful, bored, quarrelsome, and full of fears. Sophy, by now a virtual prisoner below, listened and waited, slept and planned, all the more thankful, on hearing that they were only five days from land, for the steadfastness of purpose that had brought her there.

Amidst a satisfying heap of corpses dressed in blue and red, the French flag was about to be lowered from above the fort. Victory was due to be snatched yet again by the valiant Grenadiers.

This was Tom's favourite part of the game, which was played as a ritual every day. The fort had been made for him by his father, as a study for a real one Fraser had engineered near Dublin. Every detail of it was perfect. Its outside wall, which was circular, with a parapet, could be opened on a hinge so that you could see the whole of the interior. In the cellar were all sorts of miniature weaponry and other supplies. A rack of model rifles stood at the foot of a runged staircase, and the floor was piled with sacks of provisions. The sacks themselves had been sewn by Mama from dressmaking canvas and were filled with birdseed, in imitation of grain. There was a well, whose wooden windlass worked a bucket of tiny staves bound with brass and measuring an inch across. The doorway, high in the wall up a flight of steps, was barricaded by an iron bar spanning not quite the width of Tom's hand. On the roof stood three little brass cannon, which each afternoon playtime discharged a fearful amount of ammunition into the invincible ranks of charging redcoats.

Tom was finding it difficult, though, to bring today's

battle to a satisfactory end. Bonaparte's troops, panicked at the mere sight of the British, had fired off everything they had. Even after searching under the kitchen table and reaching as far as he could beneath the dresser he had still not recovered enough shot for a final defence. Meanwhile it was unthinkable that the fort should be taken without maximum loss of life.

The ammunition needed by the cannon was in the form of a handful of black peppercorns. Tom knew he must ask permission before provisioning his fort from any of the household supplies. But Cook and the scullerymaid had both taken the afternoon off. Mary too was missing. He went in search of her.

She was in the drawing room, lying, with her apron undone, on a dust-sheeted chaise-longue. In the absence of the master and mistress this part of the house was disused, its windows shuttered and the furniture covered over. Despite the room's dimness Mary's eyes were closed. There was a line of pain between her brows. Even in that light the pallor of her face, recently gone all to bone and shadows, stood out. Though she'd been looking ill for a while now, little Tom, all innocent selfishness, had never noticed.

'Not now, Tom dear.'

Ordinary words to most children. But for Tom, at the centre of a household that had always indulged him, they were a complete surprise. Scratching the top of one pudgy leg he stood and stared at his nursemaid in bewilderment.

Mary opened her eyes and tried to reassure him. 'In a moment . . . Now, what would you like from me?'

Tom made his request, and added, timidly, 'Are you going to stay in here?' He was old enough to understand that Mary had been overcome by something unpleasant. But he was still little enough to be frightened that an adult could be troubled by anything beyond their control. And because he was frightened, he was angry.

'Are you?' he ventured, at the same moment that she shook her head and tried to smile. A mob of feelings jostled him, all of which he was too young to understand or master. Because he liked Mary, he felt confused at being angered by her. Also the gloom of the deserted room, with all its familiar landmarks covered up, was affecting him.

All this Mary knew. 'Go back into the warm, now, and I'll follow you.'

Later she seemed better, so that when, after his bedtime bath, she mentioned that she'd been unwell, he'd quite forgotten what she was talking about. It was after the maid had taken away several cans of soapy water and his tin bath, and he was sitting on Mary's lap being dried in a warm towel. When Mama had still been at home this had been his time to sit in her busy embrace, being rubbed dry and talking about the day just gone, or tomorrow. Now, each evening he did the same with Mary.

'So when will Mama send me a letter?' Tom had just discovered the post office in the town, and the wonderful fact that it could sometimes produce letters between people he knew.

'As soon as she gets to New York, on the other side of the sea.'

They had had this conversation many times. It was a routine they went through to soothe the child on his way to bed. 'She and your Papa will both write you, in one big letter.'

Why one big one? was normally Tom's next question. Waiting, Mary dried his toes, left foot, then right, as he insisted she should do, going from one little toe across to the other. But instead of making her explain the cost of postage again he added, 'Was that a letter the man gave you today?'

That morning Mary had paid out several shillings in order to receive a small package, counting out the money with great care, as though each coin were a small rock.

'It was.'

'Was it from Mama?'

'Heavens, no. She would write to you first, for me to read to you.'

'Was it a letter for you?'

'Indeed, yes.'

'Where from?'

'From Bradford, which is a town in Wiltshire. It's near Cannings Fitzpayne, where your Mama comes from.'

'Who was it from?'

'Why, my dear, you must not ask me that!' said Mary, exaggerating her astonishment to show she was not really cross. 'It was sent to me, you see, not you.'

She waited for a minute or so, to make her next remark seem like a change of subject. Then, as she was helping Tom put his nightshirt over his head, she said, 'What would you say if I told you that another young lady' – Mary herself was little more than a girl, though to Tom all grown-ups seemed vaguely the same age – 'was coming to stay here?'

'What for?' He turned his head to stare at her. She avoided his eyes and went on buttoning him up.

'To help take care of you, Tom. You see – '

'Why?'

'Because I need helping here. I've written to my sister, who's looked after your Mama's young cousins in Wiltshire. They've grown old enough for school now. So your Mama's aunt Norton is very pleased to think she can do something for you, by seeing that my sister can travel up here to help. Her name's Bella. I'm sure you'll like her.'

Giving the boy's fair hair one last rub with the towel

37

she waited for him to speak. Unnerved by his silent gaze she added, 'Besides, I may have to go away for a few days, you know, Tom.'

The child went on staring at her, his face a blank. He found it impossible that she, as well as his father and mother, should go away and leave him. So much so that he actually failed to understand what she was saying. His mind blocked out the unthinkable – that he might be left, even for a short time, in the care of a stranger.

At length he asked, 'Are you going away to see Billy?' Mary had a sweetheart, a corporal in the Light Dragoons. Tom's parents knew nothing of his existence. To Tom, though, over several daily walks with Mary he had become a familiar figure.

'Of course not, you silly thing.' Though Mary's tone was light, her face was solemn. 'You know he's gone away.'

'To America?'

'No. There's no fighting in America – else your Mama and Papa would not have gone there. Billy went away to Spain.'

'To fight with Bonaparte?'

'Why, yes.'

'In his uniform?'

'Of course. Don't you remember? Last autumn, watching him get on the ship?'

'So *you're* not going to Spain?'

'No, no ... Get down, now, and put your slippers on.'

'Will you get a letter from Billy?' Tom asked, without moving.

'Good heavens, no. There are no post offices where Billy's regiment has gone.'

She was silent, half forgetting the child on her lap. Uneasy, Tom said, to get her attention, 'Who *are* you going to see?'

'I'm going on a visit to my mother.'

'Why?'

'Because she's poorly, and needs me.'

'But you're right poorly, too,' said the boy.

Mary smiled to hear how precisely he was beginning to pick up not only her words but also the rhythms of her North Country speech. Hastily, she replied, 'I'm certain I'll be better.'

'Why cannot your sister visit her, instead?'

'Because she's not altogether my sister. We have the same father, but not the same mother.'

Tom paused to take in this unfamiliar idea. All the way into bed he was full of questions about how such a thing could be. He wanted to know too about the village where Mary had grown up with nine brothers and sisters, a day's travel away, near Lancaster, in the northerly part of the country. Also about Billy, and the French – indeed, as Mary guessed, about anything that would stop him realizing that he was about to be left again.

All the way through repeating his prayers for her to hear, getting into bed and listening to that night's story, he seemed everything she'd hoped he would be: talkative enough, but calm. She kissed him goodnight and went to finish some sewing in her attic room next to the nursery where he slept.

His cry, when it came, out of a deep pit of sleep an hour later, was what she'd feared. It left her blood and nerves buzzing with shock nonetheless.

The child was still asleep – but as he lay, face up, tears poured from beneath his closed eyelids.

In a low voice, fearful of waking him outright, she did what she could to calm him, shushing him and murmuring endearments over and over like a spell. At last he seemed to sense, from whatever level of uncon- sciousness, that someone was trying to comfort him.

39

His desolate sobs became less frequent, as his nightmare faded and he slept once more a sleep of gentle bliss.

It was some time though before Mary felt free to leave his bedside. Shading her candle with one hand, she sat by him for maybe an hour, lost in thought. Her mind dwelled on the child in her care, whose soft breathing could just be heard above the sound of the wind in the chimneypots. She thought too of the wide sea just beyond the foot of the town, and how long it took to cross it, whether to America or Spain. And of her young man, who could be killed fighting in the Peninsular War, maybe years before she found out – his death going unsuspected until perhaps some comrade-in-arms, invalided home, brought a letter or message.

She thought, too, of her mistress's approaching confinement; and of Sophy's parting instruction to 'let poor Tom keep happy, if you can'. Amidst worries of her own she even had a moment's regret that though the little boy had been entrusted to her, it was a stranger who would have charge of him for as long as Mary herself would be away.

Given her real reason for going, an absence of two weeks should surely be enough. Mary had lied to Tom when she said her mother was ailing. It was she herself who would need nursing. For the maid had gone the same way as her mistress: Mary had been made pregnant by her soldier lover, and was going away to have the child in secret.

Afterwards, she would leave it in the care of her mother, to whom every month she would send part of her wages. In or out of marriage, the arrangement was common enough. Bella, her half-sister, widow of a head gardener from a great house near Bristol, had a couple of children lodging with relatives in a village

40

not far from Liverpool, whom she'd supported in the same way for some years.

Mary sighed as she sat down again to her sewing. If the child survived, unlike six of her own brothers and sisters, would it be glad to be alive? How would she herself be, a year, five years – even ten years – hence, should she still be alive? She stitched on, her face composed. For the present it was enough that the child in the next room should sleep soundly; that her lover was not proven dead in a far country; and that her fate and that of her own child were now, thank goodness, beyond her power to control.

It was Tom's first day without petticoats. Mary's sister Bella was to arrive that morning; and as a treat to mark the occasion Mary said he could start dressing as a proper little boy a few months earlier than most other lads.

The prospect of a jacket and trousers pleased and excited him. As Mary washed his face before dressing him, it smiled up at her, like a little sun being burnished to a brighter shine.

Standing still, so that she could button him into his new shirt, he asked, 'Will Bella think I look grown up?'

'Why,' said Mary, 'she'll think you're old enough to be a real schoolboy.'

As if not changing the subject, after a pause she added, 'She's very highly thought of, you know, by your Mama's Aunt Norton. And it's not as if your Mama's aunt isn't – dear me, how can I say this? – a very particular sort of body.'

Tom, staring down at his buttons being fastened, felt little interest in hearing about a relative he'd never met. It was true that he'd overheard his parents talk of Aunt Norton. With the quickness that even very young children can have, he'd guessed that they didn't much like her. In fact, Sophy's aunt had disapproved of her marriage. Mrs Norton was the wife of a prosperous woollen-manufacturer. Being conscious that her husband was 'only' in trade made her all the more anxious about her own claim to gentility. It was typical of her that when Sophy chose to marry a former working man, Aunt Norton had failed to keep silent about what she saw as the shame of such a match.

Mary helped Tom into his jacket and started carefully to brush his thick fine curls. 'Your Mama's aunt says Bella is the very best of all the servants she's ever had – '

'Why?'

'Because of the respect Bella's always shown Mrs Norton. Mrs Norton said to her, "Bella," she said, "if ever there was a member of the lower orders who could profit from contact with their betters, that person, Bella, is yourself." So, you see, Tom, from the respect and gratitude that Bella has towards your great-aunt Norton, I know that she will be kind to you, as your dear Mama's little boy, and as a member of Mrs Norton's family.'

Being in some ways childlike herself, Mary was clever enough at meeting the needs of someone the age of young Tom. But she was not always so clever in understanding the behaviour of adults. Thus it was that, in making this little speech of reassurance to Tom, she meant every word. Poor thing.

'You must do as you like,' said Bella to Tom later that day. She was a thin woman with a fussy coiffure of tight artificial curls.

Rather than pause and look at him as she spoke, meanwhile, she hustled on with what she was doing. The drawing room, on her orders, was to be restored to use. Bella, bristling with purpose, was chivvying the maid-of-all work to open the window sashes and set a fire going in the wide grate.

'But only if you know it's right, mind,' she added, her back towards him as she lifted a dust sheet to inspect Sophy's little rosewood sewing table.

Tom had wanted to know if he might pitch himself a pretend tent, as part of his other favourite game of setting up a soldiers' camp.

Armed with her permission, he went to assemble all his cherished odds and ends of make-believe on the nursery floor. The tent itself was made from one of Mama's old shawls draped over a couple of rush-bottomed chairs. On guard outside the tent stood Tom's big wooden horse. This was another toy that his father had made for him, on a wheeled frame, so that it could be ridden up and down the room like a real pony.

The main activity within the camp was always a ceremonial parade. This featured an imaginary regimental band, with Tom himself taking the part of the principal drummer. The 'drum' was Cook's littlest saucepan, borrowed from the far end of the row of utensils hanging on the kitchen wall.

It was a wretched, rain-sodden day, the more miserable for Mary having said goodbye earlier. Tom had tried in vain not to cry as she'd walked off without him down the muddy street, a tightly tied bundle of spare clothes in her hand. Alone in the nursery, it was a relief to him to be able to tell his horse all about it. Between murmured confidences, he accused him of being naughty, and hit him with his toy whip, rather more often than usual. It made him feel better, if not completely happy again. So too did sitting inside his tent. Here, for the moment promoted from drummer boy to general, he found it reassuring to sit in his very own tight, private space, out of sight of all his invisible comrades-in-arms. Listening to the steady sound of the rain on the nursery windowpanes, he pulled the flaps of his tent close against the bad weather sweeping over the camp.

All the while, in an endless low voice, he gave himself a commentary on what he was doing. He was glad Bella had left him alone. Mary, too, had always given him the privacy needed for games of make-believe.

Now, however, he could hear Bella on the stairs. As she came into the room, he looked out from under his makeshift awning, to see what she might want.

'Yes?' she said, pointing at the borrowed saucepan. Keeping her finger levelled at it, she gave him a steady look of outrage.

Bewildered, Tom stared back.

'*Yes?*' she repeated.

Not knowing how to please her, he came out and stood up, still looking at her.

'Who said you could take things from the kitchen?' She held up the saucepan and brandished it in front of him, as though about to swat a fly against his forehead. 'Well? Who told you?'

Tom couldn't say. He'd been in the habit of playing with all these things since before he could remember. He fiddled with the hem of his jacket and looked anxiously at the floor.

'And this,' she blustered, wrenching Sophy's shawl off the make-believe tent-poles, so that one of the chairs fell on its back. Bella, in proportion as she acted meekly towards her employers, was really very unsure of her own authority.

The child continued lost for words. Or, as she saw it, obstinate. His silence forced her to change tack. Bending down, she looked him hard in the face and said, 'Don't you know that counts as stealing?'

At this terrible word the boy gave a wail of fear. Bella, feeling she was partway to making a proper

44

impression, stood back. 'Now stop that noise!' she said, in the voice of someone who never stood for any nonsense.

Tom was a child who usually liked to please his elders. He was also frightened. Accordingly he fell silent.

Thinking she'd won a battle, Bella put on a tone of grim reasonableness. 'Now, I want you to listen to me. I'm sure you and I can get on perfectly well. But only if you make up your mind to be a good boy.'

There seemed little he could answer. He looked up at Bella, waiting to see what else she had to say.

'Did you not hear what I just said?'

'Yes,' murmured Tom. His face showed both wonder and hurt.

'Good. Now go and get ready for your tea. And if you want to play with the other children here, remember what I've told you.'

This was a threat that counted. Tom knew that Bella's son and daughter were shortly due to visit her. As an only child he sometimes felt lonely, and the prospect of having playfellows filled him with a mixture of uncertainty and delight.

Three floors below, having sat up at the big kitchen table with his hands and face scrubbed clean, he tried to pluck up courage to ask when they would arrive.

But before he could speak, Bella, as if their previous conversation had not been interrupted, said, 'And the first step you can take towards not being a naughty dishonest little boy is to learn to share with others.' She was cutting a large white loaf. Her face wore a look of firmness, as if the bread might come to life and tear her arm off in self-defence. 'Otherwise you'll only learn the hard way, with other children in the house, that you must let others play with your toys if they're not so lucky' – she wanted to say 'spoiled',

45

but congratulated herself on being tactful – 'as
yourself.'

'Please,' said Tom, 'when are the other children
coming here?'

Bella, having put a slice of bread before him, was
spreading beef dripping on it, with quick, vigorous
motions. That done, she demanded, 'What do you say,
now?'

'Thank you. When are – '

'As soon as it's possible to arrange, of course. I'd
hardly want to be separated any longer from my own
children! Don't you want that?' pointing to his bread
and dripping.

Tom obediently started eating, sorrowful and insecure. His thoughts being full of families and separation, he ventured at length to ask, 'When can I have a
letter from my Mama?'

'*I* can't tell you that.'

'Mary said Mama would send me one, when she gets
to New York.'

'Then that's when she'll send it.'

Tom considered the logic of this for a few moments.
'Can we go to the post office tomorrow?'

'Good heavens, you mustn't think Mrs Fraser can
get to New York that easily. She might have all sorts
of difficulties on the way.'

He thought about this too, uncertain whether he
should be worried on Mama's account.

'Mary took me there every day.'

'Well, Mary's not in charge of you now; I am.'

'So can we go there?'

Feeling her dignity would be compromised by
answering too freely, Bella pointed the breadknife at
him like an extended finger and exclaimed, 'Now
that's enough!'

But from the way he looked, even she could not

46

mistake his anxiety to do as he was told. Softening, she allowed him just one more concession.

'We'll see,' she said.

The coming reunion with her children was something Bella had mentioned several times. In fact, she really only looked forward to seeing one of them.

From the moment they entered the house, fetched by her from a nearby corn merchant's, where a waggoner from their village had set them down, it was clear that it was Robbie alone who was her darling.

It was also apparent that not only his mother, but his grandmother, in whose care he'd been, had habitually spoiled him. At nine years old he was a noisy, scowling, gluttonous child, several pounds too heavy for his age, with all his jacket buttons strained tight. Amy, on the other hand, was neglected and sly. In her desperation to be liked, she was all too ready to act as her elder brother's adoring slave.

'Say hello nicely, then.' This was said not to Bella's own children, but to Tom. Standing before them in the drawing room he was struck dumb with shyness and expectancy. The other children, giggling and pushing each other, stared back at him.

Robbie pointed and exclaimed, 'I'm not going to play with a baby!'

'We can't play with a baby!' parroted Amy. With a quick look at her brother for approval she added, 'He's too young for Robbie. And for me, too.'

'Never mind, Robbie darling,' said Bella. 'Why don't you let me give you your lunch? Then I'm sure you won't mind letting him tag along, if you want to explore your new home.'

Tom had been looking forward to showing them his favourite places to play and his most treasured toys. Meanwhile, at lunch he and Amy waited while Robbie finished a third helping of bread-and-butter pudding. With a belch whose loudness caused him to grin with pride, the older boy left the table without speaking. Tom followed him and Amy out of the kitchen, trying in vain to keep up.

The drawing room had little of interest to the two visiting children, since all it contained apart from furnishings was a number of books. Fraser's study had even less to offer, being locked. Frustrated, Robbie rattled the door handle, and Amy tried to kick as hard as he did at the door itself.

'Damn this!' he exclaimed. 'This is no good!'

'This is no good at all.'

Tom was too little to be anything but mystified at how freely they were going round his home, and jostling each other to handle everything they could. But as they peered round the door of his parents' bedroom his bewilderment turned to distress.

'God damn me!' said Robbie. 'These buggers were all right in here!' Tiptoeing in, he stared at the big canopied bed, and the walnut wardrobe the size of a sentry box. At his grandmother's cottage he, his sister and the old woman had all slept on the floor, on mattresses filled with straw.

Growing bolder, he advanced towards the tall cheval-glass that stood between the two windows. He huffed vigorously against the mirror, then stepped back to admire its misted surface. Rubbing it clear, he put his mouth up against it and blew a sustained raspberry, to shrieks of delight from Army.

Encouraged further by his daring, they both tried spitting a few times at the mirror. Then they decided to try out the bed, at first sitting on it and bouncing tentatively up and down. The likelihood of going unpunished was making them more unrestrained by the minute. Robbie yelped with exultation at this new entertainment.

'Get off, now – get off,' he instructed Amy, 'and I'll show you something. You watch this!' Dragging Sophy's dressing-table stool over to the bed, he tried it out as a springboard. First, by standing on it and jumping. Then, with a run-up across the room and a whoop of joy as his shabbily booted feet landed squarely in the middle of the eiderdown.

In the doorway Tom looked on amazed. Only on his best behaviour, and as a special treat, was he allowed to sit beside Mama in her and Papa's big bed. 'Don't,' he pleaded.

They ignored him.

'Don't! Don't!' cried Tom.

'Don't! Don't!' mimicked first Robbie, then Amy, as they bounced up and down on the bed.

At length they looked around for other fun. The wardrobe was the next most conspicuous thing, and they were soon burrowing to and fro behind Sophy's gowns with squeaks of delight and moans of pretend fear at being in the dark. Robbie, putting his foot through a hatbox, pulled out a ruined straw bonnet trimmed with blue ribbons, and tried it on in front of the mirror. 'Ooh! Ooh!' he exclaimed, affecting delight at his appearance and mincing about in a parody of Tom's mama.

Next to be pulled about and exclaimed at were the drawers of the tallboy. Tom's father's shirts were pushed to one side, as uninteresting. But Sophy's things were fascinating.

'Hey! Hey – look at me! – look at me!'

'Look at this, then; look – '

On to the floor tumbled petticoats, stockings, garters, gloves, nightcaps, and a cashmere shawl that had been thought too valuable for Sophy to take with her. At all these Amy hooted with delight, brandishing them for her brother to look at.

Tom ran up to Robbie and hit him. Wailing with

49

rage, he tried to drag at the older boy's arm. Robbie ignored him, pushing him to one side as he went on rummaging through the tallboy in search of one particular thing.

Finding it, he shrieked with triumph and waved it aloft. It was a pair of stays, stiffened with whalebone and cut low in back and front.

'Let me – let me!' Carried away by his delight, Amy tried to wrest the garment from him.

'Get *off*!' he cried. There was a sound of fabric tearing.

At that moment Bella came into the room. Tom shrank back. If she was cross when one tried to be good, how much worse her anger must be when it was deserved.

'Oh, but you're wicked, you children!'

As Bella glanced nervously at the wreckage about them, there was no mistaking the forgiveness in her voice. Already she had grown afraid of her boisterous son, whose self-satisfaction could so quickly change to sullenness. He despised her fear – but all she could do, in the hope of being liked, was to spoil him even more.

Amy hung her head. But Robbie, to test his mother yet further, reached into a drawer with exaggerated furtiveness and snatched up a lace handkerchief. Seeing her take no apparent notice, he thrust the handkerchief at Amy, grinning and miming secrecy.

Amy eyed her mother anxiously and pushed away his fist. Bella, in order to ignore them both, snapped at Amy to clear up the room, before they went to play outside in the street. 'And then – just today, mind – you can take this,' holding out a sixpence for Robbie to seize with the hand that wasn't clutching Sophy's handkerchief behind his back, 'and buy yourselves something from the cakeshop.' Her words were meant to be firm, but her tone was thick with appeasement.

50

In a dutiful little voice, Tom, standing ignored behind her, said, 'Thank you.'

'You needn't think *you're* going anywhere!' Instinctively she tried to compensate for her weakness by a show of being firm with her new charge. '*You're* going to bed. Right now!'

'But I haven't done anything!' cried the child.

Bella evidently felt this was no reason why she should be seen to falter. 'I don't care if you didn't. You're not old enough to go into the street on your own. And if you don't go to bed right now you'll get tired.'

Tom obediently turned away, to clamber up the stairs to his nursery. But Bella had not finished with him. 'And,' she'd started to say, '*And*' – showing by her tone what she thought of his rudeness – 'I hope you weren't trying to tell tales against anyone. I don't allow that kind of thing in this house.'

The child stared at her with a new expression. For the first time, he knew what it was to feel justified rage against an adult. The shock of it left him dumb.

Even Bella must have guessed what was in his mind. Quickly, to avoid him answering back in front of Robbie, she said, 'And, in any case, I do *not* – ' fixing Tom with her eye – 'I don't *ever* – have favourites.' And hurried to get out of sight while her dignity was still intact.

Behind her back, Amy smirked and Robbie tittered out loud. But, unless you counted Tom, it was a victory for everyone. Only for Robbie was there a small disappointment: he'd got his way without having to fight for it. To compensate himself, he put Sophy's handkerchief in his trouser pocket and then slipped back to the dressing table. Quickly and quietly he pulled open a drawer, and helped himself at random to a necklace strung with cornelian and gold beads. Strolling back across the room past Tom, with a show of indifference to the child he put the necklace in his pocket too.

With his face reddened and quivering from tears, Tom watched Robbie depart. Then, alone on the landing, he raised his voice and wept as loudly as he knew how.

When Bella reappeared, to shout at him for not having gone upstairs, he threw the first outright tantrum of his life. At first, seeing his features turn corded with veins and mottled like an old man's, she tried smacking him. Then, as his screams woke an answering rage in her, she tried hitting him harder. Only when this had made him yet worse, so that he turned blue and seemed to have stopped breathing, was she frightened enough to humour him. So that by the time he was tucked into bed, both of them subdued and trembling, Bella was as anxious to please him as if he were her own son. Had Tom been older, much of his grief and anger would not have been so new to him, nor so terrifying. He would also have realized – did he but care – that he too had won a victory.

If Bella had had more sense, she would have kept her own children apart from Tom. Though he suffered no physical injury from them, they were quick to find ways of tormenting him. Above all, his repeated questions about news of his long-gone parents were not lost on them. As soon as any adult was out of earshot, it was Robbie's delight, with Amy at his back, to corner the child and intimidate him with tall stories of what had really become of his mama and papa.

One rainy day in June, when the streets had been turned unseasonably muddy, they'd had to pass the whole day by playing indoors. The older children were particularly restive in their search for entertainment. Back in the village there would have been no such

52

problem. Both were old enough for paid employment, whether at bird scaring, stone picking, or helping with the animals. But here, since they had to spend so much more time shut up indoors, their chief occupations centred on Tom himself, a fact that he learned to dread. On such days as this he would try to lurk in the basement, where the servants were likely to be at work and he could feel safe. Failing that, by being as quiet as he could, he would hope to play unnoticed in the drawing room, which Bella had usurped as her own.

But today they had once again been told to stay out of her way and play on the stairs or in the passage. The other children had gone off to confer on some game of their own, and Tom, standing alone at the window of the first-floor landing, was passing the time by huffing on one of the panes to fog it up, and drawing on it with his finger.

Suddenly he became aware of Amy standing behind him.

'We've got something for you,' she said, with a quick look at her brother. Robbie was standing at the bottom of the stairs, holding a paper of some sort.

Tom, not old enough to be completely distrustful of them, began to climb carefully down the stairs towards him, seizing hold of a banister support with each step he took.

'You've got to guess what it is,' said Robbie.

Tom went up to him and held out his hand, his face clear of everything except curiosity.

Robbie put both hands behind his back.

'But first you've got to guess what it is,' he said.

'It's part of the rules, isn't it?' said Amy.

'That's right. You can't play if you don't keep the rules.' Robbie twitched the paper just out of Tom's grasp.

'You said it was mine!'

Amy jeered. 'Robbie! He can't even tell what it is!'

'Don't you know writing when you see it?' said Robbie, holding the paper higher.

'Robbie! He can't even tell it's a letter!'

'What's the matter?' asked Robbie, keeping Tom off with his free hand. 'Don't you know your letters yet?' He had been angered to find that Tom, half a dozen years his junior, could already stumble through the alphabet nearly as far as he could himself.

'What's he waiting for?' said Amy. 'Do you think he doesn't want it?'

'I don't think he does!' Robbie said, dancing out of reach. 'He wants us to keep it!'

'He wants us to keep it, and tear it into pieces!'

Distraught, Tom ran at the older boy. Robbie and Amy scurried, laughing, into the dining room. Tom heard them whispering, as they held the door fast from inside.

'It's from your mama!' yelled Robbie.

'It's from Mama! Crybaby!'

'Come and get it, if you want it!'

'For heaven's sake, boy, what is it now?' said Bella, as Tom ran into the drawing room.

Standing before her was Cook, to whom she was giving the next day's orders. Like Mary before her, Bella also held the job of housekeeper.

Tom was still little enough to identify people from the knees down. He answered without raising his eyes to look her in the face.

'Robbie said what?'

Bella's tone was as stiff as her posture, but Tom was too desperate not to speak on, however much his voice trembled. The cook looked away. She was a young woman who looked middle-aged and whose sympathy with children had run short long before she'd finished raising a houseful of her own brothers and sisters.

'*What* did Robbie tell you?' asked Bella, full of her own reasonableness.

Tom, about to reply, looked up at her —

And was speechless. For a moment he stared, not believing what he saw. The voice was hers, right down to the false gentility with which she struggled to pronounce 'what' beginning with an 'h'. But silhouetted against the tall drawing room window sat — his Mama!

'Tom, if you've come in here to tell me something, it's not polite to keep Cook and I waiting.'

Gazing at her, the child darted out his hand to point; looked doubtful; then, more or less understanding, repeated, 'Mama! Mama! Mama!'

It was partly an explanation to himself, and partly wishful thinking. The face, too, was Bella's. But some of what she wore had been familiar to Tom since before he could remember. The woman before him *was* Bella, whom he feared and whom he was learning to hate. And yet she was also his adored Mama.

Cook, speaking in an undertone, as if Bella would hear but not Tom, confided, 'It's that lacy cap, I dare say. That and the shawl.'

Bella, with a look of roguishness, said, 'Well, good heavens, what if some of these things do get an airing? She's not going to know, is she?' Carefully she smoothed Sophy's shawl and added, 'Wherever the poor woman is now.'

'Mama,' repeated Tom, as if saying her name would mean it really was Sophy by whose chair he stood.

'Yes, well, for the time being your Mama's things are on loan,' said Bella firmly. ' — What is it, darling?'

In the doorway Robbie and Amy were watching, bright-eyed with the effort of keeping quiet.

'He's got my letter,' exclaimed Tom, pointing.

'Tom, I wasn't talking to you. Robbie dear, what letter does the child mean?'

Robbie, glowering and satisfied with himself, said nothing. At length Bella had to fill the silence for him.

'Are you making up tales again?' she demanded, turning to Tom.

He hesitated. The injustice of 'again' confused him. From the day of Robbie's arrival he'd been far too wary of the older boy to risk denouncing him.

Before Tom could speak, Robbie, backing off in readiness to retreat, tossed the piece of paper on to the floor. He fled, followed in high excitement by Amy.

Tom picked up the paper. Going up to Bella, he held it out. He said, 'Please, Bella, will you read my letter to me?'

'It can't be a letter,' said Bella patiently, 'because I haven't been to the post office.' She leaned forward and spoke slowly, as though he were learning to lipread. 'To get a letter you have to go and fetch it.'

He went on looking at her, expecting some further explanation.

'Well, give it me, then!' She held out her hand.

Tom, bewildered, hesitated.

'Come on,' she added, more crisply. 'Give it me, if you're going to.'

He handed over the paper without taking his eyes off her. She'd deceived him, by wearing Mama's clothes. But if only, by reading him the letter, she would speak with his mother's voice – why, then he would forgive even that.

Bella unfolded the paper as boldly as if shaking out a bedsheet. She was only half literate herself, and her face showed a mixture of uncertainty and self-importance. Taking opposite corners of the paper in a daintily pincered forefinger and thumb, she held it up close to his face for several moments. First one blank side, then another.

'You see? I told you it couldn't be a letter. You know, Tom, when I tell you something is true, it's your duty to believe what I say.'

* * *

56

With reminders like this, Tom was unlikely to grow forgetful of his parents. It was now half a year since Sophy had sailed for New York, and even in the servants' quarters of the house in Castle Street there had been talk of the outbreak of war with the country for which she had been bound.

None of them could think to afford a newspaper, even though in Liverpool all the news was two days older than in London itself. Nonetheless Robbie's favourite new game – after showing his disdain for Bella by thieving from among her things – was playing at the war with America. This, with much sallying across the border that he imagined to exist between the United States and Britain, had at first involved Tom, usually as a sneaky American prisoner. Tom's role, supposedly, was to try and break free, so that Robbie could then tie him up in the coal cellar and leave him there till he said he was sorry. He was quickly left out of the older children's games, after a tearful refusal to make even the faintest attempt at escape.

Such exclusion, only a short time before, would have had him beside himself with grief. Now, however, he was merely relieved at being left alone, to play in the attic or the passageways in merciful solitude.

High summer had come, and Bella, mindful that she should expect news of her sister's confinement, walked out one day to the post office. She returned with the news that Mary, after three days' labour, had suffered the still-birth of a little girl, but might yet survive herself.

Bella's response was melancholy but sage. 'You can't deny she's had a hand in what happened,' she informed Cook. 'Though I must say, to get news like that, I'd rather not have paid out quite so many shillings.'

In its way, her moralizing tone even had an effect on her children. 'Aunt Mary can't have liked you,' whispered Amy to Tom, 'or she'd still be living here. And if your parents cared about you, they wouldn't have gone away either. Ma says she thinks they're both going to die in America, the same as Aunt Mary is likely to die.'

Amy's own home life had grown harsher, after her mother had become a widow. It was possible too that at second hand she had sensed the disapproval of Bella's employers towards Sophy's choice of husband.

A few weeks earlier Tom might have responded to such calculated torment as this by throwing himself face down on the floor and howling until he was too wretched and shaken to stand up again. But now he just stared back at Amy, with the vacant expression small children have when taking in every word, and spent the rest of that afternoon looking more subdued than ever.

Towards supper time he was playing alone in his nursery. He had set out the toy fort, with all his soldiers in formation, and was trying to pretend that everything was at least as it had been before Mary had gone away.

Robbie appeared in the doorway, followed by his sister.

'She' – this was how Robbie referred to his mother – 'says you're to let us play.'

Tom knew he had no choice but to let them handle whatever toy took their fancy. He looked up, and waited to be told what his part would be in their game.

But immediate cooperation was not what Robbie had come for. He waited until Tom had been silent long enough to give him the cue he wanted.

'If you won't say we can play with you, then you can't have the letter from your mama.'

Tom, hearing this deception for a second time, was

too distressed to stand up and fight. He seemed to shrink where he sat, and tears welled up in his eyes.

'This one's got writing on,' volunteered Amy. Her voice was urgent in its sincerity. Loyalty to her brother made her genuinely anxious to be believed.

'I'll go and tell *her*, if you call me a liar,' said Robbie.

In his hand, this time, he did have something that might be a letter. With a calculated look at Tom, he let it fall to the floor.

Tom, still young enough to move sometimes like a toddler, put his hands and feet to the floor so that his bottom stuck up, and stood upright. Going to where the paper lay, he picked it up.

He turned it over and over, slowly, frustration swelling within him.

Before mastering any other spellings, he had been shown how to read and write his own name. So he could see well enough that on the outside of what he held were included the words 'To Master Thomas James Fraser'.

Amy glanced at her brother, then snatched the letter back. 'Can't he read, then?' she asked, pleased at her question.

'We'll have to help him.'

Tom looked from one to the other of them, uncertain whether to feel hope or fear.

With a look of officiousness that he fancied was thoroughly grown-up, Robbie found out at length how to open the letter.

'"My dear darling, dearest, darling boy".'

Tom held his breath and gazed at Robbie.

'No – "My dear, dearest, darling, *nice* dear little boy".'

'No – no – let me – ' cried Amy, trying to wrest the letter away. Without looking closely at it she recited, '"My dearest, dear, darling, nice, fat-face little boy".'

They laughed until their own merriment made them

59

totter. Robbie read on, affecting a feminine falsetto. '"I am living in a big new house on a street in America now, and I think I will stay there. Now I think about it some more, I think I will stay there for ever and never come home".'

He paused, and looked more closely at the letter, which he had discovered among his mother's things. It was written in a clear, careful hand, such as a grown-up might use for the benefit of a child who was just learning to read. Thus there were words, and even the odd phrase, that he could in fact understand. He mouthed a few syllables experimentally under his breath.

Amy edged up and looked over his elbow. Some of the letter she could follow more readily than her brother did. Comprehending a whole line from the second paragraph, she read aloud, '"The news that I am soon to have".'

'What?' asked Robbie. 'Where's that? What was that you said?'

They murmured together, conferring.

'There. That's where it says that.'

'There? What of it? That doesn't make no sense, that does.'

'It does!'

'It does not, you dumb sow.'

Amy tittered nervously at her brother's wit. 'It does make sense. Look right there,' pointing to the next line. She grasped the paper and read in a loud voice, as if reciting to a public assembly, '"A baby brother or sister for you".'

Robbie, feeling upstaged, pushed her aside. Holding the letter at both arms' length in the posture of a town crier he proclaimed, '"I have had a baby brother and sister for you, but because this means there will be too many of us I am going to live in America for ever until I die in the war. With love from Mrs Fraser".'

He held out the letter to Tom. 'If you don't believe us, read it yourself!' Tom was too distressed to do anything but stare at him, aghast. Impatient at this lack of response, Robbie added, 'It says your father's dead already in the war. He must be dead or there'd be two names written down at the bottom. He was killed,' pausing for inspiration, 'in an attack on a fort. Like this – ' Darting to the open toy-cupboard he picked up a cricket ball, then drew back his fist until it was level with his shoulder. 'Bam!' he exclaimed, and smashed the ball down on to a drilled square of toy soldiers.

'Stop it! You stop it!' yelled Tom.

Robbie ignored him. 'Pow! The cannon ball has killed them all. Dead! Dead!' – stamping on them and kicking them about – 'All smashed to pieces and bloody. All bloody smashed!'

The soldiers, which were made of painted lead, were strong enough to survive being dropped; but they were too finely made to resist being stepped on. Several dozen had their heads snapped off; others lost their base or an arm or leg.

Seeing this, Tom let forth a shrill scream and ran again at the other boy. Robbie had no trouble in holding him off with one hand, while using the other to continue his assault on the fort. 'And now the cannon balls are getting nearer – and they're falling – bam! – boom! – right in the enemy's fort!'

Tom, weeping noisily, scrabbled to retrieve some of the soldiers. Meanwhile Robbie, picking up the cricket ball, brought it down, hard enough to stone a rat to death, on the fort itself. There was a sharp crack as the hinged front was splintered and the little well, with all its winding gear and bucket, was reduced to matchwood.

'And the enemy are trying to stand up again,' shrilled Amy, kicking at the scattered soldiers to prevent Tom from salvaging them, 'but they're being too badly beaten!'

'And now our men have got into the fort. And our men are stopping the enemy from being unfair and hiding any provisions for themselves,' shouted Robbie as he took the sacks of birdseed that Sophy had sewn and hurled them across the room. '*And* they can't cheat any more by firing their cannon at our men. Because our men,' snatching up the model brass guns and putting them in his pocket, 'have captured them for themselves, our men have.'

Dodging Tom's upraised fists as the shrieking child tried to stop him, he climbed astride the wheeled horse and, with his toes just touching the floor, he propelled it towards the fort. 'Tah-rah-rah-rah! And now the cavalry have come! And they're going to crush the enemy. They're going to crush them completely! They're going to go . . . crash!'

The violence of his impact was wonderful.

The better to appreciate the damage, Robbie dismounted; and he and Amy stood before the wreckage of the fort, marvelling.

'Eh, look – look at that! That rack of guns is all busted! Just like that!'

'Ooh, Robbie! You broke down all that wall! Except that bit there – look!' In making the fort for his little son to play with later, to fashion it as strongly as possible Fraser had constructed the flight of stairs to the inside of the door, not by using glue, but by morticing them. This part of the parapet alone was still unbroken.

'That's nothing, that is!' And Robbie climbed on to the wooden horse once more, ready to back off for another attack.

But before he could get astride, Tom, a broken model soldier clutched in one hand, charged at him, wailing.

62

It should have been a futile gesture; but by chance the soldier's bayonet nicked Robbie on the scalp.

Blood sprang from the wound and trickled down his brow. Amy stared, fascinated – as her brother would have done if the injury had been someone else's.

As it was, Robbie was astonished when he put his hand to his face and it came away smeary with gore. A wail of dismay broke from him at the discovery that one side of his vision was momentarily bleared.

'Hey, Robbie. You've bled into one of your eyes. You have!'

Timidity was replaced by wrath, as Robbie found how little he was really hurt. 'All right, then,' he said, turning to Tom, in an imitation of grown-up deliberateness. 'All right! So you want a fight, do you?' Grim righteousness glinted in his eyes as he made as if to size up to the little boy. Tom, too enraged to feel fear, stood and howled.

'What in heaven's name is all this? For pity's sake! Robbie, dearest – what happened to you?' Bella, hurrying into the room to complain at the noise, changed in an instant from truculence to cooing sympathy at the sight of her bloodied offspring. 'You poor boy!' She circled him, awkward and anxious. The years of separation from her children had made her self-conscious as well as over-ready to please. 'What happened? Tell me, quickly.'

Robbie continued to glower at Tom. Amy looked at her mother, apprehensive. She feared Bella's disapproval almost as much as her brother despised it. Pointing at Tom, she said, 'He did it!' She tried to imitate Robbie's thunderous expression of disdain towards the hysterical child, then sneaked another look at her mother. She ventured, 'He broke the toys, too. Robbie tried to stop him, and he made Robbie all bloody.'

Bella's face fluctuated between anxiety for her boy

63

and concern at the room's disorder. 'Is this true?' she demanded of Amy.

The girl looked down, as if reluctant to mention such wickedness. 'You'd better not be deceiving me, my girl. I don't allow falsehoods in *my* house.' Bella habitually showed her daughter all the sternness she dared not direct at her son.

'He did! Ask Robbie!'

Bella threw a fierce look of compassion at her son. In her most uncompromising voice she asked Amy, 'Are you sure?'

'Of course I am!'

Amy's voice was thin and fraught. But the sight of blood had left Bella too indignant to notice.

'Because if I'm being misled – now stop that noise!' turning on Tom. 'Robbie, dear – Robbie, I insist – tell me what happened!'

The boy went on glaring at Tom without speaking. Bella felt forced to add, 'Is it true what your sister said? If it is, darling, just tell me; say "yes" or "no".'

'Of course it is!' snarled Robbie, without taking his eyes off Tom.

'Of course it's true!' echoed Amy, taking heart at her brother's support. 'Look – he's still got the toy he did it with, when he hurt Robbie's head.'

Tom feebly hurled the broken lead soldier at Robbie. With his face turned blindly upward he stood, shaking with sobs.

Bella bent down and picked the soldier up. 'Did you hit my son with this? Did you strike at my son?'

Every one of their faces showed disbelief at his wickedness.

'Did you?' she persisted. '*Did* you? – Now stop that noise and answer me, if you know what's good for you.'

The child struggled to draw enough breath, so that he could speak. All that came were convulsive gulps, as fresh sobs tore themselves from him. Bella smacked him hard across the face. 'Enough! I said, that's enough! I'll lock you up! I will. I'll shut you in a cupboard, if I have to.' Daunted by the child's lack of self-control, she was genuinely persuaded that this might be for his own good.

Tom was terrified. This was a punishment no one had even hinted at before. He sobbed faster, almost inaudibly, like a dog panting. His face turned from red to a blotchy pallor. The other children stared, to see how his eyes rolled up into his skull.

'I warned you,' muttered Bella. She too was breathing hard. Panic and rage combined to give her strength as she half carried, half dragged the child, by now rigid with hysteria, out of the room.

Up on the landing the two elder children were too excited to move or speak. They waited, avoiding each other's eyes, until, four flights below, a door was heard to shut, followed by the turning of a key.

Safe though they were from their mother's anger, they were still not inclined to go and torment Tom by baiting him through the coal-cellar door. In any case they knew, after listening at the keyhole, that there would be no further sport from him now. He was no longer enraged, but just weeping quietly from dread. They mimicked him briefly, for appearances' sake, then went off to play elsewhere, leaving him alone for the rest of the day.

If Bella had any doubts about locking him up, she showed them only indirectly. All through supper, and an extra hour of play in the drawing room, she was full of concern for the happiness of her own dear ones. Whatever it cost to be firm as well as just, she was determined that Tom should only be allowed to join the other children when he was properly quiet and cheerful. The candles were lit – nine o'clock came, then ten – and she could still tell, from down the

65

passageway, that he was neither of these things. By midnight no one was around to notice him, not crying, nor falling into scraps of wretched sleep, but wandering in his mind, as if from a fever. It was past daybreak before Bella came down and opened the door.

CHAPTER THREE

Kate was travelling in the best style these difficult times allowed. With a change of horses every ten miles, she need stop nowhere for more than a few minutes, night or day.

All she could think of was that she might arrive too late. On opening Sophy's letter, dated some weeks before in New York, she had left Richmond in no more time than it took to seal up a note for her husband and kiss the children goodbye. Her maid had taken ten minutes to pack, and the travelling carriage had been brought round with the coachman still in his shirtsleeves.

Joseph was away on business, arranging for shipments of oak to be rafted down the Susquehanna at short notice to a dockyard in Baltimore. He would be worried to the point of anger, for rumours of invasion by the British were talked of at every dinner table and street corner in the city. But to Kate such a threat was nothing compared to what might happen if she failed to reach New York by the end of the week.

Sophy's plight was urgent. Might it prove terrible? There was no way to tell, until after Kate could join her. It was desperate enough that Sophy, alone in a strange city, should be nearly nine months pregnant and about to run out of money. But where was Fraser?

Where was he? Before the outbreak of war had ruined trade by sea, he had achieved much. He had had to postpone trying the prototypes of his new vessel in some of the conditions he'd had in mind, especially the shoal-ridden waters of the Mississippi and Ohio rivers. Nonetheless the sea trials, from a purpose-built shipyard near the port of Norfolk, had been successful. Then, a month before Sophy had been due to reach New York, Fraser had sailed to join her – not reckoning that his ship was bound towards a horizon ringed with dangers.

Since then, nothing.

It had been dusk when Kate had departed, leaving astonished faces peeping from the hallway and the servants' quarters. Accompanied by her maid and two armed footmen, she had taken the road north from the city still wearing pearls and satin for a formal supper party she'd been due to attend. Just as everyone else was preparing for sleep, they left the last houses behind, and entered a countryside of utter darkness.

Brimming with helpless alertness, there was nothing Kate could do but sit and try to wear out her fears for Sophy by running them through her mind over and over again. The carriage toiled along, with the driver only able to see the atrocious road by the light of two feeble headlamps. At any other season the turnpike would have been axle-deep in mud. As it was, the great barge-like coach was jolted ceaselessly, over a surface of felled trees half submerged in dried-out mire.

Every so often the coachman would shout louder – 'Hey – hey – hey – tsst – yah!' – and they would be charging at a canter towards the foot of another hill. Three changes of horse into the night, Kate noticed that they were floundering up a long slope of road in silence. She realized that the driver, with the other servants outside, had fallen asleep. Towards dawn she too slept, her unconscious face turned sideways into the coach's upholstery and her cloud of dark hair loose about her elbows.

She was roused two changes later, on hearing her name spoken by her maid. It was still early, but already the light was sharp and the air was hot. They had stopped at a small town where the inn, like the highway itself, was full of unusual activity. The road here ran near the coast; and the war, which in Richmond was merely talked about, had filled the turnpike with militia and with military waggons and trains of artillery. There were even sightseers, gathered to stare at the fortifications going up above a nearby road to the sea.

Kate, light-headed from fatigue, took a hasty breakfast at the table that ran the length of the hotel dining room. The talk around her confirmed her suspicion: most other civilian traffic was bound in the opposite direction, south from the countryside around Washington. The city had been panicked by reports of a British naval squadron off the mouth of the Potomax.

At one point an open door revealed a group of military officers hastily conferring. One, in the uniform of an infantry lieutenant, was masked from head to heels with dust from the road as he stood at the elbow of a superior officer examining an unrolled map. The other officer, half undressed in chemise, silk stockings and pumps, had evidently just returned from a ball.

Kate rose and hastened back to the carriage. Already, feeling like a sleepwalker, she had the illusion of having travelled for days.

Another departure, to shouts of 'Go ahead!' from the ostlers holding the new horses; a great lurch as the carriage rejoined the road, and yet another stage. Once more their vehicle was bucketing along unsteadily like an elephant trying to shake its rider loose. More scattered wooden houses with their blinds down against the heat; more orchards. More cornfields as blisteringly bright as the sea itself, with the stumps of grubbed-out trees still showing above the crop like sinking hulls. More coppices; more exhausted, half-barren tobacco fields.

With each change of horses the contrast grew between the cleanness of the new team and the filthy exterior of the coach, which now looked like a giant dirt pie.

Topping a rise they came within sight of Chesapeake Bay. Outside a tavern a group of people stared towards the sea. One, looking like a well-to-do planter, watched from astride a grazing horse. Beside him stood a black servant in livery and bare feet. A young fiery-haired washerwoman ignored her two children squabbling in the dust as she too strained to see if any ships along the horizon might be marauders from Admiral Warren's blockade.

At sea the war might still lurk invisible. But on land, as Kate travelled further north, the signs grew more frequent. Some eastward roads were being hurriedly barricaded. Several had been blocked off with rows of earth-filled barrels, and the tops of trees with their branches lopped at a sharp angle. Others, where groups of citizens milled about in anxious inactivity, were closed off with makeshift piles of lumber and household effects. Kate saw chairs, tables, bureaux and a pianoforte with a jaggedly missing leg, all hastily pulled out into the road and heaped up. Along one stretch of several miles the road was so crowded with army waggons and their escort that the carriage had to leave the highway and be driven along the unpaved verge. They passed a field blackened in patches by a raiding party from a British vessel, who had set up false camp fires as a decoy. The field, from which a crop of wheat had been partly harvested, had been far more battered by crowds of excited onlookers than by the invaders.

Another dusk like bathing in warm milk. Then

70

another night in which it was impossible to distinguish the blackness inside the carriage from the darkness framed by its windows. An hour too early for the dawn, a red glimmer showed, above something that might have been either a forested horizon or a cloud. One league further on, their horses whickered at the whiff of scorching. Some distance across the darkened fields, a village had been raided and set alight. Every building in the settlement was on fire, including the church. From the highway all that could be heard was the creak and clinking of the carriage and its harness, and the night breeze in the roadside trees. The smoke was lit with an ugly glow, and the church's wooden steeple was a hundred-foot pinnacle of flame.

At the next inn, still in the lifeless hour before the first light, there were few people about. Looking from doorways or pausing while leading out the horses, all seemed intent on some other calamity further north. Kate, as she climbed from the coach with the door held open for her, looked out into the night. At first, nothing. Then, a sound – so faint that one might almost have willed oneself to hear it. An echo of something, perhaps, in the form of a continuous booming. The wind must have shifted; for suddenly it could be recognized: the steady, rolling sound of cannon fire, distorted by miles of shoreline and jumbled countryside.

They drove towards it, as the world began to dissolve into shapes and then colour. At a fork in the road, beyond a ford with a wooden footbridge, the coachman called to his team and pulled up. With no other sound but the snorting of the horses and the daybreak's first birdsong, the guns sounded much closer. The river, the surrounding woods and the horses all steamed.

Kate let down the window and leaned out.

'Shall I go on, ma'am?' asked the coachman, indicating with his whip the northward road. There was a smell of burning. It was hard to tell how much of the mist in the hollow where they stood was really smoke.

Kate tried to look uninterested in the sound of gunfire. In fact she hadn't felt as suffocated by fright since the first time she'd been about to give birth. 'We are civilians. And we can hardly be taken for spies. Drive on; and if there is evidence of danger, we shall stop.'

As the sun rose on the third day of their journey the clamour of artillery had ceased. They came within view of the skirmishing ground to find it deserted. On the far side of a valley of maize fields and scuffed pastures a thirty-acre stand of corn had been set afire by a spark from one of the guns. The hillside bore a triangular smear of incineration, down to where the flames had faltered among the tussocks of a patch of marshland by a shallow stream. A charred post and rail fence had been burned away at one point. Nearby was something that looked like a scorched tree stump, on its side with all the branches pointing up and outwards together. Closer to, it was recognizable as the carcass of a horse. One or two hillocks like split sacks of coal must have been men. Their corpses, with the ground on which they lay, were shaven bare by the fire. The morning mist was waist deep about the stream, so that nearby cattle looked half submerged, like swimmers. Above the field rose a column of thin smoke. It bore sooty particles of leaves, straw, flesh, horsehair and polished harness up into a brilliant sky.

Otherwise the little valley was as peaceful as ever.

Kate called to the coachman to drive on, and sat back again, having raised the window against the smell of burning. Think of it this way, she told herself. Quite apart from Sophy's urgent need of help, it would not do to come to harm: her sister-in-law Euphemia would be too pleased.

One of the reasons Kate had left so hurriedly had

been the risk of having to explain herself to Euphemia. She could imagine every word.

'You can't take that carriage. What if it's the one Joseph wants to use when he returns?'

Or, 'Surely you don't propose to travel without stopping. It will be the Sabbath before you reach where you say you're going.'

Joseph himself habitually travelled on any day of the week he pleased. But from the first hour of her arrival from England Kate had learned that the rest of the world offended Euphemia precisely in proportion as her adored brother was supposed to be without fault.

At least under Euphemia's supervision both the children would be well cared for. In the eyes of their aunt, little Harriet, as Joseph's firstborn, and baby Henry, as his only son, were infant gods. On one occasion in the nursery she had been seen gazing down at something on the floor with such bright intentness, like an aggressive Madonna, that Joseph had instinctively stepped forward to share her admiration – only to find nothing more than one of his son's dirty diapers. Not even her brother's clear, heartless laughter had made Euphemia see the joke.

The truth of it was that no wife would have been thought good enough for ugly Euphemia's handsome elder brother.

Kate grimaced, remembering another incident. She and Euphemia had paid an afternoon visit to one of Joseph's numberless family connections: an aunt of his deceased mother. She lived alone on another of the city's hilltops in a mansion unchanged since before the Revolution, all bare walls and polished floors and unfashionable colonial furniture. The little group of women were sitting out in the cool beneath the dignified housefront. Harriet had clambered up on to Kate's lap; and the nursemaid had carried the new baby out on to the verandah for everyone to admire. With a rare smile of self-forgetfulness the old lady had leaned over the infant and said, 'And which of our fine-looking parents do *we* resemble, eh?' She looked up at Euphemia, in whose lap little Henry lay with his tiny features screwed up against the outdoor light, and added, 'Which one do you think?'

The question was a mere formality. Like his sister, the baby already had Joseph's chestnut curls as well as his merry brown eyes, and showed hardly a trace of their pale, dark-haired mother. But Euphemia, stiff in a purple and turquoise silk gown whose brightness was meant to offset her big nose and chin, hesitated.

Kate knew that look. It was one of reluctance in having to admit that it had taken two parents to breed Joseph's children. In some part of Euphemia's imagination she surely saw both babies as the work of no one but their father.

'I shouldn't care to say.' With her great-aunt's eyes still on her, Euphemia blushed angrily and concentrated on tracing a pattern on the floor with the toe of her shoe.

The aunt, who took everyone straightforwardly, looked in puzzlement at her overdressed niece. 'Why, how should that be? I'll allow he doesn't feature his mama so very – '

'Then my opinion is not needed!'

There was a general ripple of surprise. Like many short-tempered people, Euphemia had a high opinion of her own correctness. Nobody present could recall ever hearing her interrupt one of her elders. In a tight voice she added, 'If it's obvious, I should have thought there was no need to ask such a thing.'

Such scenes had happened several times. In the discomfort of the carriage, Kate, thinking about them and about Euphemia's chilliness towards herself, could almost believe she was better off where she was now . . .

The British raiding party had not retreated after the battle in the cornfield. Ahead, a group of villagers had gathered to stare at something by the roadside. A black field hand was kicking a dog away as the creature tried to sniff at it. It was a corpse, the body of a red-coated soldier who, in the thick, unfamiliar heat, had died on the march from exhaustion. Like all his comrades he'd been carrying a forty-pound pack, a rifle and ramrod, and eighty pounds of ammunition. Over the next few days his equipment and clothing would quietly disappear, an item at a time. Already he was mainly visible as a pair of bare feet sticking upward from a ditch.

A short way on there was evidence of another British loss. A group of cheering lads and children were chasing a loose cavalry horse. In the last night's fighting his rider had been smacked to the ground by a cannon ball, one shoulder struck away and part of a lung exposed; and then accidentally burned to death when the cornfield caught fire. The wounded man must at first have tried to cling to his steed, for the bridle had a snapped rein trailing loose. Meanwhile the horse cantered to and fro, an empty scabbard banging against the bloodstained saddlecloth. Overtaken by the carriage, he trotted alongside for half a mile, wheeling off when they passed a cart going the other way to amble aimlessly back the way he had come.

Hours more passed, towards another night. A landscape of streets without buildings, and fields containing nothing but weeds and the odd grand classical building, turned out to have been the city of Washington.

On the dusty Philadelphia turnpike the heat was so damp one could feel it against the back of one's mouth. Kate, bareheaded and unveiled within the privacy of the coach, could taste the dirt of the road on her teeth. Below the flowing hem of her dress the uppers of her shoes showed a sweat stain in the shape of each foot,

75

with every toe visible. The inside of the carriage was as hot as if its leather upholstery were still the hide of a living, fly-tormented beast of the field. Kate sat, her palms braced against the seat and her head hanging to lessen the impact of each jolt. Eyes closed, she dreamed of coolness and wondered what dangers lurked astride the highway further north.

As the day dwindled, the breeze was no longer hot enough to make anyone seek shelter from it. The road led through fields of maize, across a shallow slope above a creek. The waters of the creek were blackened by flocks of canvas-back ducks, so that it looked, under the setting sun, like a river of glinting tar. At the entrance to a roofed wooden bridge they were stopped by soldiers. A waggonload of sawn pine and a drove of cattle had also been held up. The mules pulling the waggon each rested a crooked hind foot, and the cattle, straying all across the highway, tried to graze. The sergeant in charge of the soldiers, and a couple of herdsmen, were standing beneath the entrance to the bridge, watching something in the arch of light at the far end. Below, the creek brimmed with mellow radiance. Apart from the splash and squawk of a waterfowl and the sound of cattle tearing up mouthfuls of grass there was silence.

At the end of a minute the group of men stirred and went about their business. The timber waggon heaved into motion like a house that has learned to creep. Inside the bridge the cattle made a noise like heavy rain as they pattered along its timber floor. It took the carriage some while to cross, edging through the darkness a few yards at a time. At length the walls lightened and the din of their wheels grew less.

Kate was leaning out of the window as they emerged into the late sunlight. She felt a tall shadow cross her face. Having half overheard a remark from the sergeant to her coachman, she was not quite unprepared for what she saw. Even so, she was hard put not to exclaim.

Two roads led out from the bridge. From a tree that stood on a patch of scuffed ground between them, a man had just been hanged. It was clear that he had been executed as a spy. Not only was his death the work of soldiers; instead of being cut down, his corpse was to be preserved, and left there as a public warning. A group of militia were at work on him even now. One was holding the man's feet to keep them from twitching. Another was busy with a long-handled tar brush. The hot tar steamed in the bright evening light, so that as the man was pulled and twisted this way and that by the soldiers he was enveloped in a golden vapour.

His back was towards the road as the carriage passed, so that his face, laid along one shoulder, could only be guessed at. There was no reason, so many miles from home, that this should have been anyone Kate had known. Nonetheless she could not help looking. Part of him had not yet been tarred, and she noted a head of thinning black hair. Yes; a stranger.

Kate sank back into her seat, suddenly fatigued beyond all measure. She sighed and leaned her head into a corner of the coach. The present was frightening; the immediate future, too, made her shrink with apprehension. She could not wait to reach her destination – yet she could scarcely bear to think what she might find if she were late in reaching her sister, at the disquietingly shabby address that Sophy had given, in the little Dutch city at the end of New York island.

CHAPTER FOUR

Sophy had waited too long for her husband.

She hadn't admitted it to herself at first. Fraser had told her to stay at a particular address on Broadway, there to await his arrival. If he were not in New York already, then allowing for contrary winds he'd expected to disembark from Virginia in late July. It was now the second week in August, and over the last few days Sophy's stock of money had been halved, then rapidly halved again.

A time came when she knew she must part with her jewellery and all her good clothes. It was not such a hard thing to do – once Fraser arrived, he could easily afford to redeem them, or buy replacements. Only a few items made her sigh, as she handed them across the counter of a nearby pawnshop. One muslin gown with gold embroideries had been bought for her by him on the day she told him she was carrying Tom, their firstborn. She remembered putting it on for the first time, for the dinner celebrating Kate's engagement to Joseph; never had she felt so confident of the long, happy future that she and Fraser were to share. Sophy could not help looking thoughtful, too, while parting with her pocket watch. Its case was gold, engraved with a pattern of columbines, and its figures were set in a dial of rose and amethyst enamel. Her father had given it to her, shortly before he'd died.

Coming back out into the street, she had encountered her landlady – so suddenly that she'd had to step aside to avoid the spokes of the other woman's open parasol. The landlady, a stooped, energetic woman who looked older than she was, inclined her head in greeting and walked on. Only later did she give any sign of having seen one of her paying guests at a pawnshop. After supper, as Sophy, with the slowness of advanced pregnancy, was leaving the hotel dining room, the landlady came up to her.

'A word with you, Mrs Fraser, if you will.'

As the other guests made their way past them she lowered her voice. 'I don't recall, madam, when you said your time was due.'

'The baby is expected in four weeks.' Faced with climbing the stairs to her room, Sophy was glad to stand still.

'Well – ' said the landlady, with purpose in her voice, 'you'll want to be moving soon to somewhere more suitable, will you not?'

'My husband arranged that we should meet here.' It was hard, in this heavy late-summer heat, to speak patiently to anyone. Sophy tried to pick her words carefully. 'It was on his recommendation that I chose to patronize this hotel.'

'Yes, well, I'm very appreciative of that, and very grateful. But now, since your husband was already expected here a week since, I'm sure you'll be thinking of moving to an address more suited to your coming confinement.'

Sophy knew well enough that there was no such place. She could give birth at a decent lodging, where a capable doctor would be prepared to attend her – or she could throw away the child's chances of survival, and most likely her own, too, in the fearful squalor of a public hospital. Privately she reproached herself for her mistake. She should have taken care to conceal her lack of money, and taken her things to a pawnshop somewhere on the other side of the city.

79

The landlady watched her. 'Shall we say, by the day after tomorrow?'

Sophy made an effort to sound calm. 'I'm a stranger in this city; I have no acquaintance here.' Thank goodness a seaport town like New York was full of recent immigrants, who sounded as British as she did. Since the outbreak of war, there were rumours everywhere of spy scares. She said, 'I cannot risk going anywhere my husband may not find me.'

'Mrs Fraser, this establishment is perfectly competent to forward your mail. If, that is, you leave adequate instructions.'

Next day Sophy moved, to another boarding house where she could go on waiting at less expense. Not in a poor part of town — there was no reason to think things were that serious — but at a modest address on the Bowery, in a narrow house between a corn merchant and a printing works. Her new lodging would have been a depressing place, had she planned to stay for long — the wallpaper was torn, and the window looked down four storeys on to the premises of a cats'-meat vendor. But Sophy, though she took the precaution of writing to Kate, still hoped that Fraser might arrive at any instant.

That is, until another week had passed. Meanwhile the more concerned she became to hear news of his ship, the less she was able to find out. For it was now unthinkable that she should spend money on anything as expensive as a newspaper. Any information would have to come from hearsay, or from discarded newssheets several days old.

She took to walking each day to the waterfront at South Street, where Fraser's ship was due to berth, to see what new vessels might be in harbour. Also she began daily to eat only one meal, bought cheap from street vendors towards the end of their day's sales:

80

pickled egg and raw cabbage, or salt cod and stale bread.

One hot morning she put on her only remaining bonnet, its ribbons clammy with a varnish of stale sweat, and went out to look for some way of earning money. Her first attempt was in the dining room of a nearby hotel. The proprietor, who was busy breaking ice with a hammer, heard her out. He looked her over; then, pursing his lips, he shook his head and went on at his work without a word.

The next place she tried was a milliner's workshop in a basement on a neighbouring street. Two dozen women, mostly Irish immigrants, were at work behind an iron grill that protected their dirt-encrusted window from the wheels of passing vehicles. Inside, the room was as hot and claustrophobic as the belly of Jonah's whale. Here too the woman in charge gave Sophy's state of pregnancy an appraising glance. 'Pardon me,' she said, 'but I'm sure you'll understand. You see . . . we do only have work for several weeks at once. If you take my meaning.'

Sophy tried several similar places, all in vain. She understood too well why no one would give her even a day's work. On every major street one could see people newly arrived in the city. All of them were as poor and anxious as she was, and most of them had the advantage that they weren't about to give birth.

A few yards down the street from a private mansion whose housekeeper had just refused her employment, she sat down on the kerbside. She was breathless from having walked beyond her strength. A couple of pigs rooted near the hem of her dress, where a half-eaten pie nestled in a copy of last week's newspaper. The paper's main headline had nothing to do with Sophy. Yet she shuddered at it as though it held her fate in every word. 'Dreadful Calamity of Ship Wrecked in Storm Off Massachusetts Coast' it said, above an item about the foundering of a vessel out of Boston. Sophy had been at the quayside when the survivors had been brought ashore. The waiting relatives had greatly out-numbered them. Afterwards one, a girl holding a bewil-dered young child, had walked to and fro howling with grief, indifferent to anyone who might see or hear her.

From the entrance to a timber yard across the way, two prostitutes were watching Sophy. It was not safe for a female to loiter alone in the street, especially in the more prosperous thoroughfares, where the trade in women went forward so briskly. There flashed into her mind a memory of someone glimpsed in a London street who'd been as ragged as Sophy might soon be. Charity Michaelmas, the swineherdess from her own village of Cannings Fitzpayne. Where was she now, with her little girl who, Kate said, had looked so like their younger brother George?

A few dollars remained in Sophy's purse. She could think of nothing now but her final desperate plan to keep them, for when the baby was born. Back at her lodging she collected her remaining things into a bundle. She'd recently pawned her big leather bag, knowing that as she grew shabbier, she might be thought to have stolen it. Then, after a rest on the bed, meant to last ten minutes, but which became a dream-less two hours' sleep, she gave notice of her departure, and set out for the edge of town and the Manhattan countryside beyond.

Walking up Broadway, she passed her previous lodg-ing, in a suburban area of windmills and truck farms near Greenwich village. Soon the street opened out into a country road. She knew it was wise, being destitute, to fear everyone. Were there highwaymen here? Did the law punish vagrants? Trying not to look lost or aimless, she toiled on, and by the time dusk concealed the spires and orchards of the city, she was

82

five miles away, in a region of scattered farms and marshy woodland.

Sophy was too exhausted to feel hungry. She turned aside from the road, into a wheatfield broken by granite outcrops the size of a house. The corn had been partly harvested; around the base of each great rock the reapers' blades had left the ground looking as closely shaven as a man's face. The night air was so hot it felt like something to be eaten rather than breathed. Sophy made her way to the nearest boulder and lay down on the bare ground on the side hidden from the road. She fell asleep instantly, dreaming that the earth had closed over her like the waters of a pool.

She awoke next day beneath a humid sunrise. Beyond the neighbouring fields, and the fierce gleam of the river, the wooded New Jersey heights shone in the sun. The furthest distances were as clear as if painted on glass, and the foliage of the roadside trees glittered like tin.

'You can't stay here, you know.'

It was a woman who'd spoken, a fieldworker. A dozen other labouring people were coming into the field, bearing scythes and binding gear. The woman was evidently employed to tie and stook the loose corn. The skin of her arms was raised all over by thousands of tiny scratches, and her palms were as toughened as the underside of a horse's hoof.

'The farmer, he'll be riding this way soon.'

Sophy got to her feet and picked up her things without speaking.

'No – wait, now.' The woman fumbled in a bulging handkerchief containing her breakfast.

Taking the food thrust upon her, Sophy muttered her thanks and picked her way out of sight past the other harvesters. Looks of dumb curiosity followed her, and a couple of sniggers at her pregnancy and destitution.

83

She walked on. After a half-mile, the road looped round the head of a little wooded combe. Edging down through the trees she found a spring, where she drank, and washed her face and hands. Once she no longer felt parched, she was able to think of eating. The food she'd been given was two pieces of cornbread pressed together. Inside was a lump of bacon. Realizing that the woman must have given her the whole of her breakfast, Sophy felt her eyes stinging with tears of gratitude.

Eating slowly, she felt a little of her strength return. At the foot of a rock in a drift of dead leaves she lay down, careful to stay out of sight of passers-by on the road above. The hours drifted by. It was too hot for her to feel very hungry; and she was too tired to do more than drowse, or watch the leaves flap feebly on the branches above.

At sunset she was awakened by a shuffling sound. A couple of deer were at the spring, their tails twitching as they drank. Seeing her there, they leaped away as if at the noise of gunfire. Sophy eased herself to her feet and made her way up through the trees and back along the road to the newly deserted cornfield. The western hills, across the Hudson, were a dark silhouette; but facing away from the glow of twilight it was still possible to see almost as well as by day. Taking off her bonnet, Sophy hastily crammed it with ears of corn snatched from one of the stooks.

Back in the wood she lay down again on the ground to sleep. She was past all fear of such a place, on account either of other people or of wild beasts. So deeply did she fall asleep that later she noticed not a thing, as the darkness began to echo to a new sound. The noise of footsteps grew clearer, but Sophy just groaned, curled around her unborn child, and went on dreaming muddied dreams.

Meanwhile the road above her sleeping head

resounded to the march of unseen infantry: one-and-a-half thousand troops, going south to the defence of the city. By the light of waggon-lanterns and a clear night sky they trudged, their feet stirring puffs of moonlit dust in the rhythmic pace of near-exhaustion. Only when they had passed did Sophy start awake, at the silence they had left behind.

Next morning she forced herself to eat, rubbing the stolen ears of wheat between her palms to rid them of chaff. She could feel herself growing weaker, and at noon, when few people were likely to be about in such heat, she forced herself to go in search of some other food.

Luck was with her: not far along the highway was an orchard. A herd of pigs snoozed in the roadside shade, too overcome to go on snuffling for windfalls. The boy minding them was asleep too, curled up beside his wide-brimmed hat and a big stick.

Sophy furtively filled up her bonnet with fallen apples. In the shade of a nearby hayrick, she sat down and forced herself to eat nearly two pounds of the cidery, half-rotted fruit.

In this way she passed another three days. On the fourth morning she knew she must no longer stay where she might not be found. Taking her purse from where it was concealed among her clothing, she counted out five cents, before walking back along the road to the nearest farmhouse. There, she spent the money on a cup of milk and a slice of bread, to give her strength for the journey back to the city. The farmer's kitchenmaid let her eat and drink, and rest for a while, in the shade of one of the barns. Then she set out once more, for the south end of the island and the distant steeples of New York.

Partway there she had to rest again. Sitting by the road she took out from her bundle of possessions a pencil and a piece of paper. On it she wrote the names she had decided on for her child. If a girl, Harriet; if a boy, Edward George, after her brother, last heard of serving as a naval lieutenant in the Mediterranean. Addressing it to no one in particular, she also gave her own name, and that of her husband. She thought better of revealing her nationality, not knowing whether she or Fraser might be considered enemy aliens. Instead she described the child as her sister and brother-in-law's close relative, giving the address of Joseph's household in Richmond and promising a reward of several hundred dollars to whoever should restore the baby to its nearest kin.

Having done what she could for the infant in case she should die, while it lived, she concluded, 'And I pray for the blessing of our just Creator on whomsoever safeguards the life of this child, for whom I beg, before all other things, the rite of Christian baptism . . .'

She secured the note in a pocket. Then, having rested, and done what she could to look less dirty and dishevelled, she walked on. Fearing with every step to feel the first pangs of labour, she travelled slowly in the scorching evening sun. The country road became lined with grand villas, then disfigured by the odd brickfield. At length she was back among the stony streets of the town.

Even at nightfall the pavements were crowded. Amid rumours that the British had cut the roads to the south of New York, there were soldiers everywhere, quartered in the city itself, or waiting to be ferried across to the dockyard at Brooklyn.

By the time Sophy reached her lodging, just as the streetlamps were being lit, she felt jostled as well as footsore. In the blackness of the third-floor landing the first contractions took hold of her, suddenly, so that she had to kneel, grasping the bannisters, her head

86

thrown back. The pain was so great, it was as if the rest of the world no longer existed.

Then it faded, leaving her shuddering with relief. She got to her room, arranged it as well as she could for her coming ordeal, and lay down on the bed to wait stoically for the next bout of anguish to seize her.

It was then that she discovered her purse was missing.

Steaming like bonfires, the horses were led away, and the carriage was manhandled on to the deck of the ferry. It was bright morning. Amid the country quiet of the New Jersey shore, Kate was on the fifth day of her journey. Across the Hudson River the houses of New York City were hidden behind a tangle of ship's rigging along the waterfront. A cluster of church spires rose from the crowded streets, which reached inland half a mile from the seaward end of Manhattan island.

The little steam ferryboat was like a shallow box with a stove built into one end. So small was it, the heavy travelling carriage looked like an extra deck. There were a few market carts to be taken on board, and a number of foot travellers. Waiting to embark, people on deck raised their faces to catch the faint breeze coming off the ocean. Among folk who regularly made this journey there was a noise of general conversation.

Then the boat's unwieldy engine started cranking into action, so violently that everything close at hand looked blurred from the vibrations. The din, as they pushed out into the slight swell of the river, was like the interior of a forge.

Inside the carriage, its empty shafts resting on the deck, Kate had been feeling as dirty and tired as a carthorse. But now, dwelling on a half-understood snatch of talk that had been drowned out by the engine starting up, she forgot her discomfort. She leaned out of the window.

Her coachman, placed where he might obey any summons instantly, hurried up to her. 'Madam?'

'While the new horses are being put in, have a newspaper purchased.'

Coming ashore into the sunlit streets, Kate felt weak with dread as she waited for the newspaper to be handed up to her. It was brought; and she found the item that for hundreds of miles she had feared to see.

Through a muddle of streets where half the people seemed only to speak German or Italian the coachman finally got instructions to the narrow Dutch-gabled house whose address was on Sophy's letter.

A crowd of dirty children were playing on the steps and in the hall. Inside, one of the tenants, a woman with four more young children staring from the room behind her, told Kate where Sophy was likely to be. Nerving herself for whatever she might find, Kate set out to climb the stairs to the top of the house.

Inside Sophy's chamber the sun shone through a small window, so fiercely that the corners of the room seemed in darkness. There was a stink, both fishy and sweet, compounded of excrement and stale blood. The loudest noise was the buzz of flies.

Kate went towards the dim shape on the bed. For some reason, the possibility that she was approaching a corpse made her tread even more gingerly than in a sickroom. A floorboard creaked, making her flinch.

On the bed, Sophy lay with her eyes closed. There was a tiny baby in the crook of her arm, its red face creased with newness. Kate leaned over them, still holding the newspaper with its terrible announcement. Its ink, mingling with her sweat, had left purple stains on her white silk gloves.

They were sleeping. Kate gestured to her maid, who had followed her, breathless, up the stairs, and together they lifted the bloody sheet that covered the mother and child. Neither figure on the bed gave so much as a twitch.

It was hard to tell how many hours had passed since the baby, a boy, had been born. On Sophy's legs and belly, on the sheet, and on the nearby wall, the blood and other body fluids had dried some time since. The mattress was still sodden, as was the rug by the bed – it was only when she felt her hem dragging in the blood that Kate remembered she was still dressed for a formal occasion. There was even a dark crust around Sophy's mouth. It took a moment for Kate to connect this with the fact that the baby's cord had been severed: Sophy had had to use her teeth to separate herself from the child. The stump of the cord still protruded from his belly like a unicorn's horn. Dried gore crusted him all over and made spikes of his thin hair. Flies tried to settle on every opening of their bodies.

Kate pulled the sheet back over them, frowning with urgency as she pondered the best thing to do. Her fears, and her own experience of birthing, had actually prepared her for worse than this. Nonetheless, without the guidance of a doctor it was impossible to know what still endangered Sophy and her child. She motioned to her maid to come out on to the landing and gave a rapid series of instructions.

The maid hurried away. For the present Kate was helpless. She drew up a chair beside the bed and set herself to wait, still clutching the newspaper that told of Fraser's ship, and its disappearance at sea with all hands.

*　*　*

'What?' said Kate, later. She hadn't expected to hear a voice in that room.

Sophy spoke again, in a whisper. 'I know,' she said, moving her eyes to indicate the newspaper in Kate's hand. Her hair, straggling on the pillow, was so dirty no one could have guessed its true colour was fair.

'The people whose house this is — they told me, just before the baby came. They said I'd have to leave later today because they knew I wouldn't be able to pay them for the room . . .' She paused, welling with tears. Kate, guessing what she was about to say, took her hand and held it hard. Not in grief, but from anger.

'They said they knew I wouldn't be able to give them what I owed, because my husband was dead!'

They wept together. After some time, when Sophy had slept once more, and woken, there came a tap at the door. Thinking this might be the landlord or his wife, to whom she meant to speak her mind, Kate jumped up.

Sophy, from where she lay, could see no one. Her gaze rested on the tall smudge of soot above the little fireplace as she waited, expecting to hear the calm, hard voice Kate used when she was angry.

There were murmurs on the landing; then Kate returned.

Her face was bright with encouragement and hope.

'Mrs Fraser?' It was the voice of a man, introducing himself as a doctor. Kate, acting on what she knew of her husband's acquaintance in New York, had lost no time in finding out help.

Sophy was too weak to be aware of much. She noticed a very white shirt-frill, and a voice whose blend of authority and respect made her eyes swim with tears of relief.

'Are you able to answer some questions?' It was plain from the way he spoke that he already knew about the terrible thing announced by the newspaper.

90

Shortly afterwards, he pronounced her well enough to be moved. She found herself surrounded by other half-seen careful strangers, all speaking in lowered tones. Someone was wrapping her in a clean blanket. Then she was being lifted, the walls and ceilings of the house tilting and turning about her as she was carried downstairs through the stuffy dimness, in which each landing had its own smell of stale cooking. There was a splash of street noise and white light; then she was being lifted up into the hot interior of a carriage. The strangeness of knowing there was nothing more for her to say or do was like a drug.

And beside her, against Kate's shoulder, was the strangest, most unfamiliar sight of all: the alert, unfocused stare and wrinkled brow of baby Edward.

There was a short journey, during which the rumble of the carriage faded, then suddenly grew loud again, as by turns she dozed and started awake. Then there was more fierce sunlight; there were curious faces in the street, more dimness, and a broad staircase whose cornices seemed to revolve above her. She was aware of other voices, anxious with deference, as Kate gave more orders in a subdued voice, this time to some of the servants in their new lodging. Sophy was placed on a canopied bed, its sheets fragrant with cleanness, in a room whose shutters were closed against the heat.

Other attendants were introduced to her. A housekeeper, whose services, like those of the other staff, were rented with the house. Two nurses to care for her, turn and turn about. And for the baby, two nurserymaids, an under-nurserymaid, and a wet-nurse. Some of them Sophy perceived as a nearby shape or a rustle of stiff clothes; some as a face or a turn of speech. Mostly she noticed the chandelier in the middle of the room, done up in sheeting like a giant roosting bat. At some point two servants came in, quiet as cats, and the device was lowered for its covering to be taken away. She was washed in tepid water, feeling as if she were a kitten being pushed to and fro by its mother's tongue, and put into clean muslin nightclothes. Then there was food, and something to drink with chips of ice in it.

Throughout, her sister was someone Sophy had never seen before. Kate had left England as a quiet-spoken, self-possessed girl whom marriage had rescued from a mean existence as a governess. Since then, motherhood, a far country and mighty wealth had turned her into someone who looked not only calm, but invincible. Sophy watched as, shaken to the root by fatigue, Kate sat perfectly upright on a settee between two of the windows, her hands folded in her lap. One by one the upper servants of the house stood before her as she gave her orders unhesitatingly, like an actress in a well-rehearsed play.

Sophy wondered how much she herself might have changed in recent months.

At length the room was empty of all but the two of them. Kate kissed her, with a wan smile, and withdrew. The shutters had been opened, and there was a glimpse of tiled rooftops and a tree filled with evening light.

It was time to remember where she was, and what her future held.

'Tom,' she murmured.

The little boy's name, spoken aloud, loosed in her a storm of pity. She thought of his small soft body and his child's world of intense, private games, and a swell of feeling made her eyes smart and her breathing grow harsh. Sophy pressed her face into her pillow and wept as if she could never cease – at the bright, bland look of trust in the eyes of her new baby; from sorrow for her lost husband; and above all from tender-heartedness at the thought of Tom, with one parent gone for good and the other separated from him by an ocean of warring fleets. How could she have risked being parted from him for so long? And how many more months would pass before she could return?

Also Mary had promised a letter, which they'd told her today had not arrived.

As soon as she could stop up her sobs and wipe her scalded eyes Sophy reached out to ring for the nurse and send for writing things.

How was she to reach England, from what was now an enemy port? Tears of feebleness went on leaking from her as she lay back against her pillows and thought. The news of her husband's disappearance had filled her with obstinate purpose. To do nothing but mourn would be unbearable; instead, she must find her way back to Tom without delay.

But how? The whole world seemed in arms to prevent her. A sea passage to Canada would be impossible. And along the northern border of the United States, hostile armies skirmished and laid siege, in forests and on inland seas, across a front a thousand miles long. In the Atlantic, the British navy was being bloodied by American assaults, from the Virginia coast across to Africa. Nor was there a chance of reaching England via any European port. On the one hand the entire continent was held by the French; on the other it was cut off by a British blockade. Just over the western horizon, off the coasts of France and Spain, a thin line of King George's ships hung on, through tempests that sometimes lasted months.

But no matter. Whatever the dangers, she would find a way home.

She began to write, pouring all her best and strongest feelings into a message of reassurance.

'My darling Tom, it is not enough just to tell you in a letter how much I love you. I need to be back home, to show you properly how dear, how very very dear you are to me. I want to be at home with you in

England, so that I can be close by you and never pass even one more night away from you . . .'

Sophy said nothing about the disappearance of his father's ship. Probably the loss of one parent would make the child think his mother, too, might never return. Besides, poor Tom was too young and vulnerable to be given such news by letter. Sophy was also tactful enough to guess that by the time she was home his memory of his father might have paled. Please God, it would help to make his sorrow that much less.

Twelve hours later, and two hundred miles off Delaware Bay, a small group of men were being swept to the top of a long ocean swell, there to catch their first sight of that day's rising sun. The salt spray had long since made their beards and hair as stiff as rock. Each man's eyes were so sore that he felt as if his eyelids had already perished. Their mouths were swollen and split, caked with a line of dried blood.

Originally their boat had held more people. Five others, including two women and a boy of twelve, had so far perished, and been pitched overboard into a thrashing crowd of sharks. Even with some gone they were cramped. To stay afloat, they had to sit along the sides of the boat, each leaning forward to clasp the man opposite in a semi-embrace. No one knew how far they had drifted, or in which direction.

From the first day they were cast adrift, Fraser had been determined not to guess their chance of rescue. Watching his fellow survivors, he knew that the ones whose hopes had been the most insistent had been the first to despair and die. He himself had little hope. But still he felt the truth of every word of love he had written in his letter to Sophy. He also remembered that he had promised Tom he would come safely home. It was the thought of them that made him cling to life as steadfastly as anyone there. For Sophy and Tom, and as a matter of honour, he had decided that he would be the last to die.

The sun had risen and set some dozens of times more. In the house that Kate had taken for herself and Sophy at the southern end of Broadway, Sophy's sickbed now lay empty. The baby, Edward, was being walked up and down in his nursemaid's arms in the garden at the back of the house. The autumn sun, much cooler since a heavy rainstorm the previous night, shone through the leaves of a big elm tree. Edward had grown just old enough to smile, twisting his head from side to side in pleasure. Every time he glimpsed the tree, with the light caught in its branches and the breeze making it curtsey, he beamed ecstatically, as if at a friendly human face.

In the broad hallway, a pile of luggage was stacked for a journey of many weeks. Enough for Sophy, for the needs of little Edward, and for his nursemaid, a sixteen-year-old Irish orphan taking this chance of returning to her surviving relatives on their farm in County Wicklow. Kate, again acting through Joseph's business acquaintances, had secured a passage home for Sophy in two stages, via a neutral port. It had taken time. Not only had Sophy been slow to regain her usual shining good health. Kate had had to act initially through her husband's various branch offices, way out of town in other states. Only recently had New York become as important as the cities where his business was already established: Boston, Baltimore, Philadelphia.

At the big open window looking down from the drawing room on to the garden, Kate and Sophy were sitting, watching the movements of light and shade across the baby and his nurse. Kate wore a gown of heavy figured silk, in grey and lavender. On a chair

95

nearby lay her bonnet and parasol. Sophy, in black, was also dressed for travelling. Over the past weeks the sisters, always close, had re-established their habit of sharing every feeling and thought. Now, getting ready for another long separation, they were already halfway apart in spirit. Gazing down into the garden, they were both preoccupied with the first part of Sophy's immense journey. They spoke to each other only at intervals, without looking up, as they waited for the hour when she had to leave. She was bound for Africa, and the port of Tangier.

As the bright afternoon dwindled, baby Edward was brought indoors. The garden filled with shadow and the big drawing-room window was closed against the dusk. At last the carriage was announced, to take them to South Street and the waterfront.

After their departure, the roof of their vehicle burdened with boxes and trunks, the house suddenly became busier. Beds were stripped, floors were swept and shutters were closed and barred. In the drawing room, scroll-backed armchairs and claw-footed settees were shrouded over. Silver serving dishes were locked away, gilt-framed mirrors were covered, chandeliers were dust-sheeted once more. That evening, only Kate's bedchamber and the sitting room next to it were to have a fire lit and candles brought. Having waited until Sophy's ship was just a speck of lantern light beyond the busy waters of New York harbour, Kate herself was to return to the house for only one more night.

Meanwhile the carriage from which she watched was a long time on the quayside. Occasionally one of the horses would toss its head with a clatter of harness or rest a hind hoof, while the coachman sat, hunched and motionless. At length Kate gave the order to drive home.

Their journey was short, but slower than might have

been expected. There was much excitement throughout the city that evening, in dimly lit taverns and on dark thoroughfares. Within the hour the reason for it was in everyone's mouth. A fortnight earlier a New England merchantman, homeward bound to Boston from Martinique, had rescued a half-dozen shipwreck survivors, almost passing their boat without noticing it in a fierce squall of rain. Since the vessel that had been lost had been bound for New York, the merchantman was entering the harbour now, to put ashore the remaining crew members and one passenger.

And on its deck, his thick hair bleached almost white by weeks of sun, and his face scorched and furrowed by harsh weather, stood James Fraser in a borrowed coat. His expression was intent. Forgetful of every terrible thing he had suffered, and by turns anxious, then overwhelmed with hope, he was trying to will himself forward in time, to the moment when he could disembark, to be reunited with his wife.

CHAPTER FIVE

Even though he was thousands of miles away, Tom did sometimes hear of his parents.

'. . . she was alright to work for, though. It would save a deal of bother, for myself, if she does come back. I mean, not looking for any other position.'

The cook's words, spoken in a low voice to Bella, were just within earshot of the boy. He was alone at the kitchen table, his feet far above the floor, eating a corner of cold bubble-and-squeak that had been left for him. Nowadays he was kept almost entirely apart from the other children, having his meals separately and being made to find his own solitary amusements in one of the rooms at the top of the house, which was also where he now slept.

Originally, he had been made to leave his own comfortable bedroom, and avoid Amy and Robbie, as a punishment following his fight with Robbie over the smashed fort. Since then this arrangement, more or less by accident, had become a habit. One day Tom had asked Bella, with the steady look he now used when facing up to grown-ups, when he could have his old room back.

'When you're good,' she had said. In fact, she had no idea how she could persuade Robbie to give up Tom's room and several of its toys, which he had meanwhile taken as his own.

Once, Tom would have looked bewildered and held his tongue. Not any more.

'When will that be?' Answering back was almost the only human contact the lonely little boy now had.

'Good heavens, only you can answer that. Can't you?'

Meanwhile his Mama's latest letter, written the day his brother was born, had reached Liverpool, after a journey of only two months.

There, however, a few moments' walk from the house in Castle Street, it was held up.

And why not? There was no reason Bella knew of why she should traipse off to the post office every blessed day. Just in case the boy's parents were still alive, all that way from home. Or fool enough to try sending letters, when everyone knew there was a war going on.

One day Mary came back, walking up the street on a beautiful autumn morning with the lightness of good health newly recovered.

'Why, sister!' Bella exclaimed, coming out into the hall. 'I had no idea you could be so much better!' Her face was a mixture of welcome and dismay. With Mary returned, what of her own place in the household?

Mary was smiling with pleasure at being back. Above all she was looking forward to seeing Tom.

'Where is he – my little lad?'

'Oh, he'll be somewhere upstairs.' Bella was thinking that if she'd known her sister was coming back, there were some details of the house that she would have arranged differently.

Mary ran up the stairs with a look of expectation. Tom would be in the big playroom, where most of his toys were kept. She opened the door, ready to greet him.

There was dust everywhere. Tom's smashed fort had been swept up into a corner and left in pieces. The toy cupboard was open and its contents were strewn across the floor. Tom's big wooden pony on wheels had been knocked over and lay with one big painted eye staring patiently at the ceiling.

Mary, peering round the door, was puzzled, then anxious. She hastened to look in Tom's bedroom. It was a scene of squalor, the bed unmade and piles of clothes dropped on the floor. She was shocked to realize that not a thing in the room belonged to Tom himself.

There weren't many other places where she could look for him. With a suddenly quickened heart, she ran up the attic stairs. 'Tom?' she breathed, more to herself than to him. Not knowing why she was so uneasy, she peeped in at the nearest door.

The little boy didn't see her at first. He was kneeling on a chair by the deep dormer window, running a finger round the edge of one of the panes in apathetic silence. It felt colder in the room than out of doors. There was a rank smell of stale urine.

Mary had just a moment in which to hide her dismay before he turned and looked at her. His face had been framed in blond frilly curls when she had seen him last. It was paler now and someone had cropped his hair down to a stubble. He stared at her, as if not understanding.

'Oh, Tom!' she said, embracing him. 'It's me, dearest; I'm back. And soon your Mama will be home too. Back again, to take care of you herself, for good.'

Mary was not in a position to give Bella any hard words. Her own absence had been too much her fault. Besides, it was she who'd asked Bella to take her place.

But, shaken at Tom's neglect, she couldn't help making a few remarks.

'Oh, that,' Bella said, when Mary mentioned that

100

Tom's bed stank. 'Well, good gracious, the child had started wetting himself. He had to be corrected, didn't he? I told him he was perfectly free to have his sheets changed, just as soon as he stopped fouling them.'

'But, sister, why that little room?' Mary spoke mildly, full of guilt. 'And his hair used to be so beautiful.'

'Oh, it stands to reason the boy does better in that room. He can feel safely out of the way there. Since he's so quick to get into fights with my own little ones. And as for his hair, he had lice. It was disgusting, it was — if I hadn't taken him in hand properly, he might have passed it on to my son. Or the girl.'

Mary looked dismayed. 'And besides,' she added, the possibility only just occurring to her, 'you know, it mightn't have been just me, coming back. Mrs Fraser might not be able, like, to send us word. I mean, before she comes home herself.'

Bella said nothing, and both sisters looked thoughtful.

So a visit was made to the post office after all, and Bella came back with two letters. Both bore Tom's name, in a clear, careful hand.

'My, what a lucky little boy,' she told him. 'Two letters, then.'

'Nothing from Wiltshire?' Mary asked. Bella's return south was to be put off until she heard from Sophy's aunt, her employer.

'Oh, no. But that means I can pass more time with my own dear children. Now, Tom,' holding up the letters as if making a dog beg, 'do you want these?'

'Yes please,' said the boy in a little voice.

'"Yes please ma'am". And I've told you before not to stare back at me.'

'Come with me, Tom dear,' said Mary hastily. 'Bella' — with a glance at her sister — 'will have a fire lit in

101

your nursery, and I will help you read your Mama's letters up there.'

As punishment for some offence Tom hadn't quite understood, the playroom, like much of the rest of the house, had been put out of bounds. Mary, hearing this, had given orders for it to be swept and tidied, much more snappishly than was usual with her. Meanwhile, in the big chair by the fire, Tom was put on to her lap, and the letters, both of them from Sophy, were taken out to be read. Hearing her spell out the earlier one, written four months before in New York, his face kindled with interest for the first time since Mary's return.

Picking up the second letter, Mary looked at its envelope, frowned with surprise, examined it again, then exclaimed, 'Bless us, she's here in England!'

Seeing the boy's face turn up to her with a look of wonder, she collected herself. 'Why, Tom, isn't that good! Your mama – not three days from here, I dare say.'

The letter had been franked in Cornwall, at the port of Falmouth. It was there that Sophy had finally disembarked, after a vile, storm-battered journey north from the Mediterranean. Just crossing the Bay of Biscay had taken a fortnight. She had booked a seat in the early mail-coach, having paused only long enough to write ahead to Tom, and seize four hours' sleep.

The letter was read several times. By Mary, aloud to Tom; by her again, in private; and by Bella, standing halfway down the stairs to the kitchen with Mary anxiously looking on.

'But she might only be a few hours behind this,' Bella said, indicating the letter.

Both were thinking how they would prefer the house to look when Sophy arrived.

'She might have been here already, if she'd paid to go post.'

Sophy had still made no mention of her husband's disappearance. Neither Mary nor her sister had reason to think their mistress lacked for money.

Mary hesitated, then said, 'About your boy Robbie. I've meant to speak all along, you know. He should be packed up and made ready to go back to his grandmother's, this very day. He should, really; and so should his sister.'

Bella's look of harassment didn't escape her. Even Mary had guessed that she had less control over her own children than she might have. Mary added, 'I know you've not met Mrs Fraser. But' – lowering her voice – 'she can show a right temper if pushed the wrong way, never mind how easy she reads in her letters.' She stepped aside as she spoke, to make way for Hal, the footboy. Hal, overhearing, grinned to himself in agreement.

They were still in discussion when Robbie came in from the street with Amy. He shoved his way past, going to the kitchen to look for something extra to eat.

'Robbie darling,' said Bella, 'Mrs Fraser is due home at any time. You must be a good, generous boy and leave your room, and be ready to go home in the morning to your grandmama.'

The boy looked at her long enough to show that he had heard, and walked on without answering.

'Or else,' said Mary, quickly, while he was in earshot, 'you can have Hal see to it that you've left your room.' The footboy, because of his inferior position, had been bullied endlessly by Robbie. Bella herself had some idea of how badly Hal, who was fifteen and large for his age, yearned for an excuse to do him violent harm.

'Yes, darling,' she said bravely, 'we can always tell Hal to help you.'

⁎ ⁎ ⁎

So it was that as the Excelsior mail coach bore Sophy and half a dozen other exhausted passengers out of the darkness of the Lancashire countryside and into the tight little streets of Liverpool, her house was being made almost perfect. In the drawing room, lamps were ready, and a fire had been lit, to be met by dozens of reflections: from shining wall mirrors, spotless damask upholstery, and rosewood furniture smelling of new polish; from brass fire-irons, from crystal glasses, and from translucent porcelain carefully washed and dried by Bella herself. In the kitchen, amid the smell of cheap candles and roasting meat, a choice of supper dishes was in a state of near-readiness.

'Mary,' said Tom. They were in his mother's bedroom, where the sheets were being changed and warmed.

'Yes, my love?' Mary looked up, breathless from helping the under-housemaid tuck in a counterpane. She was relieved to see him come and speak to her. Even though he hadn't looked openly cheerful at the news of his mother's return, at least he appeared to be curious.

'What time will my mama be home?'

'Tonight, or early tomorrow, depending on how fast the horses can go.' He'd asked the same question twice before, so she tried to look especially patient and encouraging.

'When Mama is home, will Bella still be here?'

'Only for a few days, until she has a letter from your mama's aunt in Wiltshire.'

'Was it my mama who said Bella had to live here?'

Mary glanced in the direction of the maid, then dismissed her. 'No, dearest Tom. That was my fault.'

'So Mama didn't know Bella was here?' His mother, at least, should have meant him no harm.

'Not at first.' Kneeling down, she took the child in her arms. 'Tom, I know you've been unhappy while your mama has been away. But will you make me a promise?'

He nodded, staring up at her face.

'Promise me you won't tell your mama you've been miserable. It would make her – well – ' and here Mary had the decency to blush at her own deceit – 'she would be very unhappy – even more than you have been – if she found out.'

At ten minutes to midnight the Excelsior swayed into the yard of the Royal George Inn and put down its frowsy passengers. A salty wind shivered the chimes of the church clocks and beat clouds of dwindling coal-smoke back down from the rooftops. Above the pavements the lamps swayed, rocking huge shadows to and fro.

Sophy, in black, and followed by her servant and the porter pushing her luggage, walked up the empty street with the baby in her arms. As she hurried forward, hope, fear and regret swelled within her at the thought of all that she had risked and suffered for so little – for nothing. She turned into her own street – after so long it was odd to see it quite unchanged – she was climbing the front steps – she was knocking at the door of the house.

'Welcome home, Mrs Fraser!' It was Mary, taking her hand and laughing with genuine pleasure to see her safe at last. Behind Mary, like her wearing a cap and apron clean enough to stand up on their own, was Bella, smiling resolutely and dropping a violent curt-sey. There were murmurs of pleasure at the baby, still asleep as he was taken upstairs to the room prepared for him. Bella, anxious to meet every wish in advance, whisked away Sophy's soiled outdoor things with the deftness of a magician.

Going into the drawing room, Sophy felt both relief

105

and dismay. The warmth from the fire was enough to make one's face tighten and flush. There were freshly plumped cushions, the smell of hothouse fruit, and hot sweet wine offered on a silver tray. With no breadwinner, however, these were not luxuries, but extravagance and loss.

But what of her other lad? She turned to speak to Mary, who gave a steady smile and said, 'Tom's in his room, asleep.'

'Of course.' Sophy brightened, though with tears in her eyes, at the mention of his name. 'How is he?'

'He's well, madam,' Mary replied, following Sophy as she hastened into the hall and toptoed upstairs.

Tom's room, in comparison with the chilly stairwell, felt as warm and fragrant as stepping into a bath. In the grate the embers of a fire still glowed. A nightlight flickered beside his bed. On a table nearby were arranged several obviously new toys.

The child's breathing was the softest, sweetest sound imaginable. His thick eyelashes cast shadows on his face, which glowed from cleanliness and deep slumber. Sophy could not resist taking hold of a warm, limp little hand, in its ruffled linen sleeve, and tucking it beneath the counterpane.

'We did have to cut his hair, madam,' said Bella, who had also crept into the room. She did not trust Mary, left on her own, to tell the right lies.

From being full of hushed delight, Sophy was suddenly attentive. 'Yes?'

'We thought it might be the beginning of a fever, madam. But then we found we'd acted too hastily. The poor boy, he only had a cold. I hope you can forgive us.'

Sophy breathed a long sigh. She was relieved beyond words that all seemed well. 'I'm certain you acted for the best.'

106

Downstairs she asked later, 'Whose were those child's shoes on the kitchen stairs? The large ones?'

Bella, anxious for her character in the eyes of her own employer, explained. Her dear children were visiting her – just for that night. In particular, her own sweet boy did miss her. They were only in the attic, and no one but herself should notice that they were there, so well behaved were they.

She was all too glad when Sophy, her mind elsewhere, nodded and changed the subject, saying she had something solemn to tell the household.

Mary had kept the other servants up late, so Sophy, wanting the news of her husband done with, went down to the kitchen and told them all. She spoke as briefly as possible, bracing herself to ignore any signs of sympathy.

Bella saw an opportunity here. Speaking for herself, she said, she was so much affected by the loss that had befallen Mrs Fraser and her dear little boys, that she herself would willingly continue in Mrs Fraser's employ, to help as Master Tom's nursemaid for as long as her own mistress saw fit – in return for nothing more than her keep. Sophy, exhausted and overwrought, thanked her with tears of gratitude.

Next day Bella was up at dawn. It had been her intention to see Robbie and Amy down to the nearby waggoners' depot and away first thing, before the mistress of the house could be too much aware of them.

But she was not the first out of bed. As she passed Sophy's bedroom, taking a bribe of hot chocolate upstairs to Robbie and his sister, the door opened, and Mary came out. She was carrying a tray of empty breakfast things and moved carefully as she shut the door.

Sophy, already dressed, was sitting in an armchair with Tom on her lap. They had their arms bound around each other, and she was talking steadily in a low voice. The child nestled against her, hearing her tone as much as what she said. It was easy to see why Mary was gliding about as though pretending not to be there.

The other children were half coaxed, half threatened out of bed. They were tumbling downstairs in their outdoor things, all suppressed excitement, when Sophy came out of her bedroom holding Tom by the hand. Seeing his enemy almost run against him, Tom flinched.

The little boy's anger and fear were more than Robbie could resist. He rushed past, aiming a mock blow at Tom and glancing defiantly at the terrified Bella.

Sophy looked confused as well as irritated, realizing that these were the model children Bella had described. But since they were moments from leaving the house for ever, she merely ignored them, as she would a catcall in the street, and detained Bella with some question about the household accounts. Bella replied, nodding like a clockwork toy and anxiously smoothing her gown. With subdued haste she tried to shepherd her children out of sight.

Tom watched them going downstairs. Suddenly, in a voice that only Sophy could hear, he asked, 'Mama, before he goes away, is he going to give back your gold necklace?'

A host of feelings flitted over Sophy's face, of which the strongest was uncertainty. In a controlled voice she called to Bella, 'One word more, Mrs Bettingly, if you please.'

Three guarded faces turned towards her, and Bella fairly scampered back upstairs.

'Yes, madam?'

'Before your children leave, would you send them to the kitchen. Cook can give them something for their journey. I need your help to find something – that is, I seem to have mislaid a piece of jewellery.'

Bella, solemn and flustered, did as ordered. Sure enough, the necklace was not in its place, and she and Mary set about helping to make Sophy's bedchamber thoroughly tousled in the search for it. Sheets and blankets were stripped from the canopied bed, shoes were shaken upside down, and every garment was taken from the big wardrobe to have its pockets turned out.

Bella, who had guessed the truth, was nearly weeping.

'Madam, it's such a small thing – it might have slipped out of sight anywhere – I swear it must!'

Sophy looked at her, torn between pity and mistrust. 'I expect it has,' she said, keeping her tone even. 'Meanwhile would you please call your children – '

'Oh no, madam, no – I promise you – it can't have anything to do with them – '

' – in case they can help us – ' persisted Sophy. She had to raise her voice, to be heard above Bella's sharp noises of fear. For thieving something as valuable as this, any magistrate would make sure that Bella's son never saw her again.

Robbie and Amy, when they reappeared, clearly knew as much. The boy, wiping his nose on his sleeve, was weeping noisily. The search spread, and soon every room in the house was crazily disordered.

At the end of two hours, however, nothing had been found. Sophy, heaping the contents of her writing desk on to the Pembroke table in the drawing room, was wondering what to do next, when Bella, who'd been searching one of the glass-fronted bookcases, came across the room, trembling with urgency.

'Look, madam!' She gestured towards the top shelf, whose books were by now mostly stacked about the floor. 'I haven't disturbed it,' she said in a beseeching voice. 'I wanted you to see it, first.'

The necklace was indeed there, thrust behind a fat leather-bound history of engineering in the original French. It was impossible to say how it had come there, except that Tom, even by standing on a chair, could not have been the culprit. Sophy gave brisk instructions for the matter to be forgotten, and everyone else went about their business trying not to look glad.

But she distrusted Bella's children nonetheless. It made her uneasy to think Tom had spent perhaps a whole day in their company.

Robbie himself regained his usual boldness almost instantly. If anything, knowing he might have been in terrible danger made him cockier than ever. Just before he and Amy were due to leave, he caught sight of Tom peeping out into the hall, where they were loitering alone. Punching his sister to get her attention, he cast a look at Tom and stage-whispered, 'Good riddance to piddle-pants!'

Yowling with rage, Tom ran at him. In the drawing room Sophy, looking up from tidying the writing desk, had never heard him make such a sound.

Robbie snickered with glee and dodged behind Amy. 'He wets his bed!'

Amy joined in, chanting, 'He wets his bed!'

Knowing Tom would never hit a girl, Robbie thrust her forward, muttering, 'He's lousy, too!'

Amy joyfully took her cue. 'He's lousy, too! That means he's got lice. He's lousy, all in his hair!'

Her careless treble carried further than Robbie's voice. It left Sophy, unseen next door, rigid with attention. The pain of beginning to understand was written all over her.

It also brought Bella running. Seeing Tom she cast

110

him a frightened glare; then turned on her own children. 'Good God!' she hissed. 'Don't either of you know what you're doing?'

'Tom,' called Sophy, in a low, harsh voice.

The child stared back at Bella, then withdrew. In the drawing room his mother took him by the hand. Kneeling down beside him, she looked him closely in the face and asked, 'Yesterday, Tom – when did you see the necklace taken?'

'It wasn't yesterday, Mama.'

'The day before?'

In the moment's silence that followed, Bella knew the boy must be shaking his head.

'Have these children been here before?'

Another silence.

'So – Tom, dearest, I'm not angry with *you* – how long' – with a hitch of emotion in her voice – 'how long have they been here?'

In the hall the other children looked on fascinated as their mother clasped her hands, and screwed her eyes and mouth shut against tears.

'A long time . . . ?' Sophy knew she could trust Tom's word. She looked, as if seeing them for the first time, at the boy's scared eyes and delicate shorn head. 'More than a week?'

On a nearby table there stood a small brass bell which was used to summon Mary. Hearing it ring unusually loudly, Mary hurried into the drawing room, fearful and breathless. Her eyes widened still further at the sight of her mistress. Standing with her back to the door, Sophy was still wielding the bell, as violently as if beating something to death.

'I hope,' she said, without turning around, 'I *can* safely entrust my son to you for half an hour. Those other children are to go to the kitchen. And bring their mother to me.'

Mary scuttled past her sister, eyes averted. There

111

was no need for her to pass on the message. Bella swallowed a whimper and tiptoed into the room. Fixing an idiotic stare on the floor, all she saw was the trimming on her mistress' petticoats as Sophy turned towards her.

It was Mary, closing the door, who saw Sophy's face.

CHAPTER SIX

London, 1813

By the following spring Charity Michaelmas and her child were several new homes beyond the villa in secluded Knightsbridge. All that little Georgiana knew of the latest one was a nursery of exquisitely dressed dolls, a basement kitchen full of servants, and the staircase joining the two, broad as a village street and five storeys high. By day, holding her nursemaid's hand as she was taken to play in the square outside, she liked to look up at its oval ceiling, all finely moulded with garlands and seashells in white on an azure background, or down at the hall floor of black-and-white chequerboard marble. By night the staircase was a gloomy highway, lit only from candles held aloft by the footman who accompanied them both upstairs.

Unless, that is, Mama was entertaining. Then the way to bed lay past brilliant crowded rooms full of heat and noise from all the people who had come here to see each other and be seen.

For Charity, after being thrust out into the muddy Knightsbridge lanes with nothing but a trunkful of splendid clothes, had not sunk in the world. Her two begging letters, delivered the night they had been penned, had both brought an instant response. From young Pettifer, the dilettante designer of country villas and fine monuments, there had been a passionate reply by return. He begged her to permit the use of her body as his mistress, on a handsome annual allowance. Her other potential keeper, though, the scholarly Milsome, had outbid him, arriving in person at midnight after the briefest excuses to his family and servants.

Installed in a neat house overlooking a new Chelsea square, Charity had set about teasing the appetites of her new protector with a little adultery and a great deal of hard study. The result was that he had been as pleased with her, and as devoted, as he was with his clever, handsome wife and four fine children.

It had not been easy, however. Latin poets and German philosophers posed no problem for Charity. Milsome himself, though, flushed with early-middle-aged ardour, had needed careful handling. A simple task done right, such as conjugating an irregular French verb, and he would be kissing her hand with tears of pride in his eyes. On the other hand, too much good progress, too easily made, and he would no longer be able to congratulate himself on how hard he was working at her education.

The day came when he caught sight of a diary she was keeping, for practice, in Italian, and could find not a thing wrong with it. Confronted with its fluent phrasing and tasteful choice of words, he gave a decidedly cool response. It was time for another change of address.

Nowadays Charity was kept by a politician. Not a great man, but a rising one for all that, with a successful family business based on woollen manufacturing, a knighthood in view, and a safe Tory seat in a little rotten borough with only five registered voters, all of them cheaply bought. In a lesser way, Charity had risen with him, to the point where she now had her sights on the real thing – a statesman, indeed, from one of the country's lordly Whig dynasties.

She was also beginning to draw income from investments of her own. This meant that no longer was she shut up in seclusion as one man's possession. Her social circle grew wider every day – within the world of men, if not of their wives and daughters.

Little Georgiana remembered scarcely any of her former homes, and understood even less of what went on in them. Recently, whenever there was company she had been taken to and fro by a narrow back staircase, unseen by anyone except the servants. It was not that Charity was ashamed of her presence. Rather, Charity wanted Georgiana protected from *her*. It was for her daughter's own long-term good that Georgiana had been banished to the meaner parts of the house. As yet Charity's ambitions for Georgiana were vague, depending as they did on the uncertainties of her own fate. She knew only that one day it would be as well for the girl's origins to be concealed. If necessary, from Georgiana herself.

So there were no other children in Georgiana's life. It was a novelty, one morning, to be taken down to the kitchen – 'for a change, and a bit of company, poor thing' her nursemaid said – there to be treated to leftover peach tart and allowed to peek at a strange little boy.

Normally the nursemaid would have been dismissed in a breath, were Georgiana seen talking to another child. Out in the square, among the gravel paths and young plane trees, only other rich children were allowed. They were members of a close little world that Charity was determined her daughter would one day grow up to join. But as something more respectable than the offspring of an increasingly successful whore. What their class of people owed Charity, by God, she'd see her daughter paid – a hundredfold.

But the little boy in the basement, though respectably dressed, was only the son of a would-be servant. Sitting at the scrubbed kitchen table, with a slice of the peach tart and a favourite picture book, he was waiting while his mother was being considered, upstairs, for the post of housekeeper.

Both children, the boy in mourning clothes, and the girl in a white silk dress and frilled pantalettes, were too well behaved to stare. They were also shy. And the little boy, though polite, seemed unusually mistrustful towards strangers. At length he was persuaded to show Georgiana the illustrations in his book, while the grown-ups were able to turn away and gossip among themselves.

'This is the best picture here,' he told her, as they sat side by side at the table, their feet not quite touching the floor. He pointed to a scene from the destruction of Pompeii. Across an elegant town square – rather like the one outside, only with more pillars – a number of citizens were fleeing, their hands raised in horror at the sight of flames spurting from Mount Vesuvius. Every one of them was richly dressed, in togas or ornamented tunics, with hair dressed suspiciously close to the styles in fashion now.

'I like this one best because tons of dust fell out of the sky and covered the buildings and killed all the people' – here Georgiana peered more closely, with a child's unfeeling interest in death – 'so that all the bodies and ruins are still there. That's how you can be sure it all really happened. Though my papa used to say the buildings couldn't have looked exactly like that, or they'd never have stood up to begin with.'

'My mama doesn't want a new butler as well as a housekeeper,' said Georgiana. 'Is your papa dead?' It didn't occur to her that the book was rather expensive for a servant's child to own. But she understood perfectly how things worked below stairs. Her mama's housekeepers either had no husband, or they were married to an upper servant in the same household.

'Yes, he is,' said Sophy Fraser's son in a quiet voice that could have meant anything. 'This picture's nice,

116

too. It's a little Christian baby being fed to some lions. Mama says, now that we've got no papa this is the best book I shall ever have.'

Sophy, upstairs, was regretting the rashness that had brought her to this house. Seeing the position of housekeeper advertised under Charity's name, several things had nudged her into answering. Now that she was here, in the subdued luxury of Charity's boudoir, none of them seemed justified. Neither desperation nor curiosity. Least of all, past connections.

'In whose establishment were you last employed, Mrs Fraser?'

Charity, at twenty-one, was unrecognizable. Sophy had never in her life spoken with her before. But in the Wiltshire village where they had both grown up, she had known her well by sight. As a foundling, Charity had been put to work early on one of the local farms, living in conditions where she had done well to stay alive. But from the calm assurance of her manner, the woman who now sat across the room from Sophy could have been fifty and a marchioness.

Not that life had coarsened Charity's looks. If she had the dignity of a matron, she had the eyes and mouth of a sexually precocious child.

'The last household I supervised was my own.' Sophy's voice sounded oddly in her own ears. She realized that – somehow – she should have added, 'madam'.

How could she even have considered coming here? It was a mercy that, having changed from an ignorant miss to a grown woman in widow's garb, she too might now be hard to recognize. She described the workings of the household in Liverpool, trying to make them sound as complicated as possible. As she talked, she tried to hide her growing unease. She had almost no

117

money. The house in Castle Street, with all its furniture, had only been rented, and now that Sophy had come south to look for work, she and the children were lodged in two small rooms in a house off the Edgware Road. But anxious as she was at the threat of poverty, she was also hotly embarrassed at how badly she was handling this encounter.

'Describe to me, if you would, your experience in housekeeping before that time. You were married for how many years?' Charity was dressed very simply, in a cap, and a grey muslin gown with a high frilled collar. But her stateliness was that of a woman wearing diamonds.

'Certainly,' said Sophy, and gave a detailed answer. 'I was married to my dear husband,' she added, 'for four years.'

She sighed as she spoke – and immediately wished she hadn't. Charity, her hands folded in her lap, looked at her steadily. Her expressionless face suggested that such things as affections of the heart were – what? Embarrassing? Vulgar? Purely imaginary?

Sophy squirmed, her own hardships forgotten, as she recalled the little she knew about this queenly young woman, got with child in a barn six years ago by her feckless brother George. In Charity's world everything – friendship, pity, love – was priced according to what the market would bear. To make such a world tolerable for herself, was there at least one person for whom she made an exception? If there was, Sophy hoped that that exception was Charity's little girl.

Even as these thoughts ran through Sophy's mind, her husband, not half a mile away, held his younger son for the first time, his eyes shut fast to hold back tears of joy.

In recent months Fraser too had changed. His features had been harshened by hard weathers, and the weight of his responsibilities while working in America had brought about a subtle change in his bearing. For the first time, he looked old enough to suit his habitually earnest manner.

The baby was still too young to be fearful of strangers. Held out at arms' length by his father, he responded with a gape of pure pleasure, waving his little fists and feet like a sea creature out of water. At length Fraser, holding the child against one shoulder, wiped his eyes and turned again to the landlady, who was standing in the doorway, amazed at such a turn of events.

'. . . But if my wife left the child in your keeping, she must have told you where she could be found.' His voice was sharp with frustration. Since setting out on his long journey north to Liverpool from the Pool of London, where he'd finally disembarked, he'd several times believed that he and Sophy were only minutes from being reunited.

'Why, yes sir, of course,' said the landlady, overawed by the young man's good travelling clothes and impatient manner.

'Depend upon it, she did,' added her husband, who, equally curious, was loitering behind her.

'But sir – ' as Fraser passed her the baby with fumbling care and snatched up his hat as if it might bolt out of reach – 'might she not return at any minute?'

The pair of them were anxious to help, however, being partly intimidated by their visitor, and thoroughly intrigued by his story. The twelve-year-old girl who did the heavy work of the house was chivvied upstairs, as hastily as if Sophy might vanish yet again, and given a message by both her employers at once. Tying on an old floppy bonnet and a shawl gritted with coal dust, she set out with instructions 'to bring back Mrs Fraser by return'.

As she hastened through the streets, dodging traffic and mud, she repeated under her breath what she'd been told, being not quite sure she could remember it all the way there.

At the grand house in Grosvenor Square the area door was opened to her by an out-of-uniform footman. Not knowing what to make of her garbled message, he passed it nonetheless to one of the under-cooks, who went with it to the steward, who approached the butler, who sent it upstairs via Charity's personal maid.

'A Mr James just disembarked via Lisbon?' said Charity, as the maid stood dropping a curtsey just inside the door. The room was a spacious one, but Charity spoke across it as though she'd never raised her voice in her life. 'Describe him, Hortense — Mrs Fraser, pray excuse this.'

'He is not here himself, madame; he has sent a servant.'

'Then instruct Mr James' servant to tell him when I shall be at home, since it seems his business can only be dealt with by me.'

The little house off the Edgware Road was the one place where Fraser could be sure of not missing Sophy yet again. But the nearer the time came when she must surely return, the less he could bear to wait. Trying in vain to escape the landlady's attempts at conversation, he fidgeted about in Sophy's bedroom, becoming more restive by the minute. With his hat still in his hand, by turns he sat down — then went to the window, with its view of a washing line and some sooty market gardens — then stalked to and fro. He stared intently at where an unfamiliar bonnet and gloves belonging to his wife lay on a chair, as if challenging them to prove they really belonged to her.

At last he stood up once more with a sigh, excused himself to the landlady, and went downstairs. In the narrow dark hall he was met by raised voices.

'That's not what we told you!' The landlord was shouting at the scullery-maid, who had come back near to tears. 'You'll have to explain yourself a deal better than that to the gentleman,' he said, looking anxiously at Fraser.

'No matter,' said Fraser, with grim forbearance. His greatcoat still unbuttoned, he strode out of the house and up the street, determined no matter what to go himself to the house in Grosvenor Square.

The interruption from the lady's-maid had been a welcome one. As she tried to answer Charity Michaelmas' questions, some of which were very detailed, Sophy's discomfiture grew. She had pretended to be a stranger, ignorant of who Charity was. If she were recognized now, as the former Miss Byford from Cannings Fitzpayne, how would it look?

She cast her mind again through what she could remember about the young courtesan to whom she was offering herself as a servant. When Charity had fallen pregnant, she had been a kitchenmaid at Cannings Fitzpayne Hall. She had of course been dismissed. There had also been an unpleasant rumour concerning the girl's treatment by Lord Fitzpayne's nephew. And by the time there was a chance of a reconciliation with Sophy's brother, Charity had refused all contact with him.

Oppressed by her tactlessness in not having said who she was, Sophy could only sit, her hands folded and her back straight, and hope her own likeness to poor old George was not too strong. How could she have planned to appeal to Charity on his account?

'. . . As to references, I can provide testimonials of character,' she said.

Charity examined the proffered letters of recommendation. She asked, 'Have you ever resided in Wiltshire, Mrs Fraser?'

One reference, Sophy now remembered, gave an address not five miles from her childhood home. It had been written by one of her husband's former employers, who had engaged Fraser as chief engineer on a nearby trunk waterway.

'For some time I was – ah – at school in Salisbury, Mrs Michaelmas' – for so Charity styled herself.

'You tell me that before you married you oversaw your mother's household. Was that in the neighbourhood of Salisbury?'

'Well – approximately.' There dawned on Sophy a little of what was in Charity's mind. To be sure of concealing her early life, on no account would Charity engage someone from her own part of the country.

'Mrs Fraser, I have no objection to employing any persons whose circumstances, as I see yours have been, were formerly more prosperous. But it might help me to appreciate your qualifications if I knew where, as well as how, they were acquired. Where precisely near Salisbury was your mother's home? And your father, when he was alive – what was his occupation?'

Sophy shifted in her chair and replied, 'My father was an attorney. He died near Bath.'

'By accident, did not you say?'

Charity's expression had not changed. But in her voice Sophy recognized a grain of suspicion. Lawyer Byford's death had been a local sensation: he had been blown to pieces in a gunpowder explosion on the waterway. Across half the county, sermons had been preached describing the incident as typical of what the

122

quiet Wiltshire countryside could expect from a new development such as a canal.

But Sophy had not mentioned any accident.

There was a silence as the two correct young women looked at each other with feigned calmness. Sophy saw it was pointless to deny the truth. Now that Charity realized who she was, she was not about to hire Sophy anyway. Sophy tried not to sigh aloud. Would she ever find work with which to provide for her widowhood?

'Mrs Michaelmas – '

Charity reached out and rang for one of the servants. Thinking she was dismissed, Sophy got to her feet. Charity ignored her, however.

Her maid appeared, looking flustered.

'What's happening, Hortense?'

Had Sophy not been a stranger in that house, she too would have noticed an unusual noise. Two floors down, in the marble-paved hall, there was a commotion.

Below stairs, too, the people of the house had realized that something extraordinary was going on. In the kitchen Tom and Georgiana looked up from where they were playing together. The two children, seeing the grown-ups in a tizzy, were themselves confused, then excited.

'Madame!' Charity's maid exclaimed. 'The man, he has been told definitely that no one is at home!'

Charity hurried from the room. From the landing there could be heard scuffling, and shouts of anger. Sophy followed, her thoughts taken up with their conversation. Her mind was still elsewhere as she looked down into the broad stairwell. From below, her pale face, framed in a black bonnet with its veil put back, showed only the faintest curiosity.

Seeing the two women, the men below fell silent.

A flicker of emotion passed over Sophy's features,

123

before they went blank with shock. Furious, out of breath, and pinioned by three menservants, her husband stared up at her, in a trance of disbelief that almost matched her own.

CHAPTER SEVEN

Paris, 1815

Charity had just entered the fallen city of Paris as the most presentable camp follower in Europe. In the year of Our Lord eighteen hundred and fifteen it was early spring. Over another two years her fortunes had changed and enlarged again. She was still known to a small, exclusive circle of political grandees. But now – however briefly – her life of whoring had carried her close to social acceptance.

The reason for this was that, at present, no man could boast of spending himself in her expensive body. Her days were passed in tender friendship, and her nights in ingenious perversion, with the bookish Countess of Tadcaster. The Countess, authoress of a well-regarded translation of Petrarch, was rumoured to have kept her marriage to the Earl unconsummated. Her tastes in lasciviousness were perfectly matched with his, however: what she liked to do, he liked to watch. So it was out of wifely affection that she would open her body to the breathtaking doings of her dear Mrs Michaelmas.

Thus it was that on a particular night during her first month in Paris, Charity was to attend a function at the American Embassy, in the guise of a socially blameless young widow.

The Tadcasters were only a small part of the migration of pleasure-seeking foreigners that had entered the city after its conquest by the Allied armies the year before. With the fall of Bonaparte, no longer need the Grand Tour be just a memory of men in their middle years or more. Along the straight new roads of the wide French countryside, with their endless avenues of poplars, a stream of *diligences* and private carriages had brought businessmen, well-born sightseers, fleeing debtors, and noble youths with their tutors. It seemed every kind of traveller was hurrying to Paris, which for so many years had been the heart of a forbidden empire. At last Bonaparte, having marched up to the brink of world dominance, was now beaten back and dethroned. He had left a continent across which, from Moscow and Lisbon, from the Baltic and the Mediterranean, a trail of wreckage led to his former seat of government, in Paris.

Thus, late one afternoon in March 1815, as Charity's maid was beginning to dress her for that evening's reception at the Embassy, two people, both typical of that time and place, passed close by each other in the rue Rivoli.

One of them was astride an unshod pony so shaggy that even its belly trailed a wispy mane. The rider's innumerable layers of filthy furs and other garments were stained with the blood of German peasantry and French townswomen, and with mud from nights spent on the bare ground with only a blanket coated in clay to keep out the cold. He was a Tartar, from Bashkir, who had fought in the service of the Tsar armed at first with a bow, later with a stolen musket. Looking about him with the placid curiosity of a conqueror, he rode down the street and out of sight.

As he did so, the crowds of pedestrians under the rue Rivoli's elegant arcade included another kind of invader new to Paris that year. Miss Euphemia Lee, of Richmond, Virginia, was dressed with great care and terrible taste, in a walking dress of crimson silk that brought out the natural sallowness of her complexion and clashed with her rouge. A frilled chin-strap secured an extraordinary flounced bonnet. Behind her walked a footman, who carried her folding stool, an umbrella, and two lady's workbags.

Euphemia was making her way back to her hotel from the public art gallery in the palace of the Louvre. Her education had been one of the most expensive in the state, so she was not prepared to waste the cultural opportunities offered by the French capital. Now that the fabulous collection of paintings looted by Napoleon was available for all to see, she was applying her energies to a giant copy, entirely her own design, of Veronese's 'The Marriage at Cana' in coloured wools.

If Euphemia was in Europe to see its sights, her brother Joseph, who had also brought his wife, Kate, was here on business. He was one of many expecting to do well from the rebuilding of Europe's devastated economy.

Euphemia herself, as crabbed in her prejudices at twenty-two as if she were an old woman, had arrived with little expectation of enjoying anywhere so far from home. Two things had brought her to Paris. It was what people did; also the thought of her brother alone for so long with the woman he'd married made her prickle with secret dismay.

But now that they were here it made Euphemia no happier that she could still only go into company chaperoned by Kate, a beautiful woman, some seemed to think, and only three years her senior.

Tonight they were due to dine at the same reception as Charity and her protectors. Back at the hotel, Kate, who'd avoided her sister-in-law on the pretext of having letters to write, was nearly dressed.

The Lees were lodged in one of the former town palaces of the *ancien régime*, a building that had recently had a succession of new owners. Horses had been stabled on the ground floors, and been ridden up the huge staircase for sport. The original owner and his family had been kept under guard in the stables, on their way, after three years of imprisonment, to the guillotine. Their mansion had later become the property of one of Napoleon's generals, a former lawyer's clerk. After a string of victories he had married the bereaved and impoverished niece of that same Monsieur le Vicomte whose house it had been before the Revolution.

The general too was gone now. He had been last heard of in the south with a unit of the new Royalist army which had been sent to ensure that Napoleon, in leaving Elba, remained no more than a private citizen. Meanwhile a wing of the building stood broken open and disfigured by fire where a troop of invading Bavarians had cooked their rations in the middle of the library. For fuel they had used a heap of calf-bound first editions and a stack of tulipwood cabinets inlaid with hand-painted porcelain.

The Lee's entourage had taken half the first floor, with a view of a porticoed courtyard and a narrow main thoroughfare. Down in the street, cavalry paraded, Britons, Austrians, Prussians, Swedes, Russians and Spaniards, their helmets and lances glittering in a sunlit cascade. There too, every brisk waiter or sullen crossing-sweeper was a veteran of some great, far-away victory. The hotel's register, in recent weeks, had been filled with the names and titles of Englishmen who, with their elegant womenfolk, their servants and their family carriages, had flocked into post-war Paris like a single migrating tribe. There was even, Kate had noticed, a Wiltshire Fitzpayne of Cannings Fitzpayne.

Within their suite, Euphemia's room was vast, centred on a bed the size of a cathedral altar. Every night she prayed dutifully for a long list of family connections, for a cherished spaniel whose loyalty she recommended nightly to the Lord, and for the success of the United States' army and navy, in case there was any corner of the world where they were still embattled. Then, aquiver with curl papers and topped with a cap like a ruched haystack-cover, she laid her head, with its anxious eyes and sharp nose, in a bower of exquisitely embroidered pillows. As she slept, she was framed by twenty-foot-high damask draperies above a scrolled bedstead whose lines had the grace of a waterborne swan.

This evening, once dressed, they waited in Kate and Joseph's sitting room for the carriage to be announced. Kate, in flowing *poudre de rose*, looked both lissom and dignified in a way to make any husband's heart stop dead with pride. Joseph had married her as a young widower, his first wife having been killed by yellow fever. His former marriage had not been a success, and in his adoration of Kate there had always lurked a hint of relief. He was delightful and guileless, but he was also hopelessly impulsive, and Kate had come to feel grateful that some other woman had borne the business of showing him what marriage was about.

If Kate's appearance this evening was subtle as a fine perfume, Euphemia was dressed with dogged magnificence. Following the French craze for plaid, her silk dress was strongly coloured, with a ruffled hem and neckline. On her turban, sprays of egret feathers waggled, almost with each breath.

She was not prepared to enjoy herself very much. In the carriage, she asked Joseph, 'Is it safe to drive by this route? Have you asked the driver, to make sure?'

'What worries you, Effie?' he enquired, with a broad wink at his wife that Kate knew would be held against her. 'There are no revolutionary sympathizers in Paris now.'

Euphemia blushed and frowned. She had never mastered the art of being teased.

'Effie, you walked home this way only today.'

'I had a footman with me, from the hotel.'

'Ah.' Joseph had his suspicions concerning the tall young man who carried Euphemia's woolwork for her. As it happened they were not too far from the truth. Two years before, among the cold, flea-infested villages of upland Spain, he had cut off the ears and scalp of a ten-year-old girl, to spite a comrade who'd wanted to take first turn at raping her.

'Then that's all right,' Joseph said, with a cheeriness that left his sister torn between pleasure and uncertainty. 'And just to show you, dear Effie, that there's not a brigand left in the whole of Paris, I *shall* ask our driver.'

As they were being set down at their destination, Joseph duly looked up at the driver and stage-whispered, 'Vive l'Empéreur! Vive Napoléon!'

'Mais non, monsieur: vive le Roi.' The driver looked uncomfortable.

Joseph was enjoying himself, the more so since Euphemia was distraught. He raised his voice. 'Vive l'Empéreur Napoléon, le bon ami des américains!'

The driver broke into a sly smile. With a quick glance about him he exclaimed, 'Bien entendu, monsieur: vive Napoléon, l'Empéreur des français!' He was grinning broadly as he drove off.

Euphemia was furious, mainly at being confused. Her understanding of politics was muddled, just as her feelings about it were strong. Being intensely conservative, she never quite understood how she could be living under a government established by a revolution. To her, George Washington was a respectable slave-owner of substance, who stood for the rights of property and adherence to the law. King George, in her imagination, had somehow become a renegade whose only object was to cause public disorder by supplying arms to rebellious Indian tribes.

The reception was held in an oasis of splendour and

light, amid muddy streets full of wreckage. Out in the courtyard, braziers in wrought iron baskets flickered and hissed; voices of unseen passers-by rebounded off the dark walls, and horses gave off clouds of steam. Inside, guests passed through marble-floored halls where their own breath was visible and the newly bared arms and shoulders of the women turned to gooseflesh in an instant. Entering the grand saloon was like stepping through a door to another continent, so sudden was the gust of heat from two hundred elaborately dressed and perfumed bodies, and a thousand candles. The orchestra, made up of French military bandsmen out of uniform for the first time in their adult lives, sweated as they sawed away at the unfamiliar tunes of peace.

Many of the guests were known to the Lees, whether from Virginia, England or Paris itself. There were representatives of most European governments. Several were former supporters of Napoleon. And nearly all were gorgeous in the military uniforms of one or other newly restored monarchy. A few were well-connected prisoners of war, recently liberated. When, after a brief interlude of peace a dozen years back, war had broken out again, several hundred English visitors had been arrested, and kept in various fortress prisons ever since. One Member of Parliament present this evening had escaped across the border with Flanders, disguised as a serving woman. Another, less fortunate, had been seized at the moment of boarding ship at Dieppe. He had spent the rest of the war growing vegetables and getting up amateur theatricals in a castle by the Rhine.

Joseph, as a prelude to a more important after-dinner negotiation, was soon deep in talk with a grand young man from the French civil service. Having retreated to the quiet of a side room, they made a contrast with the other people there, a crowd of gossiping elderly females like a clutch of bedizened hens. Two of the grand

131

young man's colleagues, to help with the talk of road tolls and rates of exchange, took charge of Kate and Euphemia. The one conversing with Kate made a point of looking unself-conscious about being so close to her lovely neck and shoulders. Euphemia fell to the one who was junior in rank, who, seeing she was a fright, made an heroic show of gallantry.

Two other women, though, were the most conspicuous there, as well as the most feted. One, her presence astonishing to Kate, was Charity. The other, she had expected automatically to see. Lady Augusta Fitzpayne, the chatelaine of Cannings Fitzpayne Hall, had, back at twenty-two, fulfilled many a woman's highest hope. In rapid succession she had been orphaned, made destitute, and married to an elderly husband whom she detested. Within a few months of marriage she had had the good fortune to see her husband buried, to announce the conception of his heir, and to hear his will read, according to which she was to inherit everything, so long as she should be with child. Almost everyone marvelled at how well she had done; and everyone else said how amazed they were that his ailing lordship had been capable of begetting a healthy son.

But gossip, to the young dowager, only gave relish to the freedom she had gained through the awful gamble of her marriage. She had beauty, being of that auburn-haired type that can combine fashionable pallor with rude health; she had just enough wit; and she had an aggressive self-confidence that made her company, to many people, like warming oneself before a roaring good fire. She wore yellow diamonds tonight, and ivory silk cut with prodigious cunning. 'The lady isn't clothed by all that drapery,' was one murmured comment. 'She's merely not naked.'

Kate only knew Lady Augusta by sight. Back home in the Wiltshire countryside there would have been no question that as the daughter of a country-town attorney she should ever have met her ladyship socially.

But she had – just once – met Charity Michaelmas, six years before. It had been Kate, nervously skirting a different kind of social chasm, who had tried to act as go-between for her feckless younger brother and the courtesan who was now queening it on the far side of the saloon, dressed with a magnificence that made conversation falter.

Euphemia stared at both women. Not with jealousy but like a would-be lover. Kate knew what her sister-in-law was thinking: please, please, let me be just a little like them.

Euphemia disdained plain faces with a passion that only other ugly people could share. And only others who'd once been poor could identify with her ferocious snobbery. But it was not just the wealth and beauty of Charity and her ladyship that influenced her. What made her doggy with admiration was the look they both had of being at once exciting and serene.

Looking past Kate with bright eyes and a cool voice, she said, 'I suppose you can't introduce me?'

'I think I see one of our acquaintance,' smiling and beckoning to an embassy aide, 'who can.'

Euphemia, eager as a thirteen-year-old, was led up to Lady Augusta. Kate was suddenly accosted by someone from her husband's wide circle of Parisian connections, and could only see Euphemia without hearing what was said. It was easy to understand what was happening, though. Lady Augusta, having found out who Euphemia was, swiftly ignored her. In response Euphemia became even more ingratiating. It was her tragedy to hanker after the type of handsome people who detested looks like hers.

Taking pity, Kate later seized the first opportunity of saying, 'If you like, I believe I can introduce you to the dark-haired woman wearing emeralds.'

Charity, on being approached, was gracious but guarded. Because of a slight indisposition on the part of the Countess, the Tadcasters had stayed behind at their hotel tonight, leaving her to attend the reception alone. 'Indeed I remember our last meeting,' she told Kate. 'You were kind enough to call on me, were you not? As a neighbour.'

Kate had been no such thing. Recalling the villa in Knightsbridge and the baby just old enough to sit up on its mother's lap, she wondered if she were free to ask about Charity's daughter. 'I heard that you had the misfortune to be widowed,' she lied. 'Am I not right?'

Charity, regarding her calmly, took her cue. 'That is so, I fear – some time since.' Looking at Kate very directly she added, 'My regret is that I lack the most important thing by which I might remember my dear husband. It is a cause of sorrow to me that I shall never have known' – pausing to fan herself and sigh – 'a mother's pains or a mother's tender joys.'

'I myself,' Kate ventured, also fanning herself rather fast, 'am duly thankful that my union with Mr Lee has so far been blessed with two fine children.' Out of the corner of her eye she could see Euphemia looking pinched with disdain at such a tactless little speech. Uncertain what to say next, she asked, 'And your – husband – I never had the pleasure – '

'Mostly,' said Charity with composure, 'he owned sugar plantations. In the West Indies.'

Secretly Kate applauded the good sense of inventing a husband from so far overseas. She sought in vain for something rational to say about the cultivation of sugar. At that moment, however, dinner was announced. Neither she nor Charity was sorry that the conversation was at an end.

* * *

Next morning it was still dark when Euphemia over-heard her brother's servant running to wake his master. The footsteps and voices that followed were indistinct. But she could still sense that something urgent was happening.

If Joseph had trouble to deal with, she was the one who should be at his side. Hastily robed, she tiptoed through the chilly pre-dawn gloom to where lamps were being lit, in Kate and Joseph's sitting room.

The sight she met was not what she'd expected.

Her hair piled high and bejewelled, her peerless bosom shaming every ornament, Charity Michaelmas was still dressed as she had been last night. She looked calm but tense. Beside her on a sofa, Hortense, her maid, soundlessly wept.

'Could there be any doubt, do you think?' Kate was standing over their guests, looking anxious.

'My hosts had had word from two different sources. Marshall Ney was sent south merely to discourage any local Republicans. But now that he has encountered the man, at Lyons – '

'At Lyons!'

' – That far north!'

' – it appears that Bonaparte is accompanied not just by a band of supporters, but by an army.'

'But Ney was not outnumbered, surely?' said Joseph.

'Who can tell? But it seems it was from choice, not cowardice, that he has changed sides, and joined again with the Emperor.'

Hortense wailed. Charity patted her hand, an oddly maternal gesture from someone twenty years younger. As a former Royalist exile Hortense had her own reasons for being apprehensive. Everyone knew some of the stories from recent years. In victory and defeat alike, the Napoleonic armies had spared neither their enemies nor their own civilians. In the retreat to Paris even the château of the Emperor's mother had been looted. Hortense herself, the daughter of a high-ranking army officer, had lost both parents in the Terror. All of them knew what had befallen British civilians caught in France by the last outbreak of war.

Charity meanwhile had no way of leaving the city. The fact that the Countess of Tadcaster's ailment had kept her and the Earl at their hotel last night meant that, by a coincidence, they had been among the first to hear of this new danger. They had departed for the Dieppe–Brighton packet within the hour, taking only their personal servants, the Countess' jewellery, and three favourite pug dogs. The rest of their clothes and furnishings, and Charity, had been expendable. All that she had found, on being driven back to her hotel, was an empty apartment with drawers and cupboards left open, and a short, inscrutable note.

'I fear word of this will soon be everywhere,' she said.

A maid came in with coffee. Euphemia, all grim-faced sympathy towards Charity as a potential victim of those foul Revolutionaries, insisted on putting the tray before her with her own hands.

'You mean,' said Kate, 'among citizens of the Allied nations? We ourselves heard not a whisper, last night.'

Charity nodded, sipping from her cup like a bright nectar-drinking bird. Euphemia was amazed that anyone could be so cool at surely the worst moment of her life. 'Already there are no horses to be had – none at least that I can bargain for in time.'

'How close are they?' Euphemia, as she spoke, looked from Charity to her brother, as if his masculine authority and Charity's social eminence made them all-knowing.

'I think, Effie dear, they will still be several days' march from here.' Joseph spoke as reassuringly as he could. He was a soft man in his dealings with females, especially his sister, poor woman. Smiling, he added,

'In any case, you, as an American and a fellow-revolutionary, need have no fear.' What he chose not to mention, however, was that as the news spread, the city might well change sides in advance.

Kate turned to Charity. 'How may we help you?'

Charity sought one immediate favour: a private conversation with Kate while she herself hastened into the travelling clothes she had brought.

Some minutes later Euphemia, twitching with curiosity, saw them come out of Kate's dressing room. They were still talking, in low, serious voices. The sight of them, both dark, pale and slender, confused her. She had expected the more lavishly dressed of them to be the awesome Mrs Michaelmas. What she saw was mistress and maid, with Charity in a neat, dismal brown spencer and gown that she had borrowed from Hortense.

From now on, each female of the Lee household was to have a new servant. Hortense was to be a poor dependant of the kind whose role was to read aloud to Euphemia and lose to her at whist. Charity, her speech roughened and falsely genteel, was to be Kate's paid companion. It went without saying that each was a good and true citizen of the United States of America.

With the city and its ravaged provinces uncertain again of their fate, there was little reason for the Lees to prolong their visit. Joseph's first act on hearing Charity's news had been to send his valet, still in his nightclothes, to alert the hotel's chief ostler, if necessary with a bribe. By the time the sun was up their travelling carriage, heavy as a chariot of ancient times, had passed beyond the city's vile medieval alleyways and the crude wooden palisade recently put up to defend it. They were out in a bright, cold, bare countryside where the clouds threw shadows as swift as flocks of birds.

Three miles behind them, and the city became

almost invisible among the trees of its parks and avenues and the orchards and forests beyond its walls. On a hill outside to the north the windmills of Montmartre could be seen, and, below, the spire of the Sainte Chapelle and the towers and long roof of Notre Dame. Otherwise Paris showed itself only as a canopy of smoke, as though the broad valley of the Seine held, not tens of thousands of people, but a giant damp bonfire.

The fastest route was the newly paved post road to Boulogne. It was crowded with traffic heading north, and every post-chaise, carriage and mail coach was full. The travellers passed rolling hedgeless farmland, dawdling rivers fringed with alders, and oak forests along distant horizons like a dark fog. In the fields uneven rows of workers were busy planting and hoeing. There, as in the starved-looking villages, there was scarcely a man in sight. Only women had been left by the wars: scrawny, pipesmoking creatures in high lappeted caps and heavy clogs.

Half a day on, the evidence of war was worse. In some villages only the chimney stacks of the houses had been left standing, like trunks in a burnt forest. Over the last miles of the retreat to Paris, both armies had been close to starvation. At one lonely spot, where a church overlooked a beautiful valley, even the graves had been dug up, and their contents flung about, by a party of Russians in search of corpses new enough to eat.

Towards midnight they halted, at a posting inn near Amiens. Their carriage was left in the yard, its shafts empty and their baggage still strapped to the roof, while they took a few hours' sleep.

All that day, Kate had suspected that Charity had something further to say to her alone. As they were parting for the night, Charity murmured, 'A word in

138

confidence, if I might. Not necessarily now, nor even tomorrow, unless – '

A floorboard creaked. From around a passageway corner the edge of a halo appeared, cast by Euphemia's candle as she made her way to bed. Suddenly Charity was intent only on shielding her own candle from draughts. Raising her voice, she said, 'Good night, Mrs Lee.'

'Good night, Mrs Michaelmas.'

The tide was out at Boulogne, and the wind was unfavourable. Down in the old town, the harbour front was blocked with carriages due to be manhandled on to the first packet to England. They waited in a ghostly procession, their shafts resting on the ground and the salty air blistering the varnish on their panels.

Everywhere there were foreign travellers in various states of agitation. In the hours that must pass before the first vessel could embark, they loitered in anxious little groups. Some sat around in the coffee rooms of the town's hotels, saying little to one another. Others paced its narrow streets, looking without curiosity at the site where the Revolutionaries had reduced the Cathedral to rubble, or at the fortifications built by Napoleon's invasion troops, confidently named his 'Army of England'.

Walking about on the ramparts of the ancient Lower Town, the Lees and their counterfeit servant saw many people of fashion who had been at the Embassy reception. It was like watching the same cast of actors in the second of two completely different plays. There was the Member of Parliament who had only recently been released from a French prison. Alone, and ignoring all his acquaintance, he looked a generation older than he had three days before. One married couple were having a violent quarrel about whose fault had

139

got them into such trouble. The woman's eyes and nose were red from the cold up there above the town and the choppy sea. Beribboned mamas, their skirts flurried by the salty wind, sat and gossiped, preferring each others' company to that of their tetchy husbands. Some of the younger people were excited; and families of elaborately dressed children laughed and romped, ignorant of why their governess was so short with them today.

'Effie dear,' Joseph said. 'I want you to take my arm. Let you and I walk together, and defy the sight of Mrs Michaelmas' countrymen to make us miserable.' He had undertaken to keep Euphemia out of earshot of the others.

Meanwhile Kate and Charity walked on ahead.

'Before we reach London, I may have no further opportunity of speaking alone with you.' Charity paused. 'Is this a suitable moment?'

She meant, were they alone? Kate, on the pretext of turning away from the wind to put down her veil, made sure there was no one close enough to overhear among the people strolling nearby or staring out to sea. Charity herself was unwilling for some reason to be recognized with Kate. She was blinkered by a hideous out-of-date bonnet borrowed from one of the servants. Its brim, ornamented with gathers, stuck forward like an upside-down scoop.

'I had several purposes in going to Paris.'

Having some notion of Charity's business there, Kate blushed and said nothing.

'One of them was to find a good educational establishment for a young lady who is to be brought up abroad. You must know that I mean Miss Georgiana Michaelmas. My daughter.'

Joseph, chatting earnestly with his sister, glanced from time to time at the two other women. Knowing as much as his wife about the so-called widow

140

Michaelmas, he noted how well they were impersonating a lady of quality and her put-upon servant. Charity, with a good whore's acting ability, dithered along, talking continuously and never taking her eyes off her 'mistress" face. Kate was careful to look straight ahead of her, and give short, emotionless replies. The wind smoothed her veil close against every detail of her face.

'Those are the terms I offer,' Charity was saying. Her body was inclined slightly forward, miming anxiety.

'Be assured, I note what you ask,' Kate replied, trying to sound chilly and raising her voice as a group of her acquaintance approached. 'Good morning!' she added, in greeting.

It was Lady Augusta and a group of other noisy young people. 'Just think, we're emigrés now!' one girl was saying. Some of the men were laying bets on whether the town would remain Royalist for as long as it took for the wind and tides to change.

Behind walked a separate group. Lady Augusta's son, the six-year-old Lord Fitzpayne, was dressed as a miniature Guards officer and watched over by his tutor and two footmen.

At length Kate and Charity rejoined the others.

'Joseph, dearest,' said Kate, 'Mrs Michaelmas has put to me an interesting proposal. It concerns one of her god-children.' Avoiding Euphemia's stare, she looked steadily at her husband. Whether because the sun was in her eyes, or because the wind was cold, she could not help blinking rapidly as she spoke. 'She – the little girl – is a young lady of school age, whose parents were dear to Mrs Michaelmas. I understand they've both died suddenly, in the West Indies.'

Later Joseph remarked, 'Its deucedly sensible of the lady, to give the parents a West Indian address. Dying of fever is what most folk in the Caribbean seem to do best.'

Charity thought she'd done well, too. She rarely took anything in her life very lightly. But next morning, as the crowded Dover packet entered the open sea amid undignified rejoicing in the tiny aft saloon, she allowed herself a moment of cool self-congratulation. It was true that she had been considering a Parisian education for Georgiana. But now, with the city falling and the Continent closed again, this plan was better by far.

While Georgiana was growing up she must in any case be separated from her mother. She had to be kept free from the stigma of being Charity's daughter, together with the uncertainties that were part of her mother's profession. In some circles Charity might go on passing for a respectable woman – but for how long? The more wealth she gained, together with a limited kind of influence as hostess of a political salon, the more widely she would be known to polite society as a whore.

In Paris, therefore, Charity had been dismayed to meet Kate. She had thought there was no one she might encounter socially who knew of Georgiana and her origins.

But even as they had been sitting down at the Ambassador's dinner table an idea had been forming itself in Charity's mind. She knew that Kate could be made to feel a share of responsibility towards Georgiana, her brother's child. By using Kate's sense of duty to make her an accomplice, there were several things she could achieve. Georgiana could have a secure home and a blameless, if false, background. With luck the child herself might be deceived as to her birth. Above all, Kate too could be bound to a lifetime of silence.

CHAPTER EIGHT

Thus an ocean, as well as the years, came to separate six-year-old Georgiana from her mother. She was to be brought up as an American young lady, in the state of Virginia. The best schools, the finest tutors, in time the most sought-after dressmakers and milliners, together with a place in the highest social sphere – all these were to be bought for her by her mother's fortune, under the guardianship of her increasingly dear 'aunt' Lee. Georgiana, when next she saw England, would have been refashioned as a foreigner. In America even her past could be made anew.

Meanwhile, in a select girls' school in Richmond, Virginia, Georgiana came to treat Kate's family as honorary cousins, and began to dress herself as carefully as she'd once done her dolls. Time passed.

For the grown-ups, preoccupied with their young families or their businesses, the seasons flickered by as though each day's sun was a blur and the nights were as brief as a blink. Only in the grim months before the battle at Waterloo had time seemed to falter – to run backward indeed. Bonaparte's sudden return had looked certain to cancel every victory against him over the past twenty desperate years. But that threat beaten off, and the former Emperor removed for good, the world returned to what everyone called normality – though in fact a long period of peace was something only older folk recalled. Joseph Lee's European interests expanded, into a continent whose own resources had been used up by total war. Westward, too, several

143

fortunes were his for the picking up, as the use of steamships on the Ohio and Mississippi rivers made him a trader in other commodities besides timber.

As one of Joseph's leading shareholders, Sophy's husband also prospered in this era of peace and reconstruction. By Tom's eighth birthday the Fraser family had moved house several times. At first they had taken a cottage, with old apple trees and a tumbledown pigsty in the garden, in the village of Bow, just east of the City. Then came a tall terraced house on Kensington High Street with a view across orchards to the barn and stables of Earl's Court Farm. With the birth, a year apart, of two daughters, Mary-Anne and Louisa, they moved to a large old house in Southwark overlooking the Thames. Its drawing room had a bay window jutting over the river, so that the ceiling glimmered with reflected light. At high water the dome of St Paul's cathedral, just across the water, was crowded from sight by the sails of wherries.

Fraser's own undertakings, back in Europe, also swelled the family's fortunes. In his workroom in the house in Southwark the number of his assistants increased. He took an office near Whitehall, and he and Sophy moved their family to a house in Mayfair. Its dignified façade looked on to South Audley Street. From the back there was a view over high-walled gardens and mews dunghills to other cliff-like mansions in Grosvenor Square. There was an office here, too, taking up the length of the second floor, where Fraser often worked alone late into the night. On the first floor, with its marble fireplaces and double doors, was a dining room that seated twenty.

In this setting, Sophy's role changed. She was still her husband's confidante – even, as he put it, jesting but shy, his lover and wife combined. But she no longer helped to write his business letters; instead, he employed two bright young men as his secretaries.

144

Several evenings a month she now sat in a satin gown at the head of his table, while their guests dined on plovers' eggs and saddle of lamb followed by wondrously confected fruits out of season. Many people were there for pleasure, but increasingly others were invited on business.

Sophy greeted her family's improved fortunes with relief, but also with incredulity. As with many people who grew up in the war years, the very idea of being safe from hardship seemed to her a dream, a violation of nature. In transforming herself into an accomplished hostess she was not just supporting her husband; she was carrying out a ritual meant to banish all memory of bad days gone by.

If to their parents the war with France was an ever-present memory, to the children it was soon as distant and vague as the campaigns of Julius Caesar. In their eyes time passed slowly. For Tom, even the happier years of his childhood crept by; he could not believe he would ever begin to grow up.

One day, however, he ceased to do lessons upstairs with his brother and sisters and their governess. With a trunkful of new clothes all in duplicate, he was put into a hackney carriage and sent away, to school. Yesterday evening he had been a child. Today everyone, including Sophy, treated him as a young man.

Tom grew taller than his mama, even as the servants stopped teasing him with pet names and started to call him 'sir'. The months, if not the years, began to pass with wonderful swiftness. His brother joined him at school, making another impossible thing happen. Now Tom was one of the big boys.

Like young Edward, Tom was getting two kinds of education. Since Fraser had grown up illiterate, it was with curiosity and awe that he sent his boys as weekly boarders to Westminster School. At the same time, Tom began working for his father, as a part-time apprentice. Each week the histories of Pliny and Gibbon and the verses of Ovid or Virgil were reluctantly set aside. In their place, at his father's desk at home, he was made to study another curriculum, on which only geology and draftsmanship offered him pleasure.

As suddenly as they had begun, Tom's years as a schoolboy were ending. He had been successful in his studies, but less so at making himself popular. Like his parents he lacked guile, and he had failed to hide the fact that he found many of his classmates dullards and amateurs. Above all they resented his apparent friendly indifference, as an outsider in their anxious gilded world where the smallest lapse from fashion could set off titters of mocking laughter.

Nonetheless at the end of his last term he let several of them persuade him to go with them to the Haymarket, to a bawdy-house. There a couple of fair, broad-featured Belgian whores expertly disposed of his virginity – several times over, it seemed. After three hours he came back out into the world feeling used up in every way. Lust, curiosity, hope, energy, even amazement – all felt gone for ever. Tom wanted no one to do with that day of his life ever to see him again. It was actually a relief to go home, ready to start working for his father.

As Fraser's business enlarged, so did Tom's practical knowledge. By his nineteenth birthday he had helped on various projects: steam printing presses for *The Times* newspaper; forge-blowing apparatus for the naval dockyard at Chatham; a railway ten miles long, on the land of a Northumbrian colliery owner. All was done, however, with joyless efficiency, out of duty to his father instead of love of the work itself.

Sometimes Tom's efforts were only just good enough. It was as well that the railway needed only to be a crude thing, worked by horses rather than a little locomotive firebox. Otherwise its specifications might have been disastrous. Sophy, who was worried lest Tom wasn't giving his father due support, couldn't understand: upstairs, in the study converted for him from the old schoolroom, Tom had been at work fourteen hours a day.

It was only later, when she and his sisters were helping to pack for his first working visit abroad, that she found the answer. Put away separately were sheaves of elaborate drawings for a private fantasy. They showed plans for a Graeco-Roman 'Temple of the Muses', to stand in an ornamental park. It had heavy pillared porticoes above broad flights of steps, and floors of mosaic. Sophy guessed it had been based on some ruined floors the lad had seen uncovered while helping survey a new post-road through Gloucestershire into Wales.

As it later chanced, some parts of Tom's plan were to be adopted, though not in the way he had imagined. Another company, engaged on draining a Lincolnshire fen, would take his design and build it as a pumping station. But by then Tom would be far away and greatly changed.

His twentieth year brought a chance to leave home, and Sophy could see he was anxious not to stay a week longer. She failed to realize though that he was reluctant to go on the terms offered. Many of his classmates, off on the Grand Tour, had already gone to where he reckoned the best of life could be experienced. In Italy the ghosts he had glimpsed in his schoolbooks would speak to him in the flesh. Even street beggars, in Naples or Palermo, would have the same features he had seen on statues and vases twenty-three centuries old. And while Englishmen like him designed toy versions of what the ancients built, on the empty Sicilian mountainsides the ruins of the original temples still stood, as graceful and barbaric as ever.

147

But for Tom his parents had decided there was to be no tour. He was to be the manager's deputy at an ironworks in northern France, on a new river port on the Seine. Fraser, more perceptive than usual, had agreed with Sophy that the lad might do better away from home. Among strangers any youthful mistakes might be more quickly forgotten than if Tom were seen only as his father's protégé. Besides, Fraser, who had recently bought out and expanded a shipyard in Dartford, had concerns of his own that left neither him nor Sophy much room for anxiety about their son.

So one spring morning, the sun just visible through the city's fog for the first time that year, Tom was embraced by his family, said goodbye to the servants, and was driven through the streets of London to the river, there to board the steam packet to Calais.

At a quay by the Tower of London the vessel was cast off, beneath a stream of black smoke full of smuts like little devils. As they passed downstream of Tom's old home at Southwark, fleets of wherries and the odd merchantman glided by the noisy steamboat, silent as mirages. The canopy of grimy vapour in which the city seemed to float was pierced by the April sun and glittered, transformed into a veil of golden rain. Below the Tower the Thames, too, was dirty: a swirling black sludge shot with green and pink iridescence. The mass of masts and rigging clogged the banks like a monstrous natural growth, leaving only a narrow channel out to sea. Beyond the banks, warehouses at length yielded to pollard willows and flooded grazing land. The sunlight and the breeze across the water grew stronger, and the horizon broadened out.

Closing the view beyond one long reach of river, there stood one reminder of the ever-growing city just left behind. Along the bank was a line of mean cottages, whose cellars flooded every spring with putrid brine. They stood at the foot of a broad column of flame-tinted smoke, within which arose a mysterious shape. Five hundred tons of oak scaffolding shrouded the partly built hull of the Fraser shipyard's newest vessel, a wooden steamship of unequalled size, destined for trade with India. The cloud of floating cinders that also surrounded it poured forth from a ring of fires, damped down each morning as the sun came up. Throughout the winter, the site's pumps had been threatened by frost, and each night tons of lumber had been burned to keep them working. Every evening the great hull was lit up, as if it were about to slide into the invisible river on a raft of flame.

Only as the thing passed astern and dwindled from sight did Tom feel he had finally left home. Full of half-formed hopes and unwitting resentments, a dutiful child yet almost a man, at last he had set forth. Into a world that, like every youth, he imagined had been freshly made just for him. Starting, in that spring of 1828, with the city of Paris.

CHAPTER NINE

Paris, 1828

'Have I been here before, Miss Lee?'

'No. When you were last in Europe you never visited Paris.'

'But you did, did you not?'

'Certainly I did.' Euphemia, sitting opposite Georgiana in the travelling carriage, looked very dignified as she said this. It was the girl's duty to respect her chaperone's worldly wisdom.

'So will you be able to show me everything here?'

Euphemia's face grew inhospitable. 'Yes, in fact.' Her tone implied that Georgiana could hardly have said anything more ill-mannered.

Not knowing what she'd done wrong, the girl blushed. She'd never spent much time before with Euphemia. Since she'd been six years old, it had been Kate whom she'd known as her foster-mother.

Georgiana loved her adopted aunt Kate more than she could have said. From gratitude for all the kindness Kate had shown her, but also out of insecurity. Half against her conscience, Kate had agreed to describe Charity as Georgiana's foster-parent and godmother – like herself, just an affectionate surrogate. Georgiana had grown up believing this version of events, despite several haphazard memories of her life before the voyage to America. The years that followed had been calm and happy. Nonetheless there lurked within her a little girl in despair at being torn loose from everything she'd known.

So if her good, generous uncle Joseph told her to

150

respect Euphemia's advice, that was what Georgiana would do. All the same, it was embarrassing, not knowing how to deal with the poor woman's unpredictable temper.

Tentatively Georgiana said, 'I really am very glad to be travelling with someone who knows these places so well.'

Euphemia bared her teeth in a grudging smile. Reddening again, Georgiana turned to stare out at the scruffy farmland that lay on either side of the new Avenue des Champs Elysées. She often found it hard to look Euphemia in the eye.

The three carriages needed for themselves, their luggage and their servants rolled on towards the royal parks, and the hotel in the Place Vendôme where a retinue of staff was due to greet them with all the grovelling due to such visitors.

It was Euphemia's first visit to Europe since the end of the war, in 1815. Outwardly she had changed very little. She had gone through girlhood middle-aged and now, at thirty-five, she was the same only more so. This season's fashions had enlarged the rim of her bonnet, which stood up like a halo stuck with giant rosettes. They had widened her skirts, so that indoors she was a menace to any small pieces of furniture; also her broad puffed sleeves made her wider across the shoulders than any man. But the discontented creature inside all this expensive frippery had altered not a jot.

In one way, her lot had improved. She had feared that being a chaperone would be yet another humiliation. It would be a way of announcing that not even an act of God was now expected to get her a husband. She hadn't counted, however, on the fact that for the first time in her life she would be in charge. Of course all her adult life she had given orders to children and servants. But this was different. Being Georgiana's duenna meant that for the time being Euphemia was the virtual owner of the most courted young woman in Virginia – of the person who, out of all the world, she would most like to have been herself.

The girl's looks alone might have made her fortune. At every stage of growing up, Georgiana's beauty had seemed beyond improvement – until, with the passing of several months more, it was seen to have changed again, to a new form of perfection. And unlike Euphemia, whose brother and provider was a self-made man, Georgiana had of course never been poor.

Like the girl herself, Euphemia believed the invented version of Georgiana's life.

'When am I due to meet my old mama – my godmother, I mean?'

'Mrs Michaelmas will send for you as soon as she arrives.' Not answering questions properly was one way in which Euphemia emphasized her control over Georgiana.

Did she love the girl, or hate her? To be asked such a question would have made Euphemia shake with rage. If only because she didn't know the answer.

In the Grande Galerie of the Louvre the giant canvas of 'The Marriage at Cana' had not changed either. Still it looked down, a little in need of cleaning, on the place where, all those years before, Euphemia had spent so much fierce energy stitching a hideous copy of it on to a piece of fabric the size of a horse blanket. Its dozens of figures, seemingly in motion as violent as a windblown forest, stayed unaltered – while, below, it was passed and re-passed by a new generation of living people.

Tom didn't care for such an overdone piece of work. His reason for coming here, on his way through Paris, had been to look at some classical statuary. In particular he'd wanted to see some Cretan figures that he'd found illustrated in a book of engravings. His tastes tended to that sort of thing: simple, primitive, but subtle.

He'd been distracted, however. His attention had been caught by a Roman carving of the birth of Venus. Her arms spread wide, the goddess was looking up as she was lifted from the sea. She was clad in a modest tunic that, even in stone, looked wetter than Tom would have believed possible.

From there, he'd found himself wandering up to several paintings by Old Masters, also on a theme of women and holiness. After a while it had seemed to him, aged nineteen but still aware of knowing next to nothing about the opposite sex, that the whole palace was stocked with virgins in a state of rapture. One early Italian Madonna knelt before the angel of the Annunciation, in a simple room like the heart of all quietness. A Flemish painter had shown her sitting, patient, wise and magnificently robed, beside an open casement. Beyond, a view of hills and rivers stretched to infinity, as splendid as Tom's hopes for his own future. In another medieval painting, the Virgin was surrounded by maidens in waiting, bright-haired and still within a secret garden.

It was too much for Tom, finding himself overcome by lust and awe both at once. He turned to go.

On his way out, quite involuntarily he stopped.

Through an archway connecting two rooms he saw another painting. This picture was not of a saint or a maiden sacrifice. Instead, it showed a loaf of bread and a flask of wine against a background of shadows. Below, looking at something else, was one of the visitors to the gallery: a girl.

She sat surrounded by bustle, much of it to do with her own entourage. A manservant stood a respectful way off, ignoring the pictures and occasionally shifting his weight. Nearby, two maidservants were also trying

153

to look patient. There was a chaperone, all fur-
trimmed capes and trailing bonnet-strings, who fidgeted about as if wanting to tell the servants they should
look more alert. Once or twice she said something to the
girl, who answered without turning her head.

All the while a stream of people from the fashionable
world wandered by, on the far side of the archway.
Within its frame only two things didn't move: the
arrangement of commonplace objects in the painting,
as eternal as the prayer of the poor for their daily bread,
and the expensively dressed girl.

Tom wasn't sure he cared for what she was wearing.
But unlike the fussy chaperone, at least she was able
to turn high fashion to her advantage. Beneath a
cartwheel hat trimmed with plumes her neck was
bewitchingly slender. Her enormous sleeves and broad
skirts made her waist almost too narrow to be true.

She had dark smooth hair, with a warm lustre. Her
features, though calm, were expressive, like a bright
landscape in changeable weather. Tom stared, unaware
of his own rudeness. This breathing creature suggested
to him more mystery and splendour than any exhibit
in the whole gallery.

Not only was she untouchable though; she was also
not to be looked at too freely. The chaperone, catching
sight of Tom, didn't hesitate. With a swift, earnest
movement, she made as if to summon the manservant.
Tom was appalled. He had no desire to be seen by such
a girl while fumbling for an apology. Turning, he
walked away, with a burning face and a bright, foolish
look of intentness. Would she be there tomorrow? And
if so, how would he find words to introduce himself?

He sighed, so loudly that several people looked
round. And now he supposed he'd better do as he'd
promised Mama, and pay a call on some old biddy she
knew, at an address in the Place Vendôme.

* * *

Georgiana did not return to the hotel until late that afternoon. Next day, there was to be no sightseeing. Instead, she was to prepare to make an important visit.

It seemed almost nothing could make her presentable. Euphemia, anxious and snappish, had Georgiana put in and out of one gown, then two more. Hot with frustration, she had declared that anyone could surely do better than *that* with the girl's hair. When Georgiana's maid responded by bursting into tears, Euphemia's own maid was summoned, to be reduced in turn to wringing her hands and looking desperate.

All the way to their rendezvous, at a private apartment in the Faubourg St Honoré, Euphemia looked dangerous. Georgiana was bewildered. She had few definite memories of the person they were due to meet, but none of them was bad.

In a quiet, luxurious room overlooking an enclosed garden, they were asked to wait. They sat in silence for a few slow minutes. At length the door was opened again by the butler, and Charity Michaelmas walked in.

She took each of them in turn by the hand, greeting them in a steady, businesslike voice. They stood, waiting for her to sit down. As if not noticing, she walked to one of the windows and stood with her back to her guests before taking a seat. Only then did she raise her veil.

'Miss Bingham. Georgiana.' Charity looked intently at the girl. Georgiana's new surname had been chosen years before, when she'd sailed for America. But Charity spoke as if trying it out for the first time.

'Yes, ma'am.' Georgiana returned Charity's look with open curiosity. She was flattered by the interest of such a splendid lady. For Charity, at thirty-six, had one kind of complete beauty, just as Georgiana, at twenty, had another.

155

'Are you happy with your travelling arrangements? Is there any way in which you should like them changed?'

'No, ma'am – thank you.' Georgiana, as she spoke, noticed Euphemia stiffen. Euphemia had been so full of herself, as head of their entourage, that it had not occurred to Georgiana that her chaperone might be accountable in turn to someone else. Yet such was Euphemia's awe of the dazzling Mrs Michaelmas and her great wealth, that she was actually fearful of criticism from her.

'Have you much acquaintance in Paris?'

'No, ma'am. Though Miss Lee is familiar with the city – as you know, of course!'

'Indeed I remember.' Charity's voice was neutral. Euphemia looked fraught, however. In her descriptions of the exodus from Paris, back in the wonderful and terrible year of 1815, she had allowed it to seem that the rescue of her friend Mrs Michaelmas had been her own idea.

Charity said, 'As to your lack of acquaintance, it shall be remedied. Was your foster-mother well, when you left?'

Kate had recently been surprised to find herself pregnant again, aged thirty-eight. The baby, her fifth, was younger than his brothers and sisters by some years.

'Thank you, yes. Aunt Kate – my foster-mother – was well out of danger by the time I said goodbye.' Georgiana's eyes brimmed with tears. She hadn't known that the mention of her last home would affect her so.

Charity hesitated, watching her. In a low voice she asked, 'You miss her?'

Truthfully enough, Georgiana said, 'I'm very glad to be here. But I am bound to miss my family just a little' – for so she thought of them.

'I'm glad,' said Charity. Seeing Georgiana look surprised, she added, 'I should not have wished you to be anything but happy in Virginia.'

Curiosity was printed all over Georgiana's face. 'I shall be going home again, shall I not?'

Charity hedged. 'That must surely depend on whom you marry. You are not particularly young still to be single, you know.' Both spinsters, the old maid and the whore, looked at the girl very solemnly.

With a turn of her fine head towards Euphemia, Charity added, 'I hope Miss Lee finds you adequately provided for.'

'Oh – amply, Mrs Michaelmas,' said Euphemia. 'Far more than sufficient – and Mrs Lee has also – '

'I would not have Mrs Lee or her husband put to expense. Any further needs – '

'Oh, but Mrs Lee can spare it – we all can – your kindness – your self-sacrifice – too much – '

'My duty, Miss Lee, as Miss Bingham's godmother. It is also my pleasure – and my will. Consider besides that next year, from the estate of her late parents, Miss Bingham inherits' – and Charity named a sum that made Euphemia turn pale with reverence. Georgiana herself was expressionless, so far did such wealth go beyond anything she could imagine.

Taking out her watch, Charity stood up. 'We shall of course be meeting several times, while I remain in Paris. If you would,' turning to Georgiana with the easy politeness of a slight acquaintance, 'I should be grateful if, before I return to London, we might talk alone.'

Euphemia made a gesture of entreaty. 'I insist. No – no – I insist. I have not brought your goddaughter here so that I can stand between you – I would not dream . . .'

And backed out of the room, arms raised as if holding them both off by force.

Alone with Georgiana, Charity thought hard before choosing her words. Sitting down again and absently stroking her muff, she said, 'For the present, I merely wanted to ask – have you been inclined to accept any suitor? I mean, in particular, any American gentleman, Miss – ah, have you any objection if I call you Georgiana?'

'I haven't been. And please do.' The girl was trying not to look surprised. Just for a moment, the formidable Mrs Michaelmas' self-possession had seemed forced. Georgiana had been struggling to sort her dim recollections of this woman, whom she knew had once been a foster-parent to her. Now, catching a glint of feeling in those calm, dark eyes, she found herself recalling – what?

Her own face was easily read. Charity made a point of softening her voice. 'You see, I meant to say – in the most general way – that your choice of alliance – of a husband – may take you far from your last home.'

This was said more casually than it was meant. Time had not weakened Charity's plans for Georgiana; on the contrary, they were about to bear fruit.

'I never thought about that,' murmured Georgiana. She had grown up concerned for little beyond her immediate present.

'You see,' Charity persisted, 'you may find that you have chosen to live in Europe – after your marriage. If so, it may seem less strange to you if you can remember your life before Mrs Lee became your guardian.'

It was as close as Charity dared come to asking the most important question. Did her own face stand out – just a little – from the dozens of nurserymaids who'd cared for Georgiana in the early years?

But, given her plans, what answer did she want to hear? She watched the girl, torn between hope and fear.

'I don't think I shall recognize anything when we get

to London,' hazarded Georgiana. 'As for people – why, when I was little, I was bound to see everyone differently from how I do now.' This conversation was embarrassing her dreadfully. It would probably be good manners to remember Mrs Michaelmas, and everything about her, in the closest detail.

There was a hint of tiredness in Charity's manner as she stood up and gave Georgiana her hand. 'I hope in time you will understand – no – forgive – the suddenness with which you were sent away, into Mrs Lee's care.'

'Oh, but I've been happy – indeed I have!' Tears of earnestness stood in Georgiana's eyes. It was true that her uprooting, back in childhood, had deeply disturbed her, so that she had come to cling to Kate as if for life itself. Probably it was also why she could recall so little from the years before.

'There was a reason, which I hope you will think was a good one. It concerns the terms of your inheritance. Let me not burden you with talk of old quarrels, long dead. It is enough to say that your father's will demanded you should not continue to live with me . . .

'Of course, should you wish – why, I should be happy to explain to you what happened. In the meantime, let us see what can be done to expand your acquaintance in Paris.'

Georgiana felt troubled as she was driven away from her meeting with Charity. Was it her own fault that Mrs Michaelmas – the first mother she'd had – appeared so cool?

Only Hortense, Charity's maid of many years' service now, had guessed the truth of the girl's parentage.

As soon as Georgiana and her chaperone had taken their leave, Charity, though recently dressed to go out, retired to her bedchamber. With a look of suppressed agitation she gave orders that she was to be left alone.

By nightfall Hortense had become puzzled; towards midnight she was anxious. Respect for her much loved mistress' commands vied in her with concern. In the small hours, she finally acted on her resolve to knock at the door. 'Madame?' she called in a low voice.

There was a murmur of distress. Surprised at hearing such a sound, Hortense hurried in.

Years of training in discretion counted for little at the sight that met her. Charity had fallen to the floor, fully conscious. For hours she had lain in the darkening room, unable to move. She still held her muff, which lay beneath her in a patch of cold urine.

Lights were brought and a doctor was sent for. Mastering her distress, Hortense had Charity put to bed and sat down to await the morning and the doctor's arrival.

All this time Charity had neither moved nor spoken.

At length, however, she slept. It was only towards dawn that Hortense saw her trying to say something. As a gesture of encouragement, she took her hand. 'Yes, madame. I listen.'

Charity's voice was weak but distinct. Her face was scorched by tears.

'Can you guess what I have sacrificed?'

Hortense knew she was referring to her years of separation from her daughter. She shook her head sorrowfully.

'No, madame. I cannot imagine how such a thing must feel.'

'I refuse to have done it for nothing.'

Hortense was silent. She did not allow herself an opinion on her mistress' plans as a matchmaker.

Later that morning, lying propped up with pillows so that her hair could be properly unpinned and brushed, Charity said, 'You've never seen me pity myself before, have you, Hortense?' She was pale and weak, but otherwise she had recovered.

'Never, madame,' said the maid, tactfully brushing away without a change of expression.

Thereafter it was understood between them never to mention Charity's fit of hysterical paralysis. Much less the repressed passions that had caused it.

It usually pleased Tom to think of his mother. She was better looking than most other fellows' mamas, and better company too. But in getting him to visit this aunt person, he felt she'd let him down – even though he could tell that she herself didn't much like the woman. At least he'd been able to postpone the call for nearly three weeks.

But, knowing Miss Lee would be at home this time, as he crossed the Place Vendôme he looked like a small boy on his way to school.

At the same moment Georgiana was asking, 'Who is this gentleman who you said would be calling?'

Euphemia was busy embroidering a pair of slippers for her brother. Looking up, she said, 'This is not a gentleman caller. This is a young man paying his respects to me on his mother's behalf.' She went back to her sewing with the fierce, neat movements of someone impaling a doll through the heart.

Georgiana understood what Euphemia meant. After an unexplained delay by Mrs Michaelmas, her own entry into the English-speaking part of Parisian society had begun with delightful suddenness. The nights were taken up with dancing, and her afternoons had been claimed by a flood of visitors, most of whom had been young men and their connections.

Thank goodness Euphemia, far from being jealous, was eager to identify with her social success. Sometimes it was almost embarrassing. Georgiana herself

161

had been rapt with curiosity at the attention paid to her. But when Lady Augusta Fitzpayne and her son had called, it was Euphemia who had been blushing and flustered.

There was probably no knowing what this afternoon's visitor had done to displease. Poor Euphemia's black-and-white view of things was too eccentric to bear looking at sensibly.

Mr Thomas Fraser's faults were even less apparent once he'd arrived. The servant announced him and amid the usual pleasantries he took his seat on a hard chair opposite them both. He was a tall young man, bright-faced and hesitant, with curly fair hair. For some reason he looked at Georgiana, then at everything else in the room, as if he'd just been shaken awake and found himself somewhere unexpected.

In truth, the coincidence that had sat him down within two yards of Georgiana made him tremble with suppressed excitement. But, since Tom was a gentleman by nature as well as by upbringing, he did his best to ignore her. His visit, after all, was to Euphemia.

Introductions completed, he began, 'My mother – '

'I beg your pardon?' Euphemia said. She looked up from her sewing, unsmiling.

Tom tried again. 'My mother sends her regards.'

Euphemia took another careful stitch. Having let a silence establish itself, she looked up again, as if waiting.

Tom could not help sounding puzzled at her obvious hostility. 'I believe she had the pleasure of meeting you in London some years ago. While you were travelling in Europe with my aunt Kate.'

'I remember Mrs Fraser. She and I were introduced when your aunt' – putting unfriendly emphasis on the last two words – 'and I were indeed travelling in Europe. With my brother, Mr Joseph Lee.' Her tone

162

suggested that Tom had mentioned something he ought not to have done.

The young man looked at her steadfastly, at a loss to know what he'd said wrong.

'Do give Mrs Fraser my compliments,' added Euphemia, in a manner that implied huge generosity. Like a lot of rude people, she had a high opinion of her own good manners.

'My mother was particularly anxious that I should ask on her behalf after my aunt's health.' The last news to reach the household in South Audley Street was that Kate had been near her time.

With fierce concentration, Euphemia drew out a thread to its full length. 'Your aunt is well.'

Georgiana, sitting with her eyes lowered and her hands in her lap, was awash with shame. She'd always suspected the jealousy Euphemia felt towards Kate. But she would never have guessed that it would affect her behaviour towards Kate's entire family. She glanced at Tom, who showed the bewilderment of a puppy unfairly hit on the nose.

'Dear Aunt Kate has been safely delivered of a beautiful little boy. When we saw her last she was beginning to mend, though' – Georgiana paused, caught short by the memory – 'for several days . . . we thought we'd lost her . . .'

She turned her head away, the better to avoid tears at the terrible recollection of what might have been.

Tom was in agony. He'd been thrust, unwilling, into a meeting that proved to be with the creature of his dreams. Now her first words showed her as even more wonderful – more tactful, more passionate – than he could have guessed. And social form demanded that he should virtually behave as if she weren't there.

There was a silence which Euphemia did nothing to break, while Georgiana tried to breathe more easily and Tom stared at the carpet. At length, prickling with

163

embarrassment, he ventured, 'I am so glad that your news is good.' In fact, he had not seen his aunt for several years. His relief was so obviously for the sake of Georgiana herself that the girl could not help smiling. Though innocent, she was observant for her age. Just by watching and listening, she'd learned more about human foibles than most young women could by getting themselves into all sorts of trouble. It was as though, looking on from a corner, she should have been the chaperone, with Euphemia, all whims and high-handedness, as the coquette.

Her smile unmanned Tom completely. He tried to steady himself by looking at Euphemia, sewing away as if she'd got behindhand in making his shroud.

'Shall you be staying long in Paris, Miss Lee?'

He was so obviously interested in the answer that Georgiana nearly burst out laughing. Then, for some reason, the effort of keeping a straight face brought her close to tears once more. Fearing that Euphemia would snub Tom again, she interrupted, 'We shall be staying at this address for some time – is that not so, Miss Lee?'

'We are waiting on the party of a certain gentleman and his mother,' said Euphemia, with a conspiratorial look at Georgiana that the girl completely failed to understand. 'Since they – I mean, of course, Lady Augusta, and her son, Lord Fitzpayne – have been kind enough to invite us on the rest of their tour.'

Georgiana tried to look unsurprised. None of her elders had told her about this.

Threading her needle with a wool of a different colour, Euphemia was squinting hard. 'In other words, Mr Fraser, Miss Bingham and I have little idea how long we shall remain in Paris.'

She said this as though Tom's polite enquiry had been an impertinence. To make up for this, Georgiana could not help giving him a smile of encouragement.

It left him feeling as though his heart had been blown clean out of him. With the barest pretence of speaking only to Euphemia, he said, 'I myself will be staying near Paris for several months.' He named the town where he was lodging, an hour's ride from the capital, and described his position at the ironworks.

'Why are you so far from home?' asked Georgiana. 'Did you wish for that post very much?'

'It's something my father has asked me to do,' he said, as if not quite understanding. After the period of his childhood when his parents seemed to have been taken from him for ever, he had almost ceased to question anything they said or did. At some level of his mind, little Tom, the poor orphan child, as he'd heard himself several times described, had decided that he wouldn't dare. He would only be punished by losing them again. It was a habit of thought that he had yet to outgrow.

He added, 'As for work, I can't think what else to do.'

'And as for other things?' Georgiana asked, turning to face him. Tom was almost too taken with how she looked to notice what she was saying. Her dark eyes held him, steadfast.

'To spend my life as I should like, I should need independent means.'

There was a sniff of disdain from Euphemia, tugging hard on a thread. She despised lack of money almost as much as she hated ugly people.

The young folk were too well mannered not to be embarrassed. After a pause, Tom went on, 'I should need to be free. I mean, free to travel.' He started to talk about Italy. The antiquities that were being dug up there – oh, what could he tell her if he wanted to do justice to some of the newest discoveries? A few weeks ago, in the Louvre, he'd seen a Venus that he thought was – well, how could he describe her? – and

165

yet it was said that she was almost ordinary, compared to some of the works now being collected by scholarly Englishmen abroad.

Speaking of the Louvre – on that same day – the most wonderful coincidence –

Euphemia cleared her throat. Then she put her sewing aside and made a show of looking at her watch. The fifteen minutes that custom allowed for a visit like this were over.

Tom had no idea how he came away from there. Once he'd started to talk, even though she was almost the first girl he'd met properly outside his family, the words had started rushing out of him. He'd had no idea it was possible to feel so interesting. He felt like a hero of self-renunciation, saying goodbye with the same look of well-bred indifference for each woman, instead of telling Georgiana how he'd seen her before. With her chaperone standing by and watching them, she gave him her hand in farewell, murmuring something conventional and blushing with the effort of not smiling.

Back outside, in the street, the afternoon light seemed tremendous. Hawkers shouted, draymen growled and swore, hundreds of iron-bound wheels sounded against the stones beneath. The room where he'd just been received, all fresh flowers and mirrors and expensive solitude, seemed more than ever like the deepest bower of feminine privacy.

How wonderful it seemed – yet how inevitable – that it had been here, rather than on a different street, in some other city, that he had been fated to meet this girl. The whole of Paris existed only as a maze that led through those portals, across that lobby, up that grand staircase, along all those corridors, into a quiet room that had been, for him, at the very heart of confusion. He thought about the steadiness with which she'd looked at him, when they'd been unobserved by her chaperone, and the vulnerable sweep of her neck above her straight, narrow back. He had found himself; he was lost.

As for Georgiana, after Tom had left she made an excuse to go to her room, trying not to look too cheerful at meeting this new acquaintance. Once alone, she lay down on her huge bed, by turns lit by a little smile and fetching a sigh.

Then, without warning, she found she was weeping, until she thought she might choke.

CHAPTER TEN

On a hot August afternoon below London Bridge, Sophy joined a select party on a chartered steamboat going down to the Fraser shipyard at Dartford. The leading shareholders of the Far Eastern Steam Navigation Company, together with some of their womenfolk and four gentlemen from *The Times* and the *Morning Post*, were on their way to an important public occasion. To promote investment in the company's great ship, the *Albion*, they had been invited to witness the return of the vessel's smaller prototype, the *Sparrowhawk*, from its first sea trial.

The tide was near the ebb as they cast off into the crowded river. On the aft deck their elaborately dressed party was served with refreshments, under an awning designed to keep off flakes of soot from the funnel rather than the heat of the sun. At this season the whole city seemed to give off vapours, from stableyards behind each street, and from thousands of foetid alleyways. But the river was the dirtiest place. Their little ship floated on a torrent of black sludge.

It puffed a trail of smoke over scenes that had changed little for many generations. Behind the waterfront the narrow streets rose steeply, lined with elegant brick houses whose roofs gathered in a tide against the great nave and dome of St Paul's. The sky was huge, pricked by hundreds of classical white-stone spires. Beyond the ancient arches of London Bridge, through which the river poured in a series of cataracts, there stood the Georgian palaces that lined the Strand. They

168

appeared to recede into a dignified infinity, the broad flights of steps beneath their river terraces lapped by the retreating tide.

The paddle steamer fussed on, past half-timbered houses with narrow rotting gables jutting out above banks of glistening mud. The masts of sea-going vessels rose far above the houses, thick as a reed bed. Apart from their own gaudy little cockleshell, there was no other steamer in sight; every other ship was still rigged for sail. Only when they left the city behind did their surroundings become less like a scene from former times. Along the Wapping shore, huge warehouses built of brick as solid as a mountain core were going up, making a wall so dense that the fields behind might as well have been magicked out of existence.

Under a muggy grey sky sheened with bronze they overtook another grubby little steamer. It was towing out to sea a wooden man o' war whose days were now done. The fighting ship's sails were furled, and streaked with soot like melting black snow. Its wooden hull, astern, was crusted with carvings picked out in battered gilt. It towered above both steamers. In the warm air the black smoke from the two smaller boats collapsed in swirls about it.

They passed the long Venetian façade of Greenwich Palace, which rode on the water's edge like a mirage. Soon the shipyard would be in sight. Sophy strained to look across the intervening stretch of estuary. The water was rimmed with a dull gleam. On shore, in this thick, late-summer air, everything – houses, trees, hayricks, distant hills – was reduced to a silhouette, like stage scenery.

At last, beyond the prickle of masts along the Woolwich shore by the arsenal, the hull of the *Albion* was visible. It stood above the huts and scaffolding of the yards and the scrubby pollard willows of the Dartford countryside. Seen as a flat grey shape, it looked mysteriously larger than ever.

Sophy had not been to the shipyard for some time. In recent months Fraser had had to travel extensively, arranging for the provision of coaling jetties for his ship, at a berth in South Wales at Milford Haven, and in Lisbon and Gibraltar. If the *Albion* was to reach India without relying on sail power, and favourable winds, she would need supplies of fuel to take her the length of Africa and back, round the Cape of Good Hope. In his absence his fellow directors had had charge of the shipyard. Responsibility for day-to-day affairs in particular had fallen to the project's other main backer. This was Harry Anstye, a man of private means whose knowledge was amateur but whose enthusiasms seemed boundless.

They disembarked at a floating jetty beneath the shadow of the *Albion*'s copper-sheathed hull. Once ashore, the ladies, walking gingerly up the dusty slipway, paused to put up their parasols, like a flock of birds stretching their wings. Sophy looked around for Edward, her second son, who was due to join their party here.

One or two things she'd noticed in the yard made her all the more anxious to see him. Amid pleased exclamations from the visitors at the 'horrid grandeur' of the nearly completed hull in its forest of oaken props, at least a couple of other people had seen that something here could not be right.

'Between you and me, that can't be on the same schedule.'

'Doesn't look very useful, does it?'

'Ned!' Sophy greeted her son in a voice of anxiety masquerading as happy surprise.

'Hello, mother.' Edward, an angular, cheerful sixteen-year-old, dutifully took her arm. 'Shall I be

170

needed right now?' He lowered his voice, glancing around them.

Sophy tried not to smile in response to his conspiratorial expression. Free from the promptings of guilt that she still felt towards her elder son, she was always at ease with Edward.

'That won't be necessary, thank you Neddy dearest. The two young gentlemen from Mr Anstye's office take care of our party. But' — she motioned with her eyes rather than her head — 'what's happening here? What did your father say?'

Edward, who was a self-confident character for his age, had the presence of mind to be discreet as well, for once. 'He said scarcely a word. I nearly told him I didn't believe he could be so close. You know what he's like, usually.'

'Thank heavens you didn't, if Mr Anstye was with him. I take it this muddle is Mr Anstye's doing?'

'I'll say it is!' exclaimed Edward, following Sophy's look.

Beneath the bowsprit of the *Albion*, right in her path to the water's edge, another vessel was being built. The smaller ship was still a wooden frame, as though a sea creature had been dug up from the ooze in skeleton form and put together again with its vanished snout dipping down towards the river.

'Not only did Father not say much, but Anstye was as pleased with himself as only an idiot can be. I think he's an idiot. Don't you think he's an idiot, too?'

Sophy gripped his hand hard, as a signal to be quiet. Turning, as if to dwell on the view of the river and the busy shipyard, she made sure no one else was in earshot. 'Ned, don't ever say so in a public place. Not even to me. Firstly, it could put your father's company at risk. You must understand that.'

She paused, to collect herself and look carefree.

'And secondly?'

'And the other reason you mustn't talk too freely to me, Ned dearest, is that I can't bear it when you remind me of myself at your age.' She gave a grim little smile.

They walked a few yards further up from the tide line. 'Of course, Father and Anstye both said something about putting things to rights. That was the phrase they kept batting between them ... Father must really be angry with him for sub-leasing the yard. Mustn't he, Mama?'

Sophy nodded. 'But I doubt there was any "of course" about it. Mr Anstye's capital is more important to us than you realize. I take it this new work *is* on the rented half of the site?' To accommodate a ship the size of the *Albion*, Fraser had had to rent an extra quarter-mile-square area of shipyard, in addition to building on his own premises.

'I think so. Mama, shouldn't the *Sparrowhawk* be in sight soon?'

'When is the tide due to turn?' It had been planned that the prototype steamer should be seen by the visitors as she returned on the flood tide, partly for navigational reasons, but mainly to show off her maximum speed of eight knots.

'Some minutes back, I think.'

Edward was not alone in beginning to think about the time. Nearby, amid a group of shareholders and their wives, one of Anstye's secretaries was looking by turns at his pocket watch and out towards the sea. There was still little call for impatience, much less unease, but Sophy could not help following the young man's gaze down-river.

The visibility was not good. On a day like this it was hard to see where the estuary's horizon met the sky. Beyond the near distance, any sails looked as if their ship were drifting in mid-air.

'But surely it can't be hard to see your father,' Sophy

172

said, meaning his ship. 'We only saw one other steam boat, on our way down. And there are hardly any houses in that direction.' The sight of smoke over the sea, even here below London, was an unfamiliar one. Only a town could give off the same volume of smoke as a sixty-ton steamship.

They walked on to where a better view could be had. Edward said, 'I can see something there – I'll wager you I can!'

Sophy shaded her eyes. 'Are you sure?' Far away towards the Essex shore there was a vertical thread of smoke that might have been anything. 'All I can see is something that might be a bonfire.'

'The land is further away than that – I'm sure it is. It must be something afloat. Don't you think?'

'Yes, dearest,' murmured Sophy, in a tone that meant Edward should keep his voice down and not advertise any delay out loud. She watched the column of smoke for a few moments longer. It was paler than the light grey sky and rose straight up for many hundreds of feet. After a minute or so she asked, 'What fuel is the *Sparrowhawk* burning – I mean, all steam vessels produce that filthy black smoke, don't they?'

'Well, yes. She's fired with coal rather than coke. Yes, what a clever mama! White smoke, like that – it's growing, isn't it? – only comes from wood.'

They lingered briefly, looking out to sea with feigned interest and the beginnings of weariness. Sophy several times opened her parasol against the hazy sun and shut it again. Absently she prodded its tip in the dust, making patterns, as she tried to explain to Edward which of his father's business connections were due to attend an important dinner party next week, and why. Meanwhile the distant smoke flattened across several miles of sky as they waited.

* * *

Several miles down-river, the *Sparrowhawk* had just come within sight of her berth at the Dartford shipyard. To Harry Anstye, standing by the helm and pining to be less of an onlooker, the Kent shore was just a dull jumble. Here the outline of a coppice, there the faint profile of the uplands beyond. But to Fraser's eye, each distant shape announced other hills or valleys, continued underneath them on the river bed. For him, as much as for the half-pay commodore the company employed as nautical adviser, this great waterway, with its baffling gusts, its sudden fogs, and its tides that varied so much according to the season, was now like an extension of his own body. He knew it almost to the point where the wind was a solid thing you could see, and the water, changeful as the mists above, was in a sense invisible, so closely did he understand the channels and banks beneath it.

The trials had gone well; yet he was glad he had not invited many people to witness them. A smallish steamship like the *Sparrowhawk* was a clanking contraption, scarcely more than the seafaring equivalent of a stagecoach. Close to, it would give a false idea of a larger vessel such as the *Albion*. And on a voyage like this he had little time to spare for anyone who was not a member of the crew. It was nuisance enough to have Anstye along, even given that the man had taken responsibility for details of fitting out during Fraser's recent travels. Fraser was sometimes guileless in sizing up his fellow men. And, God knew, on this project he had been too busy to think of anything beyond questions of mechanics. Nonetheless he did find Anstye too apt to announce his delight at being a partner, and not nearly swift enough in coping with particular situations. He was standing now at Fraser's elbow, surveying the horizon. Every few seconds, with an air of earnestness, he would peer through a telescope, of all things. He had of course never mastered the reading of a maritime chart.

'Well,' said Anstye, as the river was narrowing to where both shores were visible, 'at least we won't have to worry about hitting any rocks.'

It was the sort of remark he tended to make when everyone around him was trying to concentrate.

Meanwhile the *Sparrowhawk*, with its heavy new machinery encased in a traditional hull of Wealden oak, was passing through an area notorious for its shipwrecks. Few men might have died here as a result of poor navigation, but any number of ships had. Along this waterway passed more kinds of goods, in greater quantity, than anywhere else on earth. From London's Thames-side warehouses were exported manufactured linens and woollens, silks, laces, refined sugar, finely wrought firearms and brassware, saddlery and harness, Sheffield cutlery, glassware and the world's most sought-after porcelain. Into them came East Indian spices, tea, American raw cotton, pine from Quebec and the Baltic, French and Italian wines and spirits, and timber, rum and sugar from the Caribbean. It was no wonder that a maritime highway like this was crowded with shipping as thick as insects in a June hayfield.

Anstye lit a cigar and hummed a tune. He was the very figure of a prosperous Englishman of leisure: fair, balding, plumpish and ruddy-complexioned. Within the confined space where they and the ship's two most senior officers stood, his cigar was making a fug. It didn't help that smoke from the funnel was apparently drifting down around them and obscuring the voyage's remaining half-dozen miles. Fraser said nothing and concentrated on the chart that he and Commodore Hanwell had laid before them.

'Fire! In the boiler room!'

It was impossible to tell who had raised the alarm.

Apart from the captain, the first mate and the chief engineer, the crew only totalled a dozen; yet instantly there seemed twice that number running to and fro in a state of dreadful urgency. Everything was happening with incredible speed. The moment before, even by straining every nerve, the group at the helm had seen nothing but perfect normality. A few seconds later, and the hatchway to the boiler room was pushing out a torrent of smoke. Running towards it, swearing, Fraser saw the caulking between the planks of the deck begin to erupt in bubbles. He could feel the heat from below through the soles of his boots.

It was as if several versions of him were responding at once. His guts were crimping with fear, and his mouth felt as dry as if he'd swallowed poison. Dimly he appreciated that the underside of the deck was on fire, and it might be only a minute or so before the only safe place would be in the water amid a mass of panicking men. At the same time it counted for nothing that a horrible death might be about to cheat him out of half a life span. The only thing he sensed, at the level of instinct, not reason, was the risk to so much that he'd striven for over several desperate, toiling years.

He took a deep breath, and slid rather than climbed down the hatchway into the smoke-filled engine room. Too late he realized he should have counted the number of men on deck. If he collided with anyone left down here in this obscurity, he would die. He had to keep his eyes open; the small space into which he had stooped was roofed with flame. But the smoke was so thick that apart from the fire, nothing was visible. Already his throat felt as if he was gagging on his own tongue. The motion of his blood hammered against the top of his skull, which seemed to have grown several sizes too tight. His eyes and nose streamed. Surely he would never find his way back.

Every inch was familiar to him, however; more than to any other man on board. Without being able to see his own hand in front of his face, he made three frantic adjustments to the controls, his features contorted in a silent scream of effort.

The result was immediate. Even at a moment like this, not knowing if he was closer to death than to life, Fraser was awed at the power he had released. The whole vessel was shaking as violently as a bottle tied to the tail of a frightened cat.

He fled. There was a risk greater than the fire itself, now, as a surge of boiling vapour sought to vent itself. But even the chance of death from scalding could not make him move fast enough on his own. As he reached for the top rung of the ladder, three of the crew seized him by the hair and clothes and dragged him across the deck with just enough violent haste to save him from being cooked like a knuckle of ham.

'Good God!' he heard Anstye say to him, as he lay choking for breath on the hot planking. 'What a prodigious thing to do!' He insisted on helping Fraser to his feet. 'What *did* you do down there, exactly? I'll wager it was fearfully hot.'

'Put on the plunger and opened the feed cocks,' Fraser croaked. 'The boiler lagging – too close to the flues – had ignited.'

'Shall I tell the helmsman what to do now? . . . What shall I say, then?'

'Run her aground.'

'But – '

'I've only put out the fire around the lagging – the timbers could still be burning.' It was hard to know if the hatchway was still belching smoke, or steam.

'Surely, though – '

'Do it!' said Fraser, in a voice like an upraised fist.

To make the ship fit for repair, it was necessary to stop her store of fuel catching fire. It was as well that, as the steam pressure lessened, it became possible to use fire hoses below decks.

After half an hour the fire had stopped smouldering. In the saloon, a wilderness of cracked mirrors and wet stinking horsehair from burst upholstery, Fraser was at last able to turn back from fighting the flames. As he splashed his way to the engine-room hatch, several inches deep in water, a falling object nearly struck him to the deck. For an instant, wearied by the fight to rescue his ship, he failed to realize he had almost been killed. The body of a man had tumbled headlong from fifteen feet above, where a rung on the hatchway ladder had virtually burned through.

'Mr Hanwell!' he shouted to the commodore, who was following him forward from the saloon.

'Anstye!' exclaimed Hanwell, recognizing the man who had fallen.

Anstye was unconscious in Fraser's arms. There was already a discoloured swelling on one temple.

'Help me get him back above.' There was no question of doing the correct thing, and leaving the man to be examined where he lay. He had landed face down in a foot of water.

'Is it just concussion?'

'Probably. I don't think his injuries are serious, otherwise.'

Assuming he lives, Fraser thought.

And if Anstye did recover, would his commitment to the business also survive?

One of Fraser's ships had been saved. He hoped his company would be, too.

'Flaunting our family assets, are we, dearest mama?' The dinner party arranged for the week following the sea trial was being held as planned. It was one of the grandest occasions the South Audley Street household had seen.

'Nonsense, Neddy dear.' Sophy was looking queenly in dark blue silk, heavy and billowing. She indicated the guests who filled the brilliantly candlelit drawing room. 'What you see here are some of your father's liabilities. And if I ever hear you repeat me, I shall know you aren't old enough to be down here.' Edward, looking improbably adult in evening dress, had been allowed to join the grown-ups at dinner for the first time.

'Deign to explain, oh best of mamas.'

'Sir Richard, over there, is from the Board of Trade. Your father's firm may need a contract to carry mail if the *Albion* is to make a profit. Nathaniel Hadleigh – that short, cube-shaped man – is a director of the Plymouth Dock Company. It's lucky that he's in town at this time of year. We – I mean, your father – may need his help in keeping down harbour dues when the time comes. And – '

'I see, I see. Never fear, I shall treat everyone present as if they were a bomb about to go off.'

'At the very least, Neddy.'

The summons to dinner came. Sophy led the company in, on the arm of an agreeable elderly diplomat who was telling her how anxious he was to die in London, so that he need never see his native Russia again. Fraser had had dealings with the Russian Embassy recently, in setting up a small-arms manufactory near St Petersburg.

Several other guests had a connection with him outside the shipbuilding business. There was the owner of a London water company, who had commissioned the building of a reservoir in the riverside marshes between Westminster and Chelsea village. And there was a young landowner, bent on agricultural improvement, who had hired Fraser to supervise the

179

draining of forty square miles of East Midlands fen, turning a wilderness of bog oak and reeds into prime arable. A cousin of the same young nobleman was also there, for whom Tom, while working from his father's office, had excavated an ancient Roman villa near Chichester.

But most of the men present were connected with the future of the *Albion*. A couple owned extensive coal mines in the South Wales valleys and in Nottinghamshire. Another was chairman of the shipping company whose rented colliers were due to sail in advance of the *Albion*, to stock her ports of call with fuel. From another, Fraser was leasing part of the area on which his ship was being built, down one side of the shipyard that bordered his own. The treasurer and the secretary from his board of directors were also there. Their help, especially, would be needed if the *Albion*, once launched, was to bring in a continuous income. While any one project was in hand, Fraser was a perfectionist. Once it was finished, however, he was all too ready to go on to the next, without stopping to claim his share of the profits.

But the most conspicuous guest was Anstye, still with his arm, which he had sprained in his fall, tied in a sling.

'So you were able to calm all the panic?' a woman seated next to him asked, as the soup course was being cleared for a choice of six fish dishes.

'Oh, there's no reason for you to think it was so very frightening,' said Anstye, in a way that suggested he was being modest. He had got a lot of credit, around town and in the newspapers, for being the only person on board the *Sparrowhawk* who had been injured.

'It must make you more determined than ever to launch your big ship.' Anstye's neighbour was the wife of one of the mineowners. Within a neighbourhood reaching from Llandovery to Abergavenny, her husband's wealth had put her at the head of local society. But, having never been to London before, she had come ready to be overawed by everything, from dining with persons of rank right down to the white gloves the butler wore. She was lavishly dressed, in a style that had been out of fashion in the capital for over a year.

Anstye gestured to the footman to serve him stewed eels, rather than crimped cod and oyster sauce. 'For the privilege of being a pioneer, one must take such risks to one's safety for granted.' He had long forgotten that it had been under his own supervision that the faulty boiler lagging had been installed.

'How wonderful it is to meet a man for whom such an undertaking can be an obsession. I must say, my own dear husband too, at the end of a hard day shut up with his managers . . .'

Sophy, in conversation with a would-be railway investor from the Pennsylvania Society for the Promotion of Internal Improvement, tried to eavesdrop.

She was not altogether happy at what she could hear.

'Oh, but you must not think I have no other concerns,' Anstye was saying, in a tone that invited further questioning. 'Particularly where my own family joys and hopes are concerned.' He nodded across the table in the direction of his son, a youth of twenty-one whose interests were fornication and trading horseflesh.

'Oh, good heavens, no – what I meant was that there's nothing I can abide less than a man with a narrow cast of mind, as I was saying to a very dear friend only last week . . .' The poor woman was evidently not made easier by knowing she should not talk so much.

Anstye duly helped her back to the subject that interested him. 'Of course, you must make allowances for fatherly fondness. But I fancy the boy is nonetheless worthy of my plans for his immediate future.'

He paused, to let her ask what he meant.

'Why, Mr Anstye, what – '

'Parliament, madam. I think it is not too much to wish. You must, as I say, permit me a prejudice or two in his favour. He is, after all, the only child of his poor departed mama – yes indeed, a grievous shock; but time is a great consoler. Parliament, as I remark, is to be my son's destiny: I am confident of it.'

Sophy, having disengaged herself from talking with the American railway promoter, asked, 'For which seat would your son stand, Mr Anstye.' She was trying to play the bland hostess, all superficial politeness. Something told her, however, that she should pay the closest attention.

'I thought, Oldbury-on-the-Hill – '

'Oh, yes?'

' – or maybe Newington Constable. Or then, again, I thought perhaps Ikleburgh Parva might serve. They're all due to hold a by-election.'

'That sounds fascinating. Do tell us both more. You must forgive my ignorance, but I don't believe I've heard of any of the places you mention.' This was untrue; all three Parliamentary boroughs were notorious for returning only the candidate chosen by the local landowner. In the Middle Ages they had still been towns. Now, none had more than ten inhabitants qualified to vote. At least one was just a few grassy bumps in a sheep-pasture.

'Lord Magnaborough,' Anstye announced, as though that explained everything. Both ladies put on a look of suspense and waited.

'What I mean is that they are all – if I may put it so crudely – his.'

The mineowner's wife again responded to her cue. 'Oh, but what if his lordship does have powers of patronage? I am sure your son could be elected anyway, on his personal merits. I mean, should it ever come to that.'

'The selfsame thought had occurred to me, madam. And – I'll be frank with you – I would be prepared to put matters to the test. I mean, should it not be the lot of young Alexander over there to accept help from his lordship – Yes, my dear fellow, we are discussing you,' raising his voice. 'Together with your prospects as a protégé of Lord Magnaborough.'

The youth ran his eyes over the ladies, pausing at Sophy, and favoured them with a smile. 'I dare say a man can't always be idle,' he remarked, before turning back to his neighbours.

Sophy said, 'Why, what other seats might you – might your son, I mean – have in mind?' She tried to sound only casually interested, knowing that without automatically being handed the kind of borough Anstye had mentioned, getting elected to Parliament could cost a fabulous sum. Meanwhile what of his commitment to Fraser's business?

'Upstowe,' he said, looking confidential. 'The borough of Upstowe, in Wiltshire, would be a virtual certainty.'

'I know it well,' Sophy remarked. 'I was raised in that part of the county.' What she did not say was that she knew to within a thousand guineas how much at least one local Member of Parliament had paid for his seat. 'But you say you're certain – of what? Do you mean your son would be elected unopposed? Or just that he's sure to become a candidate?' Uneasily she pictured the number of voters in Upstowe who would have to be bribed, whether with several days of free drink, or by help with the family business. In a small town like that, it would have to be worth a man's while, before standing up to cast his vote publicly.

'Both, surely!' Anstye's rosy face beamed with

183

enthusiasm. 'I'd stand myself, did I not have – well, other interests,' motioning towards where Fraser was listening, with gentlemanlike patience, to one of his female guests. It was not that parties like this were above Fraser, even though as a child he had been employed, at twopence a day, as a ploughboy. They simply failed, when the talk was not to do with work, to catch his interest.

'Lord Magnaborough is a Whig, is he not?' asked Sophy, still feigning ignorance. What she really wanted to know was, how well did Anstye understand the practical details of electioneering? If, as she suspected, he had failed to grasp them, it was certain to be a case of good money thrown after bad.

'Indeed he is. But that does not mean he will withhold his favour from those of us with a – dare I say? – Radical slant to our thinking.' Anstye looked roguish. The mineowner's wife tittered at the thought of keeping dangerous company.

'It must be a privilege to know him personally,' Sophy said.

'Ah – now, there I must make a confession. His lordship is as yet – well, a prospective acquaintance. But I am on close enough terms with his land agent – and with two other members of the Lower House who enjoy his goodwill. We have the very best hopes of knowing his lordship well – and if not, why, the seat of Upstowe can still be the boy's for a modest expenditure; I'm sure of it.'

Sophy tried to look impressed. 'He would give your son a seat like Oldbury-on-the-Hill, in return for having it abolished?' The fight to remove such Rotten Boroughs, with maybe half-a-dozen voters apiece, was almost the only topic in current political circles.

Anstye's cheerfulness was undiminished. 'Come now! I'm sure his lordship will understand that no offence is meant to him personally.'

'But would your son campaign for electoral reform?'

'Of course!'

'Including the abolition of his own seat?'

'Why, where would be the good of voting himself out of a position of influence, if he is a true servant of reform? But he would be for change in principle, of course. After all, it's the principle that counts more than anything else ... Ah, dear lady, the entrée! How splendidly your household does these things!'

Eleven meat dishes were followed in due course by three choices of game, and a succession of compotes and iced desserts. Meanwhile Sophy, who usually found pleasure in such entertainments, was impatient for the evening to pass. It irked her that at times like this her husband was the one person to whom she could not talk.

At length they shook hands with the last of their departing guests. Downstairs the wide hallway was emptied of people waiting for their carriages. Alone, they lingered, talking, before a glowing hill of embers in one of the drawing room's marble fireplaces. For two people who looked forward to each other's company, they nowadays spent almost no time together. In the early days of their marriage they had lived in a little house in Cannings Fitzpayne with Sophy's widowed mother and one servant. Now, their Mayfair home was almost a village in its own right, with an ever-present floating population of visitors and employees: shareholders, draftsmen, shipwrights, engineers, lawyers, political allies, importers, exporters, and contractors of every kind.

If it was as different as could be from the beginnings of their life together, it was also what they wanted. Sophy, recalling the insecurity of those years, knew that she mainly wanted to have things continue just as they were now. She had always felt relief, as well as pride, that nothing had threatened the contentment in which her two daughters and her younger son were growing up. It was even worth all the inevitable separations from her husband and from Tom.

Together they dwelt on the day's events.

'What did Neagle want?' Sophy asked, referring to another would-be railway owner who had been present at dinner. The building of a public railway line in Lancashire which was to reach all the way from Manchester to Liverpool had prompted a surge of speculation all over the country.

'He wanted me to survey a line to Salisbury and Exeter. Leaving London along the Surrey bank of the Thames.'

'Would you? Might it be profitable?'

'It would be in the short run. But it would mean that, for the sake of a quick return on investment, I should live and die with two hundred miles of defects to my name. I saw Anstye talking with you. Did it amount to anything?'

Sophy told him, mentioning her misgivings about his partner's latest enthusiasm.

To her dismay, he took her seriously.

'Damn the man. This Parliamentary nonsense may be a whim. But that doesn't mean he won't get drawn in past any hope of retreat.'

'You mean, financially?'

'How else? And I doubt he understands the political issues, either.'

'Yes – he tried talking reform with me, this evening. And the son is no firebrand, let alone a younger Pitt. I dare say he'd barely do as his father instructed, should he be elected.'

Fraser, standing by the chimneybreast, kicked absently at a fallen coal. 'Confound him! How does he think the company will get by, if he withdraws money now, to pay electioneering debts?'

'Would you have time to raise capital elsewhere?'

'There's not a chance of that. The lease would run out far too soon on the rented part of the yards.' From the start, the *Albion*'s construction schedule had been dictated by the fact that this lease could never be extended.

Sophy said nothing. The handsome couple, in their perfect evening clothes, gazed into the embers of the fire and tried not to look haunted by what was in both their minds. To complete the great ship, Fraser had called upon every favour he was owed throughout his wide professional acquaintance. He had also invested everything he possessed. One unmentionable word hung before them, as if it danced above the coals in letters of flame. Bankruptcy.

To Sophy's credit she did not blame her husband – even though she knew he need not have run any such risk. Indeed, she loved him for the very trait of character that had brought their fortunes under threat. He could have lived off his investments, or made quick profits from doubtful enterprises. Instead, he chose to be seduced by the work itself rather than the plunder it might bring. In his way he was as much an enthusiast as Harry Anstye. Only whatever Fraser attempted he did superlatively well, with inspired inventiveness and yet with attention to the minutest detail.

But for them all to be at risk, again. Sitting in her hundred-guinea gown, on a silk-upholstered sofa with gilded paw feet and lion heads, Sophy wondered how much more bold she might feel at this moment, did she not know what poverty was. It had been in their first year of marriage that Fraser, through terms of employment beyond his control, had been taken away to the debtor's prison. It had cost Sophy every scrap of loyalty to her beloved husband, to set out for London to join him there, knowing she was pregnant. It had seemed not only that Tom would be born in prison, but that he would grow up there. Now, looking at the shapes suggested in the dying fire, she dared herself to remember those days more closely. Had she really planned to commit an adultery with old Lord Fitzpayne's nephew, to buy her husband's freedom? How could she have forced herself even to plot such an act of selfless folly?

And what with those days, and the uncertainties they'd suffered later – why, what stock of courage, if any, did she have left? What could she do, should her family be in danger again?

'What sort of man is Magnaborough?' she asked. 'Since it seems we too may depend on his goodwill? Might he give Harry Anstye's son a seat with few enough voters to be cheap?' Polite London society lived in an area no more than half a mile across. Inevitably she knew his lordship by sight; not, though, by reputation.

Fraser stirred as from a dream, and ran his hand through his hair. He looked tired. 'I only know the kind of things that are printed in the Court Circulars.'

'Oh.'

There was no point in asking him about gossip in the clubs of Pall Mall or St James's Street. Fraser was in a position only to hear what was said in a number of coffee houses frequented by his fellow professionals.

For lack of anything more hopeful, Sophy said, 'Harry Anstye might yet stand by us.'

'Indeed he might.'

They were lighted to bed almost believing it would be true.

Next day, and several mornings thereafter, brought no relief. Sophy's usual occupations of running their large household or supervising the children's schooling no longer gave her pleasure. They seemed like a drudgery she was being forced through for no reason except to exhaust her. Surely the time was rushing towards them when she would have to take Edward and the girls on one side and tell them, then the servants, quite without warning, that the thing she most feared had come true. That the house was to be closed up, that they were leaving – to go where, she had no idea – and that they would have to walk down into the street with no more possessions than they could carry.

Such were her thoughts most of the time. But then the housekeeper would need her instructions in planning the week's menus, or Mary-Anne or Louisa was due to be driven with her to the dressmaker for a fitting. At such moments, shaken free of her anxiety by other people's demands, Sophy would briefly cease to feel like a housebreaker in her own splendid home, or like a girl who has borrowed her mama's beautiful clothes without permission.

The most reassuring of these routines was the Sunday morning drive to church, even though it usually caused a fluster. Somehow, despite a household of quiet, efficient servants to help them, the children could rarely get ready in time. Louisa would have forgotten her prayer book, and would bound back out of the carriage in a panic. Then Mary-Anne would collide with her in the doorway, having dithered for half an hour over the right match of gloves, stockings, bonnet and parasol. Edward was usually the last into the carriage, sauntering downstairs with an air of perfect calm while the horses and his family fidgeted. He would take his seat as though they were not to notice him. It was his way of hinting that as a more or less grown man in his seventeenth year he was intellectually above such things as churchgoing.

This morning it was Fraser who was missing. He had had a letter delivered to him by hand, which was unusual on a Sunday. But there was no real reason why he should still be upstairs. After a minute, Sophy got down and hastened indoors.

Instead of going straight into his dressing room, something made her rap on the door, as hesitantly as if it led to a sickbed . . .

As she went in, her husband didn't look up. With a piece of paper in his hand he was staring, motionless, at the floor.

Sophy, still holding her prayer book and reticule, stood in the doorway, struck dumb with unease.

At length he glanced up, as if he didn't recognize her. 'Read this. Anstye sent it.' He thrust the paper towards her.

Sophy glanced through Anstye's letter. Then she read it twice more, feeling the same numbness spread through her that she saw in her husband's expression.

Certain phrases struck her. But the meaning of the whole thing was too unwelcome to register in her mind at once. 'My son's political agent . . . yield to this gentleman's importuning authority . . . political glory elsewhere than in the train of a great patron . . . one's own pre-emptive boldness . . . seed money . . . cutting a dash before the good burghers of Upstowe . . . investment in young Alexander's future – and, dare one say it, in the future of one's country . . . not withdrawing capital, but merely being persuaded to re-direct it temporarily . . .'

'He means his son to try for a seat without patronage!' she exclaimed.

'Evidently.'

'But if he means him to stand as a Radical, why cannot they wait for a by-election that will offer them a better chance? Upstowe is an agricultural constituency. No one but the Tory candidate has ever been elected there.'

'God knows,' said Fraser, with shocked weariness.

She could see he lacked the heart even to stand up

out of his chair. Before retreating, she hesitated. Hot sunlight exploded into the room. Over the clatter of West End traffic, frequent even on a Sunday, church bells could be heard ringing from several parishes.

'He might change his mind.'

'No – no; you know all his whims are inflexible ones. I would have sought funding elsewhere, had I known what sort of man he was.'

'Shall I write to Tom, if things threaten to get worse?'

'Good God, no. He at least should be kept free of whatever happens to us. He must stay where he is, no matter what.'

After a pause Sophy said, 'None of this is a certainty. At worst we could still have months in which to act, somehow.'

Fraser nodded curtly, as if to say, of course. Two kinds of anger mastered him: against himself, and against the colleague who was so cheerfully ignoring the likelihood of ruining him. Saying nothing, Sophy put down the letter on a side-table, glanced helplessly at his averted face, and left, closing the door quietly.

She made his excuses for him, and she and the children were driven off, to a nearby Mayfair church that was not so much a place of worship as a fashionable rendezvous. It was where one saw precisely the same people that one met, during other times of the week, at private concert parties or dinners, at the theatre, or riding in Hyde Park. The church's elegant Georgian interior was itself like a lofty drawing room, with Corinthian pilasters, and cornices swagged with stucco flowers and fruit.

The familiarity of the place, the ritual of Morning Service, and the inattentive congregation of prosperous, calm faces – all at first combined for Sophy to drive away the ache of worry.

Only briefly, though. Nothing could hold Sophy's

191

attention as firmly as her concern with Harry Anstye's insecure new ambition. Round and round went her futile thoughts, as incessant as the drone of the learned Dean taking the service. His sermon was to do with the prophesies of Ezekiel. '. . . behold, I will open the side of Moab, from the cities which are on his frontiers, the glory of the country, Bethjeshimoth, Baalmeon, and Kiriathaim . . . and will give them in possession, that the Ammonites may not be remembered among the nations . . . because that Edom hath dealt against the house of Judah by taking vengeance . . .'

Sophy wanted to laugh out loud from exasperation. What were all these people doing, attending so respectfully to the savageries of some ancient desert tribes? She looked around at the gathering of sleek masculine heads, and wide feather-trimmed bonnets turned up towards the pulpit like sunflowers in a hot field. What did the Hittites or the Amalekites have to do with what she knew of the King's Bench Prison for debtors, or her children and their cruelly shrivelled prospects?

At length the Dean spoke the words dismissing the kneeling grandees from Grosvenor Square and Park Lane, together with their families and attendants. The organ started up, and the congregation got to its feet with a rustle of expensively tailored fabrics and a stir of restrained bows and nods to acquaintances and neighbours.

Among the people there, up for the Season, Sophy saw someone who was particularly in her thoughts. It was Lord Magnaborough. He was a bald, heavy-built, vigorous-looking man with a dignified wife and an air of calculated bonhomie. In a separate pew, a tutor and two nurserymaids were supervising the exit of his six young children. Glum as a frustrated lover, Sophy stared at his silk top hat and wide-collared coat. Had Anstye, after all his boasting of possible connections, even tried to approach the man? Perhaps she should try to find out.

At the west door, coming out into dust and sunlight, the congregation was bidding a dignified farewell to the Dean and his curate. Both clerics were being particularly respectful towards the wealth and personal grandeur of the parishioner immediately in front of the Fraser household. To Sophy the sight of Charity Michaelmas was as familiar at church on Sunday as the words of the service itself. In Cannings Fitzpayne, for fifteen years they had each worshipped in the little Norman church. It had been as dark inside as if gouged from the living rock. All but a dozen or so of the packed congregation had borne the marks of heavy labour – and Charity had been no exception. She had worn clean, intricately cobbled rags, and a refined beauty that had seemed frail at the time. The little swineherdess had had good bones, but also the waxy flesh to be expected on any child who was fed with kitchen waste. Now, in lilac silk trimmed with heliotrope ribbons, the splendour of her looks seemed indestructible.

The two women descended the church steps, Sophy with her clutch of tall, handsome children, and Charity followed at a distance by her maid and a footman. An aura of magnificent loneliness surrounded Charity. She was on formal visiting terms with no one among the worshippers, even though she'd coupled with several of the husbands and fathers there. Sophy, whose connection with her Charity had long since realized, also ignored her. In Sophy's case she knew it was what the other woman wanted. What use had Charity for any of her memories?

But as she made her isolated way, as if through a crowd of phantoms, most people were intensely aware of Charity Michaelmas. Several of the gentlemen currently frequented her salon, which, being a meeting place for politicians, Whig and Tory alike, was by definition favoured only by men. Her lovers, in particular, could be identified by the way they pretended not to have seen her. One such man was Lord Magnaborough.

Driving home, Sophy realized she had known all along about this connection. Hadn't Kate mentioned it, in a conversation with Sophy during her last visit to Europe, four years before? The relationship, she had said, was a long-standing one. It had served Charity Michaelmas, and Georgiana, very well.

Maybe so. But would it serve Sophy, too?

CHAPTER ELEVEN

In the countryside near Paris a gathering of expatriates was passing a summer day by the river. Beneath a perfect sky their party made a fine picture, the sort bound to make you think of lovers meeting and being happy. The sliding waters of the Seine cast reflected sunlight up into the boughs of tall, mistletoe-hung poplars, whose leaves winked and glinted in the bright afternoon. At the edge of the vista stood a group of open carriages and tethered saddle horses, their attendant grooms smoking and gossiping in half-undress. The gentlefolks sat at a picnic by the water's edge, on a natural lawn like the apron of a theatre stage.

A short distance away stood the small country mansion rented by the self-exiled Massachusetts textile baron who was their host for that day. Above a pair of curving stone staircases the villa with its closed white shutters turned a blind face towards the heat of the day. On the river, the odd pleasure boat glided by, rowed by gentlemen in shirtsleeves and light waistcoats and bearing women whose flimsy white gowns made them look like rare blooms cast adrift.

Most of the party was English, permanently journeying for pleasure between those parts of Europe where they were most likely to meet just enough of each other's cousins or old university acquaintance. One or two claimed to be travelling for their health, spending much time drinking sulphurous water in the casinos of various French or German spa towns. There was an Irish peer, too afraid of his tenants to live for long in his own rain-soaked countryside. Others, passing through Paris on their way to winter in Florence or Genoa, were maybe escaping some social taint or scandal, or their creditors. For most, a place such as this was blissfully like home – yet unlike, thank goodness.

At the centre of this scene of calm brilliance sat Georgiana, bare-headed in the faint breeze. Her gauzy, tight-waisted summer drapery made her look more slender than ever.

'How well all this becomes that fine young couple,' was one comment, from a lady sitting by the remains of lunch among the older members of the party.

'You mean that splendid-looking American miss? And the suave lad with the copper-coloured hair? He seems determined enough to please, even if no mortal being has ever seen him smile.'

'He? No, I don't mean young Fitzpayne,' replied the first speaker, the authoress of twenty trashy and immensely popular Gothick novels. 'It's not the young lady he worships; it's the notion of his own superior good manners. Maybe I could use such a character in my next.'

'He does look like a mime of social perfection, even from here. So he's not half dead with love, regardless of the lady's qualities. Have you noticed,' continued the other, a gentleman who dabbled in antiquarianism and watercolours, 'how even in this light her hair seems full of shadows?. And that profile from a Greek myth . . . Which other young man did you mean? . . . Ah. How could I not have noticed? The tall fair-haired lad fidgeting about nearby.'

'How indeed? Not many young men, even as good-looking as that, could be so intense without losing all dignity.'

'He doesn't dissemble, does he? No one can fail to

see that *he* is enamoured of the fair American, now that you point it out. Does she return his feelings?'

'I believe so – at least, from the deal of time they seem to have spent in each other's company. Despite the scowls and twitchings of the chaperone.'

'She's a quiz, is she not? Our host told me he met her once when she was a girl. He said she looked and acted exactly the same at seventeen. The poor creature's mother never let her forget that it was unforgivable to be born so plain. But the would-be lover. Young Fraser, isn't it? The engineer's son. A bit out of his depth socially, wouldn't you say?'

'How so? Even when flustered, he looks the very image of a gentleman.'

'In himself, perhaps. But not necessarily in his family. Oh, the father's a rising man, certainly. Financially and in every other way. But risen from where? Would that handsome girl look at him so favourably, were she mindful that one of the father's family was once housekeeper to that same Fitzpayne's late parent?'

'Perhaps she prefers to judge by the man himself, rather than the occupation of some grandparent. I should, in her place.'

'Madam, I had no idea you could be so susceptible. But the fact remains that the Fraser boy is not as well placed as she is to be invited quite everywhere. Surely it's not a case of secret assignations?'

'Good heavens, no! The young man is far too honest – and earnest – in his intentions, to stoop to anything like that. He can scrape acquaintance with just enough people in Paris. For example, Bishop Wharton's son, over there, is one of his schoolfellows.'

'Well, I'll allow that even without being compared to Fitzpayne, he does look as though he's got warm blood in him. If I too were the young lady . . .' The gentleman onlooker sighed, thinking really how he wished he looked like Tom. The authoress, who held strong views on women's rights, thought she too would have liked to resemble him.

'Not that the Fitzpayne boy doesn't have strong passions of his own. It's just that his are nothing to be proud of.'

'You mean he has what you ladies would call vicious habits?'

'Pray don't ask me to speak for the rest of my sex. Besides, I doubt if anyone would call gaming vicious in a boy not yet of age, and accompanied by his mother – '

'When I saw them both in Baden last spring I thought he played as if all he wanted was to lose. And the mother was no good example.'

'Well, perhaps so. What I meant was young Fitzpayne's response to that scandal about him. It was the only thing he was allowed to be known for, during his time at Harrow.'

'Oh, that old story. But how could anyone prove such a thing? Whatever the circumstances of his lordship's conception – forgive me, dear lady, but it was you who raised the subject – '

'It's the youth himself who raises the topic in people's minds, by acting as if he dares the world to find him at fault. Of course, having a mother like his would be bound to make most offspring act oddly. Sometimes her behaviour almost makes one feel sorry for him.'

'Too true. She used to be wild – she can't hear us, can she? – and now, she's merely outrageous. Who was it, anyway, who first put that story about?'

'The servants, I think. If it *was* as people say, neither man present at the adulterous deed could have blabbed. His old lordship would have been paralysed and dumb. And her ladyship's – undoubtedly vicious – nephew would surely suffer death from torture rather than tell such a story at his own expense. Her pregnancy did deny him the inheritance, after all.'

'Such a story would certainly amuse the nephew far less than it does you, madam.'

'Why shouldn't one be amused? Though the lady cuts a foolish figure now she's no longer young, you must admit it would have been a clever ploy.'

'Of course. Assuming it's the truth.'

'But of course.'

'Harold, darling,' called Augusta Fitzpayne to her son. 'Come here. I want to show everyone what a good example you are to me.'

'Certainly, mother.' The youth strode over to where she sat, with a display of manly restraint. *He* could show perfect politeness, his manner declared, even though the rest of the world might fail, in his place.

'Now, dearest boy, hold this. I want to demonstrate something that will show you in rather a good light.'

She picked up a small silver vessel used for holding ice. At that season, near the end of high summer, its contents were worth nearly as much per ounce as a rare perfume. Emptying it with a flick of her wrist, she held it out. Lady Augusta, whose red hair was nowadays dyed, wore diamonds: round her neck, from her ears, on her wrist and fingers. A cloud of midges danced above her head. Even bystanders who were slightly drunk began to look fearful of being embarrassed, or of seeing the young man humiliated by his notoriously whimsical parent.

Lady Augusta turned towards a servant in charge of a small stove on which tea was being made. 'Fill that up, would you?'

The man, seeing that he was being asked to pour boiling water into a thin metal container, sought to pass his employer a napkin, to save him from being burnt.

'*Not* that!' exclaimed her ladyship, waving back the napkin. 'Come on, come on!' she exclaimed, as the footman looked from her to her son with a worried expression. 'Get on with it!'

Fitzpayne, in a deliberately graceful pose with one knee bent, held out the vessel and looked at the ground. He was expressionless as only a man could be who shows tact from motives of disdain.

He stayed like that as the servant, with a look of suppressed panic, started to pour from a kettle, his own hand wrapped up amid a scalding cloud of steam. Fitzpayne kept so still, he might have died and turned rigid. The other guests were motionless too. The man tipped in some more water, hesitated, then, with an air of disbelief, poured a steady stream. Fitzpayne didn't move an eyelash. However, the blood drained from his face, so that his lips turned the colour of old ivory.

When the container was full the servant paused again, looking at her ladyship. Fitzpayne put it down, making a point of not spilling any of the boiling water. He stood up, to a patter of applause from his mother's silk-mittened hands.

'Bravo! You see, ladies and gentlemen! Even strong men like my son can be made to do as bid, if one asks them properly.'

Fitzpayne's face remained a mask of courtesy. Pointedly he kept the inside of his injured hand from view. Already the palm was half as thick again. A row of blisters were forming on his finger ends like pads on the foot of a frog.

'Consider yourself dismissed, my angel. I can't tell you how proud I am.'

Fitzpayne bowed, with a self-righteous absence of irony, and walked away.

200

'What was that about?' Georgiana asked Tom.

'I think it's Lady Fitzpayne's way of drawing attention to herself.' Tom was too easily embarrassed to explain any further. As she began to be neglected by other men, her ladyship was increasingly ready to flirt with her own son.

Before Georgiana could show sympathy for Fitzpayne's disfigured hand, Tom hastened to suggest a short expedition on the river.

'Yes,' she said, 'but let's go quickly, before I'm forced to ask permission from Miss Lee.'

He handed her into the rowboat, trying not to look anxious at the quantity of ruffled petticoat involved, and pushed them off.

Once afloat, it was cooler, but almost blindingly bright. Ripples of light snaked across the underside of Georgiana's parasol and cast a gleam beneath her chin. Neither of them, in their haste to be alone together, cared to glance back, in case Euphemia was signalling angrily from the bank.

Tom's face was stiff with concentration as he laboured to turn the boat around. He wanted to carry them both as quickly as possible out of earshot of the other picnickers, strolling or lounging beneath the brilliantly dappled riverside poplars. In months of striving to be invited where he might meet Georgiana, he had spent many hours in her company. But they had never been able to exchange one word without having to include someone else in the conversation.

As Tom backed water mightily with one oar, the river, the broad sky and the trees, with Georgiana in the foreground, all whirled around as if swung by a giant lever. The draught of their movement ruffled her broad sleeves. Out here, the river seemed not only more brilliant but emptier. Sated with lunch, and languid from the afternoon heat, most of the people on the bank watched them. Georgiana shifted her parasol so that she was invisible to their fellow guests; but Tom was glad to be so publicly alone with her. The more openly he courted her, the more he felt certain to succeed.

His desires made him neither timid nor desperate; he simply acted on them, unquestioning. So preoccupied was Tom, he hadn't even thought to see who his rivals might be. To him that poor devil Fitzpayne was just someone burdened with a rogue mother, an air of repressed self-hatred, and gambling debts incurred in six countries.

Thinking of the scene they'd just witnessed, after a while he remarked, 'Harold Fitzpayne's an odd fish.'

As she often did before she spoke, Georgiana considered, her face still. 'I admire his politeness. I don't mean to me, but towards his mother – even when she torments him, as she did just now.'

'He's polite for his own sake, not his mother's.' A splinter of jealousy pricked Tom's heart.

Georgiana said nothing. Tom, glancing over his shoulder in order to steer, at first mistook her silence for disapproval. They bobbed about as he pulled on the oars. He felt the cool water dribble from his hands down to his elbows, and spatter his beautiful white trousers.

With the rest of the world rocking to and fro behind her, Georgiana said, 'Lord Fitzpayne is certainly politer to Miss Lee than I seem to be.' Her own irritation with Euphemia made her feel increasingly guilty.

Tom was looking behind them again, to change course around the half-submerged corpse of a white willow. 'Does Miss Lee like you?' He had not meant to be so direct; but he had been concentrating.

'I don't know.' Just avoiding scenes with Euphemia, so Georgiana found, left one with little energy to spare for asking questions like that. 'She actually wants to be hated by some people – so that she can feel martyred. And others, she wants to serve, as the next best thing to being loved by them. You've heard her speak of my godmother, Mrs Michaelmas.'

She hesitated, her eyes on a coot's nest they were passing, piled high in a reed bed. Part of her thoughts were simply with the frank, handsome youth sitting opposite her, so close in the little cockleshell boat that her petticoats frothed over one of his shoes. Before that first, formal encounter at the hotel in the Place Vendôme it had never occurred to her that anyone's company could be stirring, and a relief, all at once.

'As for me . . . I think Miss Lee worships all that money I'm due to have – but sees me as letting down my own fortune. I'm afraid she often finds me wrong in ways I haven't yet understood.' She sighed. 'Perhaps the poor woman can't help being a snob. Her father left her and her mother in utter poverty when he died, before Uncle Joseph came home from Europe and rebuilt the family's business.'

'I can't agree,' said Tom. If he sounded abrupt it was because his impulse to confide in Georgiana was far stronger than any mere desire to please. 'My family were poor once.' True to Fraser's decision, Tom knew nothing of his parents' new troubles. Much less that Charity had since put them in her debt by duly gaining Anstye the political patronage of Lord Magnaborough. 'As children we often asked for the story of how my father was finally released from the King's Bench Prison. It was a family legend, like being read to from myths of the ancient Greeks. For that matter, Mama and Aunt Kate had a lean time of it when their own father died. But it didn't change them for the worse.'

Georgiana sat quite still, the reflected light running over her as if she were a submerged statue. Her gaze was on a distant watermill which was so deep in ivy

203

and drifts of flowering loosestrife, it might have shoved its way up out of the ground.

'I miss Aunt Kate.'

They both said nothing, dwelling on the coincidence of having a 'relative' in common. After a moment Georgiana added, 'I can always trust her advice.'

Something in her voice made him look at her more closely. Suddenly Tom felt as if his chest cavity had fallen empty, as he saw that there were tears spilling from her eyes.

Whatever the cause, to pretend nothing was wrong would have been unbearable to him. He steered them beneath a nearby willow. Leaning out to hold the boat still via a trailing branch, he waited, watching her as she strove to compose herself. Poor Georgiana felt her heart swell as though it would stifle her, at the sight of his calm, anxious face. His steady look of concern might have been that of a man twice his age.

At length she gave a shuddery sigh and tucked her handkerchief into her *nécessaire*. Tom waited, too tactful to press her for an explanation. She gave him a watery smile, and said nothing. After a pause he began gingerly pulling on the oars.

A minute passed, in which the only sounds were the river rippling past their keel, and distant voices from the bank. Georgiana felt relief washing over her, after the surprise of her outburst. Squinting into an explosion of reflected sunlight at a point far up-river, she said, 'How wonderful it seems . . .'

'What?' asked Tom, looking at her, his brow furrowed with concentration as he calculated their course.

'Both of us growing up so far apart, in England and in Richmond – '

'Yes – '

' – and all the while destined to meet, not knowing of the things we had in common.' Georgiana, hearing such lovers' talk from any other couple, would almost certainly have been satirical. She gave the ghost of a sob, and a broad smile. 'I expect you didn't even know I existed!'

'I'm sure that's not true!' said Tom, grinning with elation. 'I'm certain it's not!'

Across the water, their clear laughter could be heard half a mile away.

As the time came for them to rejoin the others Tom said, 'Shall you be journeying to England – to London – this season? I mean you to meet my family, if you will.'

It was only now, when he felt almost sure of triumphing, that a crowd of practical problems began to occur to Tom. Would his parents think he was too young to marry? Why did it seem that those around Georgiana were making it hard for him to court her? If it was possible that she would have him, whom should he ask for her hand in marriage?

Her origins, grand but vague, mystified him. He had no idea that she too found them confusing.

She said, 'I don't know where we're going next.'

They were leaning towards each other, their voices lowered as the current drew them back to the Massachusetts cotton lord's *fête champêtre*. It was growing late. Servants were shaking out damask tablecloths stained with grass and with vintage champagnes from before Bonaparte's downfall; hampers were being packed with crystal and silverware. The other guests, waiting for the carriages to be made ready, pretended not to be curious about the young couple, whose wish to be ignored was obvious.

'Miss Lee did say she'd been told we were going to Italy. My godmother owns a famous old villa there, on one of the northern lakes. But that plan seems to have been changed – I believe by my godmother. Mrs Michaelmas holds all my money in trust, I think.

And ...' her voice dropping as their boat bumped against the bank, 'I'm told she's in London now, seeing the lawyers.' Georgiana was blushing with annoyance as she fumbled to give Tom an honest answer. In her own ears, every word made her sound like a tease.

'So we might – ' she began to say. But she was interrupted by Euphemia, stalking towards them with a look of iron patience, and Georgiana's bonnet and shawl, ready for the carriage.

Driving back, Tom was both happy and wretched. He got a seat in the same vehicle as Georgiana. But he could only speak to her across the dignified profiles of her chaperone and Harold Fitzpayne, and Lady Augusta's bobbling twin masses of corkscrew curls.

Georgiana, trying like him to sound indifferent, took up their conversation again. 'Later this year we might be staying, as I remarked, near London. Of course, I may be mistaken – but I believe we are due to spend some time at a house taken for us on the river, at Richmond, Surrey. Is that not so, Miss Lee?'

Georgiana's earnest young face was a lot milder than her feelings as she tried to will her chaperone into giving a straight reply. But she was due to be disappointed, if she thought that the presence of other people would help her.

'One will have to see. Won't one?' Euphemia trembled, her face mottled. It was a solemn duty, to act as watchdog to the girl and her magnificent fortune. She was secretly elated at the chance to carry it out so publicly, and snub young Fraser before the very eyes of her acquaintances – her friends – her dear friends – the Fitzpaynes.

At the same time nothing could have been more frightful than public suspicion that the girl was being moved around the resorts of Europe in the trail of his young lordship.

Luckily for Euphemia, Lady Fitzpayne seemed to

think no flattery was too much for Georgiana and her dazzling prospects. It was something the girl had noticed in a lot of people since they had been in Paris. 'Richmond will do well enough, I dare say. But you, my dear, must surely come down with us to Wiltshire. The Hall has scarcely seen us, since my dear husband passed away.'

She cast a look at her son, full of fake-tender memory. Fitzpayne stared between the ears of their nearside horse with stony composure. Scandal or not, he knew she'd hated her husband. And the country.

She turned to Euphemia. 'It would be such a privilege to have the old place graced by someone of Miss Bingham's beauty, charm, and – though I know it's naughty of me to mention it – fortune.'

Everyone except Tom felt what hard luck it was for Fitzpayne, to be closely related to such a woman. Wanting to lessen the embarrassment he must feel, Georgiana made rather a business out of expressing her thanks.

Fitzpayne had also been thinking of getting Georgiana and her chaperone down to the country, as his guests at the family seat. He shared his mother's views on the need, sooner or later, to brace up and make a wealthy marriage. And he considered that, as a man beyond social reproach, someone like the unfaultable Miss Bingham was the least to which he was entitled.

Now, however, it was with a snap of reproach in his voice that he said, 'I don't wish you or I to make invitations on false pretences. It's not yet settled that we shall be going down to Wiltshire.'

Georgiana tactfully made a point of smoothing her shawl, to avoid his eyes. Lady Fitzpayne, her eyebrows drawn even higher by astonishment than by cosmetic art, exclaimed, 'But, dearest boy! It was your idea that I should have the place opened. It's for the shooting,' she told the company in general. 'My son here knows perfectly well how much he's been looking forward to it.'

It happened that only Tom was looking directly at her. So, for something to say, she blurted, 'And of course you must come down too – I'm sorry to say that I don't remember your name – as well as Miss Bingham and Miss Lee. Don't you agree, Harold?'

Unseen by the others, Fitzpayne shot her a look of frigid rage. In a contained voice he replied, 'We must discuss this later, mother.'

For the rest of the drive they managed to talk only about things of no importance.

Georgiana might have felt less sorry for Fitzpayne, had she heard him resume the subject of Tom in private. With a show of self-control worse than any violence he reminded his mother that in only a few months he was due to come of age. It would be he who had control of her income then, rather than the other way about. 'Thereafter, madam, there is nothing I shall not do to make you understand me. One does not extend invitations to persons of middle rank. Much less to descendants of one's family's housekeeper.'

Tom himself would not have cared less, by then. For Fitzpayne or anyone else. At last he had been able to tell Georgiana what was in his mind. In the general pother of the Fitzpaynes' departure outside their hotel, he and she found themselves ignored. Euphemia, rigid with nervous pleasure, was leaning over the side of the carriage to exclaim her farewells. So flattered was she at being spoken to by Lady Augusta and his young lordship, even the back of her neck was flushed.

Tom caught Georgiana's eye and leaned towards her. 'If you agree, I should like to write to Miss Lee. To ask if I may call upon her.'

208

In reply to this formal little speech, Georgiana nodded. Though her eyes swam with tears of happiness, in every other way she still managed to look matter-of-fact. For the hundredth time, Tom took in her firm, considered grace. Acquired, he supposed, through being raised by his beautiful Aunt Kate. Holding her gaze while Euphemia and Lady Augusta were busy gushing in the background, he swelled with pleasure at being able to picture Georgiana in ten, then twenty, years from now.

'Unless,' he added, 'you think I should speak to someone else.'

Georgiana hesitated, then shook her head. The horses, fidgeting in the shafts, jolted them to and fro.

Seeing her pause, Tom felt his heart stumble. 'Are you sure?'

She shook her head again, ignoring a jolt of uncertainty. It was hateful, not quite knowing who had charge of her affairs. It made her feel like some rich man's love-child.

Tom was determined that no social blunder on his part should hinder his chances. Looking hard at her, he said, 'You're quite certain of that?'

She coloured and glanced at Euphemia's back. 'If there is – if you should – at least Miss Lee will be able to tell you.'

Georgiana was no ditherer. And from the start she had not doubted that this serious, open-hearted youth was a man she could honour for ever. She too wanted everything done correctly. For her own sake, but above all for his.

Within the hour Tom had written to his parents, to tell them about the wonderful girl he wished to marry just as soon as her family connections gave permission. He also despatched a note to Miss Lee. That done, he found himself possessed by a huge, pointless energy. Under a balmy, broad-skied evening, he set out to wander the streets. Many twisted miles, and five hours later, he was still striding aimlessly along the riverside *quais*, almost too anxious and too exultant to know which city he was in.

CHAPTER TWELVE

Tom's letter to Euphemia arrived next day, every line stiff with respect. Towards her – but also for himself. The lad was no truckler – and if he'd known how to, he would still not have stooped to toadying.

For a day it lay unanswered, tidily placed on her writing desk between a half-finished picture in pressed flowers and a feeble three-volume novel about a heroine of impeccable virtue. Euphemia wanted to savour her own righteousness at the impudence of all fortune-hunters and of Tom in particular. Like an artillery soldier firing off ranging shots, she considered one cruel reply, then another.

In the end her answer was decided for her. At the very moment that she was taking up her pen, bright-eyed with disapproval, her maid brought in a note from Lady Fitzpayne.

Could Miss Lee and her *delightful* young friend, it asked,

> *be persuaded to advance your departure by a day or so, albeit from a scene of such triumphs (given that the number of mere mortals, their hearts sundered by the darts shot from the incomparable eyes of the divine Miss Bingham are so legion that one might almost say the City of Light has been sacked again) – oh dear, how one is tempted to run on when applying one's pen to such a subject – do forgive me, dear Miss Lee! But then, how is anyone with a feeling for fine things to restrain oneself when confronted with such qualities?*

211

Might you, in other words, find it in you to oblige
our plea, and accompany Harold and me on our
remaining travels, as our guests, back to London?
So very anxious are my son and I to have this
whim gratified, believe me we look quite foolish
with longing.

A correct little postscript from Fitzpayne confirmed
that Miss Lee and Miss Bingham would be invaluable
in helping to make the journey back less tedious.

Euphemia breathed a sigh of triumph. Going into
her bedchamber, she sat five full minutes at her writing desk without moving. Four and a half of those
minutes were spent relishing the social distinction
conferred by such a letter. The remaining thirty seconds were taken up by a painful battle with her
conscience, which had been grumbling at her, on and
off, all day. As a result, she felt more resentment than
ever against Tom for causing her such a disagreeable
sensation, even for so short a time.

It was probable that, had her nose and chin been
deliciously fashionable, Euphemia would still not have
been a good woman. Certainly, no one could have
looked more decisive, as she composed a reply for the
Fitzpayne servant to carry back.

'. . . your ladyship astonishes us both. Not only by
your generosity but by your courage, and by the brav-
ery of your son, in considering such a journey.' The
day before, Fitzpayne had been riding in the Bois de
Boulogne. A couple of wood pigeons, exploding into
flight from a nearby elm, had frightened his well-bred
but incompletely schooled horse, and he had been
thrown, spraining his wrist.

'Your offer is so magnanimous that Miss Bingham
and I accept it only upon one condition. You must, and
I insist upon this, reassure us that his lordship is
sufficiently recovered . . .'

212

To Tom she also sent a short, neutral letter saying
that if he wished to call, he should do so at a particular
time next morning.

This was done with much bustle and fierce high
spirits. Georgiana, who for some hours had been pale
with impatience, grew almost certain that Tom's letter
had indeed arrived, and that Euphemia had sent an
encouraging answer.

'Well now,' said Euphemia, coming back into the
sitting room, 'you shall be needing to make some
changes in your life. Shall you not?'

'How, madam?' breathed Georgiana. Her outward
calm could not have had less to do with her real
feelings.

'Why, you are to go to London. Mrs Michaelmas
desires that we be off tomorrow.'

The girl looked at Euphemia. Her face was blank
with suspense.

'Early,' Euphemia added, as though uttering a retort.

This fib was one of the things that had troubled her
conscience, when first she'd thought of it. But only a
few seconds were needed for Euphemia to persuade
herself that it was no lie at all. In fact, it was the full
truth. Charity herself had said, in so many words, that
wherever young Fitzpayne might be, there was no
reason that Georgiana might not appear. Particularly if
the girl could be displayed to her best advantage.

'But Miss Lee!' Georgiana could no longer hide her
distress. 'What of . . . our other commitments?'

Euphemia gave a brisk smile like the bars of a prison
door. 'You must mean this.' She held out Tom's letter.

Relief breathed through Georgiana like a summer
wind. But as she held out her hand for the letter,
Euphemia took a step backward. Georgiana found she
was being invited to read it from a distance, with her
head turned sideways. It seemed rude either to look
closely or to turn away.

It was indeed from Tom. She looked up, confused by Euphemia's expression which was as lively as if she'd been drugged.

Back in Virginia, though Georgiana had often been in Euphemia's company, they'd never been alone together. Only now was she beginning to find out what kind of woman Euphemia was. Clearly she herself was out of favour today, despite her chaperone's bright eyes and unladylike grin. Euphemia, when pleased with someone, tended to be sugary and tearful.

'Have you – forgive me, madam – but is it likely, do you think, that Mr Fraser has your reply by now?' Standing face to face with Euphemia, amid the gilt and flowers and silk hangings of their apartment, Georgiana trembled. She sensed a need for tact, but had no idea what to say.

'What do you think?' If Euphemia's eyes were fires, her voice was spiked with ice.

'Why, how can I know what to believe!' exclaimed the girl, teetering between doubt and indignation.

'So you consider that I would betray the trust that Mrs Michaelmas has placed in me?'

Georgiana looked at her chaperone. She was slightly taller than Euphemia. In her clear face, every thought could be read. 'No,' she said, in a questioning tone.

'Why, then! Mr Fraser' – whether twisting the truth or not, nobody could speak through clenched teeth as well as Euphemia – 'knows well enough by now that he should address himself to Mrs Michaelmas.'

The girl looked only partly relieved. Euphemia added, 'You can communicate with the man as freely as you like, once your godmother has permitted an engagement.'

There seemed nothing Georgiana could say without putting herself in the wrong. In a faint voice she asked, 'So Mr Fraser does know – from your letter – that we are due to leave?'

Anger at feeling guilty stiffened Euphemia's resolve. Staring the girl down, she exclaimed, 'So tell me, miss: what do you imagine?'

To make good time on the journey to the coast, they had to be away early. It was still short of eight o'clock when Georgiana, looking down into the square in her travelling clothes, saw the carriage being brought round. A white mist softened the outlines of the rooftops and chimneys, and dimmed the sun's rays. The quiet city seemed a place apart from the rest of creation, floating alone through a sea of muted glory. The only people moving below were the coachman, pulling up with their luggage already lashed into place behind him, and Euphemia's maid, who darted into the street as soon as he halted, spoke with him briefly and scurried back indoors.

Preparations for their departure could well have been left to the servants. But Euphemia, rustling about with grim good cheer, had been unable not to join in. By the time they were due to leave she was as full of suppressed excitement as a wayward child.

Georgiana, not knowing why their apartment had to be vacated so early, guessed it was to do with the Fitzpaynes' own departure. Some minutes back a man in their livery had brought a hurried letter for Euphemia.

'Well,' she said, coming into Georgiana's bedroom as the luggage was being taken down, and addressing her charge's maid, 'has Miss Bingham been dressed as I instructed?'

Georgiana's maid curtseyed as if to say of course, while Euphemia inspected the girl. Poor Georgiana was sitting at one of the windows in her frilliest bonnet, trying to be wretched with dignity. She was indifferent to how anyone wanted her to dress, whether they were to travel with Harold Fitzpayne or not.

'My dear Miss Lee,' the letter read, 'my very dear Miss Bingham, Your condition has been met! We feared he might have a trying night; but this morning my brave boy is as well as any of us, and adds his entreaties to mine that you will not delay in making us your happiest as well as most devoted . . .' Etc.

The most this hinted at was a fading bruise or so. But it was enough for Euphemia. The thought of herself ministering to a broken but strong young man from one of Europe's noblest houses was more than she could resist. In a voice already softened, she said, 'You do know, Georgiana, that we must make a detour this morning?'

Georgiana fought off the hope that this was to do with Tom. 'Indeed?'

'Lady Augusta Fitzpayne' – rolling the syllables round her mouth – 'did suggest that we might travel with her. But,' indicating the letter, 'reading between the lines, I fear his lordship may not be as well as his mother would like to believe.'

Even as she spoke, Euphemia's fantasy of tormented marble limbs and a sweat-bedewed manly brow was becoming a reality to her.

'Poor man!' A ghost of Euphemia's concern showed on Georgiana's gentle face. 'I never guessed she'd been making light of the accident.'

'It is our duty to call upon them, of course. If only to persuade them that their journey must be postponed.'

They went downstairs and were handed into the carriage. Georgiana could scarcely hide her melancholy at leaving Paris. No miracle could hinder them – no galloping messenger from someone or other, nor even sudden lameness in one of their horses. Their party set off, through streets that were suddenly coming alive. The sun, which minutes before had only reached spires and weathercocks, domes and lofty columns, now cast an early yellow light on attic windows and on the tree-tops in the royal parks. The clatter of traffic on stony streets was already growing loud as they turned out of the square.

Georgiana saw Tom. He was standing on the far side of the street, waiting to dodge between the passing carriages. At that hour, and on that street, the only place he could be going to was their hotel. He looked self-absorbed and reckless.

The colour rose in Georgiana's face, making her parted lips vivid and her eyes large. Hearing her soft gasp of surprise, Euphemia noticed Tom as well. So swiftly did she move that, before the girl could lean out of the window, Euphemia had reached across her and yanked up the glass.

'Why, madam! I *will* speak with him – you shall not prevent me – it is not right that we should drive on – ' Georgiana stared at her chaperone. Euphemia was breathing heavily. Behind her veil her eyes glittered.

A haywain went by, hiding Tom from where their carriage had been stopped by traffic. It was followed by a couple of night-soil carts, then a drove of cattle. Both women reached to seize the leather strap that lowered the window. As though she were looking on at a distance, part of Georgiana could not believe that she and Euphemia were actually struggling together. The other part of her was clawing and buffeting as shame-lessly as a back-alley drab.

The carriage suddenly pulled away, throwing them back into their seats. The window thudded down and Georgiana leaned out, breathlessly dragging her veil back from her face. At that moment, Tom caught sight of her.

She might have been looking in a mirror, so like hers was the expression on his face. He broke into a run, cannoning into passers-by as he strove to catch up

217

with them. But for some reason their horses were being whipped up to a trot.

Where their narrow street met two others, darkened by overhanging housetops, the traffic slowed again. Euphemia, full of furious purpose, rapped on the coachman's little window. As if at an agreed signal, the man urged the horses on, turning them up an empty side street even though it led away from their destination. In their haste, the off-side wheel caught against the wall of a street-corner house and left the ground, then came smacking down. Barefoot slum children cheered, and a flock of chickens scattered, as the coachman risked breaking his horses' knees by putting the beasts into a canter. In a few moments Tom, running, and looking bewildered, was out of sight.

Georgiana, despite her modest manner, was by nature proud. In any other circumstances she would have scorned to weep. But now she sobbed uncontrollably.

'Put down your veil,' said Euphemia some minutes later. They were approaching the Fitzpaynes hotel. Her voice held a tremor of uncertainty. She had not planned to bring her charge here with swollen eyes and an unmaidenly look of outrage.

Georgiana did as she was told, if only because she did not trust herself to speak.

'And you had best stay in the carriage.' Anxious to humour the girl before they met their hosts, she added, 'Surely, now – it must be obvious to you that he cannot have had my letter? If he *was* on his way to our hotel?'

This time even Euphemia would have had to agree that she was lying. But she reasoned that circumstances justified her. The girl's feelings were at stake, after all.

Georgiana looked at her with a desperate glimmer of trust. 'But – could our man not have been ordered to stop?'

Euphemia glowered uneasily. But she held Georgiana's stare. 'I'm sorry. I think he must have mistaken my signal.' She was saved from saying anything more by the carriage coming to a stop outside the Fitzpaynes' hotel.

Waiting with his mother in the spacious lobby, Harold Fitzpayne was of course unharmed and master of all about him. Euphemia would have to give up her notion of bathing his young lordship's brow all the way to Calais while he occasionally fainted against her. She contented herself with making noises that mingled sympathy with congratulation on his wonderful recovery.

His perfect health was noticed by Georgiana too. Back on the road, and once more shut up with Euphemia, she dwelt angrily on the events of the last few hours. Georgiana's life – what she remembered of it – had been happy, but it had also been limited. She had little experience of people who lied while almost believing, as Euphemia did, that they told the truth. Exaggerating Fitzpayne's condition had been a trivial thing. But since it was of no importance, why had Euphemia even bothered to mislead her? Had the woman any idea where reality – facts easily checked by other people – left off, to be overtaken by a chaotic world of pure invention?

The city dwindled behind them till it was not even a smudge of smoke on a distant horizon. Leagues of road passed by – and still neither of them cared to speak. The landscapes of high summer – crowded harvest fields, sun-struck villages with shuttered houses rising out of the dust of the highway, cool tunnels of forest – all were as unreal to Georgiana as shadow-play upon a wall. The more she turned her

219

anger around in her mind, examining it, the more she found to dismay her. By the end of that day's travel, at the Hotel des Anglais, in the cobbled main square at Amiens, her disillusionment with Euphemia, her gaoler, was almost total. After two hours of being heroically polite to Lady Fitzpayne and her son over dinner, she confronted Euphemia in her room.

'I need to ask you some questions.'

'Pray do – as soon as Simpson has finished.' Euphemia, in nightgown and robe, was at her mirror, having her hair put into curl-papers.

'Shall I leave, madam?' asked the maid, pausing with the brush in mid-air.

'Certainly not. Nor you,' she said to Georgiana. Without, however, telling the girl that she could sit down.

Georgiana took a seat anyway. She waited, hands folded, for what became an embarrassingly long time. No one spoke.

At length she and Euphemia were alone.

'Why am I to refuse Tom Fraser?'

Euphemia finished tying on her nightcap, with deliberate slowness. The longer Georgiana's question remained unanswered, the more it began to seem unjustified.

'Why should you do what?'

Euphemia spoke with her back to Georgiana. In the dim room the light from the dressing-table candles made it hard to see her reflection. But if her face was nearly invisible, the tone of her voice was clear enough. Georgiana knew that for some reason she was being humiliated on purpose.

She repeated what she had just said.

'Do what?'

'Refuse Mr Fraser,' she said once more.

'Have you been told to refuse anyone?' Euphemia spoke with chilly disbelief. 'Who told you? Have I?'

220

'Why, no.'

'Then how can you have been told to do such a thing?'

'So – am I right to think neither you, nor my godmother, would wish me to discourage him?' Georgiana frowned as she spoke. She had to ask these questions. But could she believe anything she would be told?

Euphemia said nothing. Carefully she snuffed the candles one by one, until the only light still burning was the one Georgiana had brought with her.

The girl ignored this hint to be gone. 'Madam – for God's sake – you, or someone, owe me an explanation. How can you not have wished me to discourage Mr Fraser? For months you have spoken ill of him! What does my godmother think? Does she know how I've passed the time in Paris? Does she have some plan for me?'

Euphemia did, she knew well enough. It had been impossible not to notice how she had thrust Georgiana into Harold Fitzpayne's company at every chance. But was there also some reason why the wealthy Mrs Michaelmas would care one way or another about the lord of the manor of Cannings Fitzpayne?

'As for Mr Fraser – quite apart from his character – why, he's your own relative!'

'He is not a relative of mine!' Pointedly Euphemia began to get into bed. 'And since you mention the wishes of your godmother, I think you know well enough what those are.'

Georgiana stood up, moving as carefully as if some part of her own body might shatter or spill. If she lost her temper now, she had no idea what terrible thing she might say.

'No, madam,' she replied, in a low, unsteady voice. 'My godmother has never told me anything. Either as my legal guardian or as the friend of my parents. And you – you – ' Tears came to her eyes as she gagged on her own frustration.

Euphemia let the silence grow. Then she said, 'Are you accusing Mrs Michaelmas and me? If so, I think you should tell us what your accusations are.'

Georgiana remained silent, wiping her eyes as violently as if she could stop up the tears with blows. In vain she sought a chink in Euphemia's cunning contempt.

'And since you say you don't know what her wishes are, let's hope for your own sake that you're not just trying to disobey them.' Euphemia looked intently at the girl and lowered her voice. 'Consider, miss, who your friends are. You've no claim on my brother's family. You needn't assume that because he's been generous to you, he's obliged to go on paying out.' If Euphemia knew the girl's expenses had been met by Charity, she didn't choose to remember this now. 'And if you forfeit the good will of Mrs Michaelmas, what do you hope to gain?' She paused. 'What do you hope to save, even?'

Georgiana's anger yielded to bewilderment. 'Why – why do you say that? What do you mean by that? Do you mean the terms of my inheritance? Surely I inherit unconditionally?'

But Euphemia had said enough to satisfy herself, at least. Having asserted her authority by being unhelpful she said, 'I'd like to sleep now, if you don't mind. When next you're asked to see Mrs Michaelmas, try not to harass her with questions. She'll find it unfortunate of you, to say the least, if you imply you're deliberately neglected by her, and kept in ignorance. Goodnight.'

For the rest of the journey to London they scarcely spoke to each other.

CHAPTER THIRTEEN

Just before dawn Tom got down from the Dover stage in the yard of the Adam and Eve on Ludgate Hill. London was as quiet and dark as a sleeping forest, with only the watchman's cry to be heard rebounding through some distant street. The noise of the coach had seemed enormous as it skirted the dim mountain of St Paul's cathedral and clattered under the archway of the inn. There were no other passengers about, and only a couple of ostlers, the light of their lanterns each bobbing about in a halo of steam from the horses.

For four days without stopping, Tom had been on the road from Paris. He no longer knew whether he was tired, only that he was as light-headed with astonishment and doubt as when he had set out.

Before the leaders of the Dover coach had even been unharnessed he had hired a post-chaise and set off again. The horses strained into a canter between the echoing housefronts of Fleet Street, taking him westward out of a faint dawn towards where the moon was setting in an empty sky. A night breeze whispered around open attic windows and cavernous alleys. Suddenly, with whirrings and creaks, every spire and church tower above ten square miles of streets sent out the chimes of five o'clock.

By sunrise they had passed the acres of new squares being built around Chelsea and were in the country once more, amid the orchards and market gardens of Fulham parish. At Putney the old wooden bridge thundered beneath their wheels. Below it the river poured through rickety piles, hidden in a mist that filled the valley. On the bank a herd of cattle were being driven back to pasture after milking. Moving half submerged through the cold white fog, they looked like a shoal of dolphins.

Another hour, and the road wound past the broad oaks of Richmond Park. It reached the brow of the hill that stood between Tom and wherever he might hope to find Georgiana. Beyond the trees at the summit the hillside dropped steeply to a curve of the Thames, which flowed among rich meadows and massy parkland trees. Far across the Middlesex plain stood the outline of Windsor Castle.

The village was really a group of country mansions and fine terraced houses looking down from the side of Richmond Hill. Tom had expected to find only a few lodgings grand enough to house an establishment like Georgiana's. Instead, discovering her address took over two hours of breathless enquiries, at the more prosperous shops on the twisting main street and at a couple of servants' agencies. A few of the people he questioned looked askance at this travel-stained, flustered young man. Others, noting his gentleman's manner and clothes, were positively anxious to ingratiate themselves. Eventually he found himself, hat in hand, his mind a blank, tugging at the bell-pull of a high garden gate outside a big old house by the river walk.

If Tom's head felt emptied, his heart was painfully full. He had come here with no plan, even though for four days he had thought only of what might happen now. Hour after hour, through the cornfields of the Ile de France and across the chalky uplands of Kent, he had dwelt on nothing but what she might say, and how he would answer her. Yet over every mile of the way the only thing he knew was that, whatever he imagined, what actually happened would be different.

He didn't even know, standing tense and bleary in the hot morning sun, what his own feelings were. Every emotion – hope, amazement, uncertainty, dismay, resentment – yes, and anger at his own desire – left him bludgeoned and confused. Since seeing Georgiana look out of her carriage window and leave him standing in the street, it was still too soon to know which one was destined to hurt him most.

A butler opened the garden door.

'Sir?'

Only now did Tom realize how frowsty he must look. Without thinking he said, 'I have an urgent appointment to see Miss Lee. She wrote me before we both left Paris.'

'Miss Lee is not at home, sir.'

'My appointment is also with Miss Bingham.' Tom sensed it was best to hide the fact that he wanted only to confront Georgiana, alone.

The butler did a half-second's inventory of everything Tom wore. Despite the condition of Tom's clothes, he could see that his boots had been made by the best people in town. 'What name shall I give, sir?'

Tom had not stopped to think that this would be a difficult question. The butler would have been newly hired, along with the house. But already he had probably been told which callers he should admit, and which ones he must turn away.

'Harold Fitzpayne.'

'M'lord,' said the butler in acknowledgement. He turned to lead the way.

The two ladies and their personal servants had not been expected back in England quite so soon. Consequently much of the house still looked un-lived-in. Tom was shown into a long dark drawing room. Two footmen appeared from nowhere to lift a dust sheet off a winged armchair for him, and one window was unshuttered, letting in a shaft of mote-filled sunlight.

Standing alone in the middle of the room, Tom waited to be announced. He was shaken to the core by fatigue and impatience. Knowing so little about what was really happening, did he dread the moment when Georgiana would appear? If so, whose harsh words did he fear the most – hers, or his own?

The butler came back, and indicated that Tom should follow him. 'Miss Bingham will receive you now, m'lord.'

What the devil! thought Tom. He had momentarily forgotten who he was supposed to be. What business had Georgiana to be receiving that poor dolt, in her private sitting room?

Worse – as he was shown into a quiet chamber with an old-fashioned spindly four-poster visible in the room beyond, he saw that Georgiana was alone. She was dressed in white muslin, exquisitely worked, and looked as delicate as a dandelion seed.

The door was closed behind him, leaving them alone. The butler, his duty done, went off. With the other upper servants, in one of a warren of rooms facing back into the hillside, he'd been about to enjoy a third helping of breakfast.

At the sight of Tom, Georgiana visibly started. She had not known that desperation and hard travelling could make someone so young look as haggard as this. The responsibility of being loved by him left her aghast.

He too was dismayed. How could she not have betrayed him on purpose? Every muscle in her body announced a sense of guilt.

'What happened?' Tom was beyond caring that he sounded distraught. He could not bear to stay in ignorance. He could not bear to think what she might be about to say.

Georgiana was standing before a tall window, trying not to twist her hands together. Her shadowy form was eclipsed by an explosion of light from the river, sheeted with brightness beyond the upper boughs of a mighty plane tree. He could not see that every breath brought her nearer to a surge of tears.

'I don't know what happened,' she said, more abruptly than she'd intended. She felt suffocated by shame, knowing she had no better answer to give.

'But – have you been told to have no more to do with me? Is that what's happened?'

'Not exactly. I mean – I've been given hints.'

'What do you mean? How?'

'I've been made to understand what's wanted from me by . . . well, looks. And silences.'

'But not in plain words? Do you seriously believe so?'

She shot him a look hot with frustration. 'You would, in my position.'

'You can't – I mean, you haven't even told me who I should speak to, if I'm to have a serious answer.'

Georgiana turned away from him, speechless. She put both hands over her mouth, as if by force she could keep back her tears.

Tom stared at her.

In an uncertain voice she said, 'You must believe me – I want to know what's happening, too. Oh, please! Please understand!'

'But you must know – you must! You're bound to know – it's impossible that you can't. Good God, it's our future – it's your own future – it's everything – everything could be at stake, from today right up to the minute that you die.' Wild-eyed and unshaven, he glared at her. The thought entered his mind that he should leave – just walk away and have done. Yet, inasmuch as he knew he couldn't – not yet – he was ready to hate her. How could he have been brought to this?

Georgiana turned away again, still too proud to weep

227

openly. Outside the tall window, sparrows chirped. Voices came up from a boating party on the river. It seemed to both of them that there was nothing more to be said – and that this moment's torment was all they had left to live for. How were they to fill all those years of getting up every morning, once Tom had left?

As a last appeal, she forced herself to turn again and seize him by the sleeve. 'Help me! Please!'

He looked at her, expressionless and unmoving. 'How? What can I do, when you won't tell me how?'

His stony self-mastery sobered her, more suddenly than if she'd been dealt a blow. She took the most deliberate breath of her life. 'I'm sorry – no, you *will* listen to me. And when I'm finished, then you can say whatever you like. I'm sorry I've got no parents and hardly know who I am' – it was only by sarcasm that Georgiana could still bear to speak – 'and I'm sorry that our Aunt Kate is three thousand miles away, so that it's beside the point that she – that she' – trying to stifle a sob – 'she at least would give me what advice she could. And I'm sorry you were wronged when we were in Paris, and treated with such disrespect. But I did tell you what I thought was the right thing to do – when I told you to write for permission to Euphemia. And however rude she was when – when we saw you last – I mean, in the street – well, at least she had already told you to write to Mrs Michaelmas.'

'No, she hadn't.'

There was a brief silence.

'Could – maybe the letter went astray?'

'No.'

'But how can you be sure?'

'Because what she did tell me was that I should call on her.'

'That's not what she said to me.' Puzzlement crept into Georgiana's voice.

'I was to call on her the next day. But by the hour

she'd given, you'd already left. For Calais.' Tom spoke guardedly. The hope that maybe they need not have quarrelled was almost too much to bear.

There was a longer silence in the room. Each of them savoured the significance of what the other had said. How could Euphemia have been so silly in her treachery?

Tom found the courage to ask for one more reassurance. 'But – why have you agreed to see me alone, when your man announced me as Fitzpayne?' He tried to sound calm. But his voice was hoarse with suspense.

Georgiana's heart flowered into happiness. No longer was she ashamed that tears sparkled in her eyes. 'Because – oh, because I saw you, from the window! Don't you understand that sitting up here on my own, all I could think of was when I might see you next?'

Tom had not the least idea what to do with himself. He seized her hands and looked helplessly about him, as if the corners of the room might explain to him how to contain his explosion of relief. With a dry sob he glanced down, then up at the ceiling. Then, having nowhere else to hide his face, he pulled her to him, laid his head against hers, and wept aloud.

Georgiana held him as tightly as if drowning them both. Opposing tides of feeling washed through her as her body trembled with the violence of his sobs. She was choked with anger – for him, and for herself, too. It was nothing – now they understood one another – that she had been made wretched. But it was unbearable that Euphemia should have made an accomplice of her, in behaving meanly towards a young man of honour.

What should she say? What could she do? Georgiana had not known remorse could feel like a fatal injury.

Shuddering from the shock of release, Tom at length mastered himself. Georgiana clung to him. 'Help me show you how sorry I am!' she exlaimed. 'I'll do anything – only help me!'

The poor girl had no idea how her words might be understood, nor even what she really meant. She only knew, as he kissed her hotly, that to protest would have wronged the best in both of them.

He held her by the arms and spoke very gently. 'You are certain?' From the steadiness of his manner, no one could have known that the thought of twining naked on this brilliant, vulnerable creature made him almost dead with longing and dread.

And what of her humiliation, if he refused her?

'How could I not be certain?' She was aflame with earnestness.

A new emotion shone in his face, subtle as a change of light over a kind landscape. Still Georgiana failed to understand him. He took her hand, and put an arm around her, to lead her into the next room.

Only then did she realize what he meant to do to her.

She was surprised, mainly at her own embarassing stupidity. But not for one heartbeat did she hesitate. After what had happened, how else should she honour his intention towards her, as her lover? If only she had been stronger before, and more suspicious of her elders! At least now, she could show firmness of purpose, and take this chance of purging her remorse. It might cost her all the courage she had, but still she must open herself to him.

Each knew the other was afraid. It was as well such knowledge made a bond of sympathy. Georgiana's white dress was appalling in the number and stiffness of its fastenings. She tugged and twisted at the three dozen hooks that secured the back of its bodice. Not since childhood had she tried to undress without the help of a maid. Her under-bodice had been laced so tightly, she could only escape by wrenching at it until the lace snapped. It had to be unthreaded one eyelet at a time. There were six petticoats, fastened with hooks. By the time her white silk stockings had been flung into a corner, along with Tom's rancid shirt and breeches, she was tearful with frustration.

Undressed down to her shift, she turned to face him and raised her arms so that he could lift it over her. She felt too diffident to take off her last garment for herself.

He helped her, his heart speaking in his face.

She got clumsily on to the bed. Tom felt pity at seeing a moment of awkwardness in such a graceful woman. A patch of sunlight had made the bedcover hot beneath her back.

Now that he knelt above her, she could almost be done with feeling fearful. At last, she sensed desire darting into her. How she had deceived herself! She loved this man, certainly, and honoured him, so much that she wanted to die of it. But she also ached for him, right down to the root of sensation, with mere common lust.

As he put his mouth on her cunt she no longer felt she had a body. His kiss – it took her some moments to understand what was happening – yes, his kiss jolted her beyond everything she'd known. Whatever was being done to her, it was not to be endured. Nor could she bear that it might stop. In her, heaven and hell were the same place. She was everything and everywhere. She was an empty infinity, drizzling brightness.

She didn't dare open her eyes. If she did, the god who was raping her would cease to exist. Something using her voice cried out with a terrible sound like an uprooted mandrake.

Euphemia came into the room.

Her soft gasp seemed the loudest noise Tom or

Georgiana had ever heard. They bolted apart, trembling with outrage and shame.

Only when she saw who he was did Euphemia raise her voice, in a yell of astonishment.

'Oh! *Oh!*' she yelped. For once she felt no satisfaction in being outraged. She had reasons of her own for being shamed.

Through the further door Charity Michaelmas followed her in.

'Damn you!' snarled Euphemia in an undertone. 'Damn you!' Blindly she snarled at each of them. '*Damn* you!'

Knowing Harold Fitzpayne to be staying in the neighbourhood, she had not been out of the house by accident. Her half-conscious plan had been to let him feel he had – well, not exactly compromised the girl. She hadn't wanted anyone to think she was taking risks. On the other hand she could not resist the chance of taking credit for leading him to an early proposal of marriage.

The young people cowered, their desires blasted by her intrusion.

'I'll see you damned! *I'll* have you shamed for your whoring!' she hissed at Georgiana, who was making pitiful efforts to cover herself.

'No – no – please – no!' gasped Georgiana, senselessly.

'I'll make you suffer! I'll make both of you suffer!'

Tom started cramming his clothes on, livid with shock. Even now, he would have known how to meet an attack from a man. No matter that he would have looked foolish putting up his fists while naked as a damned soul. But he had no idea how to defend himself against a flurry of feeble slaps from a woman. He fled to the next room.

Until he almost ran against her, Charity had not guessed exactly what was amiss. At the sight of a frantic young man running nearly naked from her daughter's bedroom, the dignified curves of her face stayed as immobile as ever. She was wearing a bonnet and travelling dress of heavy blue silk that caught the light like a waterfall.

Tom fumbled to button his breeches, hunched like an old man in his confusion. Euphemia followed him in.

'I can have you indicted for this!' Sensing Mrs Michaelmas's inexplicable calm, she made an effort to be restrained. But her eyes blazed with thwarted savagery. 'If her godmother wishes it, you needn't think *she*,' pointing towards the bedroom, 'can't be made to give public evidence against you!'

She turned to Charity, trying to bear with dignity her own failure as chaperone. 'Never fear, madam. I shall send immediately for someone to remove him.'

'I should prefer it, Miss Lee, if you did not.'

The lack of emotion in Charity's voice silenced Euphemia more thoroughly than any reprimand. With a ragged attempt at self-possession, she stalked back into the bedroom and closed the door.

Charity waited, looking out of the window. Tom finished dragging on his coat and paused too, though he had no idea for what. Behind the bedroom door Euphemia was speaking in a voice of quiet cruelty and Georgiana could be heard weeping.

As Charity turned, the young man looked steadily at her, hat in hand and collar awry. He had the air of a prisoner with no case, before a judge passing sentence of death.

Several things were in her mind. Tom looked much like his uncle, George Byford, at the same age. Before she had refused to see him again, George had fought a duel on account of the shame he had brought on her, and nearly died as a result. The nephew, she saw, had the same air of defiant hopelessness.

She was thinking too that she had defended her daughter's maidenhead in worse circumstances than this. Twenty years ago, in a cesspit of a street in Shoreditch, two of her potential clients had been only half joking when they had proposed a contest. They were to see which could stand and spend himself first: one in a chicken, one with the two-month-old Georgiana spitted on his member.

With a slight movement of her head, she signalled to him to go. Tom, lost in self-hatred at his own bungling, departed without a word.

As he went out at the garden gate, Charity still stood by the window, looking out. Rather than dwell on her daughter's heartbroken cries, she was trying to arm herself, with more memories.

Down beyond the high garden wall, the river and its banks were peopled with parties of pleasure. An arrow-shaped ripple spread across the water as a mallard swam briefly into view. Charity too had sailed past here, huddled in rags beneath a piece of sacking on a canal barge.

She gazed up the Thames, to where it wandered into view among flat meadows and bold English elms. Beyond that horizon were the hills where she had strayed, barefoot and big with the unborn Georgiana, asking isolated shepherds and parties of drovers if they could tell her the way to London. Having never seen a town, she had had no idea what sort of place she was looking for. Below the hilly streets and castle at Windsor, she had been unable to believe such an important place was not the capital city. And when she should reach London, she had been convinced she could easily find George Byford, just by asking passers-by if they knew his address.

Tom Fraser, with his nearly bankrupt parents, need not be a problem, even if the girl proved no longer intact. Meanwhile, though Euphemia mostly served her purpose well, Charity knew she must make herself go into the next room and deliver Georgiana from that overwrought termagant, if only for a few hours. She did not admit to herself that she could scarcely face her daughter in tears.

As for Fitzpayne, well, there were reasons why he should be increasingly anxious to marry money. Already there were rumours of the Wiltshire estate being mortgaged.

In the short term, though, her plans must be adjusted without delay. Charity turned away from the long vista beyond the window, with its bracing, terrible memories, and went to speak in private with Euphemia.

CHAPTER FOURTEEN

Twenty hours later Tom appeared at his parents' home. To a stranger he would have looked no worse than someone, say, who had just completed a long journey. He managed to be courteous to the family servants and looked pleased, if wan, on being cheerfully greeted in the hall by his younger sisters. Mary-Anne and Louisa were still at the unformed age when their horizons were bounded by governesses and an occasional steamer trip to the polite resort of Margate. To them a grown-up brother was a godlike creature, the very embodiment of freedom and adult dignity.

Edward hailed him with a show of sang-froid aimed at hiding his genuine pleasure. 'How d'you do, Tom.'

'How do you do, Ned.'

'Moderately, dear fellow.'

Sophy, hearing them all, came out of her husband's study and hurried downstairs. 'Tom, dearest! Where have you been?'

'In France, mother,' said Edward, proud of his own tolerance towards his mama's seemingly pointless question.

In manhood as in infancy, Tom had no use for falsehoods, however harmless. To Sophy he said, 'I was back the night before last.'

He seemed tired and sobered. Sophy looked at him closely, but without wonderment.

'So where've you been?' asked Louisa, a blooming girl of thirteen who was already as tall as her mother.

'I don't want to talk about it.'

236

'Why not?'

'Louisa!' said Sophy sharply.

Tom turned to his mother. 'I went to see Miss Bingham.'

'Who — ?' began Louisa's forthright elder sister, Mary-Anne. She was silenced by a look from their mother.

'I need to see father,' Tom said.

For some reason Sophy's face changed from concern to fearfulness. 'Tom dearest, he's got someone important with him. They — father's visitor — will be leaving soon. Why don't you come upstairs with us? Brannigan can bring you some breakfast.' She put a hand on his arm.

'No. I want to see father now.' Pulling himself free, he ran up the stairs two at a time. The surprised young faces of his brother and sisters turned upward to watch Sophy hurry after him.

'Tom, *please!*'

Tom thrust open the door to his father's study. Fraser and Charity Michaelmas were there, standing up to shake hands in parting.

Ignoring his father, Tom said to Charity, 'You've got to let me marry her now. After what I've done — '

Throughout a day and most of a night he'd thought only of what he wished he'd said at the time. Now that Charity stood before him again, he was remorseful, mainly on Georgiana's account. But he was also prepared to feel triumphant. Fate had been on his side after all — the worse he seemed to have behaved, the more the proprieties favoured his case.

'You've got to!' he exclaimed. 'You know my intentions are better than — you know they're better than they appeared!'

Charity looked at him with the same bland politeness as before, saying nothing.

Sophy had followed him into his father's study. It

was she and Fraser who seemed agitated. She quickly said, 'I hope you'll do us the justice of believing that our son will be discreet. From what you say, I am sure nothing blameworthy has been done.'

Charity gestured as if to say, but of course, at the same moment that Tom exclaimed, 'Of course I will, mother! What do you imagine?' His mother's words left him amazed. He had come home expecting to be chided perhaps at whatever he confessed, and worried over, too. But not opposed by his own family, to the point of betrayal.

'And,' said Sophy, as if he had not spoken, 'we consider that anyone would do our son a great wrong in entertaining the least suspicion of his hunting out a fortune.'

Tom turned on her, his face working violently. 'What is this?' His voice was thick. 'How can you? How dare anyone!' Glaring at Charity, he shouted, 'Look at this house! Look at us all, and how we live. Do you think I need to sign away my life, just to raise capital by taking a wife who's said to have money?' Rich man's son that he'd been, he almost spat the last word, so great was his disdain.

His parents avoided his eyes.

'I'm not aware,' said Charity, 'that Miss Bingham has been – as you seem to suggest – compromised, by you or anyone else. Certainly, no one in her household would be prepared to say so. And no reasonable being could doubt your word when you say that you're innocent of guile or greed. Goodbye, Mrs Fraser. I'm glad that my interview with Mr Fraser will be profitable to all of us.'

Fraser moved quickly to open the door for her. Sophy made herself shake hands, and accompanied Charity on to the landing, where a footman was waiting to escort her round the corner to her house in Grosvenor Square.

Tom was beside himself. Motioning angrily in the direction of Charity, he exclaimed loudly at his mother, 'You can't just say nothing!'

For all her pretended certainty, Sophy too was wretched. What would Tom say, when she told him how their fortunes had come to depend on Charity Michaelmas' goodwill?

On impulse, she leaned over the bannister. 'Mrs Michaelmas. Why do you not wish our son to marry your – Miss Bingham?'

Charity looked back unflinchingly at George Byford's sister. 'Your family's assets have rarely been secure, Mrs Fraser. If your son cannot appreciate what that can mean, it would be a kindness to explain.'

As soon as the street door had been closed behind Charity and her servant, Ned, still in earshot, let out an exclamation of surprise. 'Poor old Tom! Been chasing a skirt with too much money pinned on to it?'

He was astonished when his mother, running down the stairs, tried to strike him in the face before bursting into tears.

'Please, mother,' said Tom wearily, going to put his arms around her. 'Don't do that.'

Sophy struggled to calm herself. 'Forgive me, Tom. But there are things you must be told.'

Fraser could not bear to be present as Tom learned some of what had passed between his parents and Charity Michaelmas. He was an inflexible, open-hearted man, who always acted as he thought right. And even if he hadn't been so, he would not have known how to make an apology. It was a new thing for him to be deeply compromised, let alone in the eyes of his son.

But there it was, as Tom himself was quickly told after the study door had closed on Sophy and him.

Either Tom would cease all contact with Georgiana, or a quiet word from Charity would bring about the withdrawal of political – and hence financial – support for Fraser's partner.

Most shaming to Fraser was the knowledge that he desired the exercise of his own talents, and therefore the survival of his business, even more than he valued his son's happiness and self-esteem.

When Sophy had finished speaking, with as few falterings and excuses as she could manage, there was a silence. For a full minute Tom sat, looking at nothing. Eyes averted, Sophy waited, brimming with dread.

'What did Mrs Michaelmas mean, when she said our assets were insecure in the past, as well as now?'

His tone, as he looked at her, was courteous but hard. She scarcely knew him.

Now would have been the moment for frankness – when she should have told him everything she knew about Georgiana's parentage, and the true source of the fortune that the fashionable world expected her to inherit. But alas for any trust between Sophy and her elder son! It had been one of Charity's conditions that Sophy should conceal these facts. Looking him in the face she said faintly, 'Mrs Michaelmas has connections in Wiltshire – near Cannings Fitzpayne, in fact – and has known of our family for many years. She knows your father was obliged, when you were small, to leave us for a time and find business in America. And – for what it signifies – she also knows that by the time we were reunited, you and I and Ned had fallen into danger of great hardship.'

He looked at her without speaking.

A terrible thought seized her. In all the years since she had chosen her husband over her son, and followed him to America, had Tom believed that she had wronged him on purpose?

Hastily she said, 'Also she may have known at the time, just before you were born, that your father was imprisoned for debt. I know it was none of his fault. But if Mrs Michaelmas judges people carelessly, it may be that she has reasons of her own. I say reasons, not excuses – God knows, Tom, how greatly you have been wronged! But I do believe that in her youth the world was particularly harsh in its handling of Mrs Michaelmas – '

Tom gestured impatiently. He could not be doing with dim histories from his mother's girlhood.

'Listen carefully, mother. Miss Bingham – Georgiana – will be twenty-one next year. Haven't any of you thought what that means? If you're ready to put some speculative threat to father's business before the most important part of *my* life, what's to prevent me doing the same to you? We can be married anyway, as soon as Georgiana has means of her own – and then you and father can go hang!'

His mother's look of stoicism almost undid him. He stared her down nonetheless.

'Tom, even if Miss Bingham would have you – yes, which I'm sure is so – she can't. Certainly not next year. Maybe never, while your own fortunes are uncertain.'

'Why not, in God's name?' His disbelief verged on contempt. 'Tell me why not!'

'Miss Bingham's coming of age will make no difference to her. She isn't due to come into her money, at the earliest, until she's twenty-five – '

'What?' Tom exclaimed, foolish with dismay. 'Are you sure?'

'Quite.'

'But we might all be dead by then!'

' – Also, Mrs Michaelmas' powers over the estate go beyond that, should she see fit.'

Even as she spoke, Sophy was hot with self-loathing.

241

Never had she lied to one of her children – not even, as now, by leaving something unsaid.

'Please, Tom dearest – please try to see why it is that Miss Bingham, too, must want you to do as you've been asked.'

He was too shaken to speak straight away.

'If, as you say, she loves you, it may be that she can't bear to refuse you herself. From love – but from shame, too, at being forced by her guardian. Dear Tom, don't you see that if you do go on paying court to this girl, it may be even more of a torment to her than if she never heard of you again. Consider how it would be if – yes, loving one another – you did marry her. You would be doing her an unpardonable wrong.'

'How?' he said faintly. 'How would that be?'

'You would be asking her to ruin both of you.'

Tom stood up and took a few paces. Standing in the middle of the room he turned this way and that, utterly irresolute.

'Oh, mother!' His voice quaked with failed determination. 'Oh! What shall I do?'

Sophy could not bear to look him in the face. She stood up and embraced him. 'I love you, Tom. We all do. You must let me help you. I shall tell you what must be done.'

Within the hour a letter for Tom came by hand from the house at Richmond. It was from Georgiana. Sophy saw Tom turn ashen even before he began to read it. When he had finished, he turned his face away.

'Do you wish me to know what she says?' Sophie finally ventured.

'No,' said Tom – then almost threw the letter at her.

Dearest Tom,
– For so I may call you, and indeed I think I

*ought, now. I care nothing for how frankly I
describe what befell us yesterday – only that you
will forgive me, if in fact I am to blame. You I
could never blame for what they tell me to think of
as our indiscretion. The more I come to know you,
the better I am bound to love you – yes, and for
ever, come what may.*

*But now – oh Tom! – they have told me we must
stay apart, for the reasons that they say you know
by now. Yet how can I be patient, and let them
send me where they will – we are to go to Italy
after all. I think we are to leave today. Surely, had
my parents lived, it would not be thus – I would
not now be a betrayer, of my true self, and of you.
Oh, what must I say to you? There is nothing I can
do – only tell me how to find this bearable! Please
– only, please write, to say that you forgive me for
whatever I am about to do – and to tell me that, if
I do go away, you know that I shan't have done so
in silence. Tom – dearest – this is not
presumptuous of me – you do owe me this one
thing – and, even if you write by return to say that
you hate me, still the words will be yours, and they
will be deserved besides.*

*But never to see you again! You must meet me –
once more – it can be done – you cannot deny me.*

*Only, tell me what I must do, if I am to bear all
this.*

Poor girl! thought Sophy. To Tom she thought it best
only to say, 'This must be answered, you know,
immediately.'

'I know that – I know!' he exclaimed, snatching back
the letter. More calmly, he added, 'I'm sorry, mother.
It's just that I don't know how I'll bear to find the
words.'

Tentatively, Sophy offered to draft a reply, and on a

nod from him she sat down, pen in hand. When she was finished, she passed him what she had written.

He scarcely glanced at it. 'Yes – yes, I'm sure that will do.'

'But Tom – you can't just send someone else's words! Some of what you write must be your own.' Sophy was dismayed at the responsibilty that was being thrust upon her – by Tom, by her husband, by Charity. It was as if Tom's courtship of Georgiana was a mangled corpse that everyone was too squeamish to bury.

'Why should I care? If I'm to be a villain, does it matter how much of one I am? I can't despise myself worse than this – so what does it matter how much *she* despises me?'

He picked up the paper nonetheless, and looked at it again. For a few moments he set to scribbling with frantic haste, like a man rushing to his own destruction, and desperate to have done with it. He wrote,

Dear Georgiana,

To you I owe nothing but respect, and gratitude for every generous thing you have said. There is no other course; things must be borne as they are – you must depart, and I in conscience must do nothing to contradict the wishes of your guardian.

Duty bids me say no more. Except that, since there must be no further meeting between us, I hope you will be grateful one day for the chance that has separated us for ever.

Who ever am, in friendship and regard, TF

The letter was sealed up, and given to the servant who was to carry it back to Richmond. That's that, thought Sophy, hearing the street door close behind the man with a dull thud. Even Tom must know that things must slowly get better for him, now. She went up to

244

her own sitting room, relieved to turn her attention to the household accounts. The family finances had instantly ceased to be dreadful, now that Tom had done what he had to.

She would have been even more relieved, could she have avoided him for the rest of that day.

Four hours later a reply came from Georgiana.

> *I do not deserve this. You cannot have thought –*
> *as I have – yes, over and over – of what has*
> *passed. I know now that I stand wronged by you.*
> *It was I who had the courage to propose that we*
> *meet – not you – even though it is I who stand*
> *most at risk.*
> *Oh, but I shall find it in me to forget you. I must*
> *not think my future happiness is all gone, even*
> *though the past is betrayed utterly by your*
> *unfeeling letter. If your own heart is so unharmed,*
> *then so is every part of me – heart, mind, spirit –*
> *senses, too – all are untouched by you. Your letter*
> *is enclosed. I am, as you suggest, grateful that, by*
> *whatever means, we are separated. As you say, for*
> *ever.*

Going into the dining room in response to the lunch gong, Sophy found Tom tearing up a sheet of paper and casting it into the fire a few pieces at a time. He looked as if he'd recently aged about twenty years. But at least she was reassured by his air of deliberate calm.

Speaking quietly, in order not to be heard by his sisters and their governess, whose voices could be heard as they came into the room, he said, 'My letter to Miss Bingham.' He indicated the fireplace, where flames from the paper fragments were breaking and spurting among a mass of glowing coal.

245

Without thinking, Sophy exclaimed, 'But it was sent – '

'So, it has returned,' he said grimly. She stared into the fireplace, feeling a heat in her face that came from more than the flames.

He handed her Georgiana's letter. 'This came, too. You may as well read it, since you're already so deep in my affairs.' Tom did not mean to be cruel, but he felt more grief than he could contain.

'Then, if you would, dispose of it.' Even words of hate, if they came from Georgiana, were something he could not bear to destroy himself.

Still blushing, Sophy took the letter without a word. 'If you'll excuse me – '

'Of course, Tom dearest – '

'I have another letter to write.'

Sophy went to join the others at table, reading as she went. Only on reaching Georgiana's signature did she look up at what Tom had just said.

She ran after him into the hall. 'Tom – surely – you're not going to answer this? Please don't – not in anger!'

'You all wanted the thing finished, mother. And now I'm going to conclude it properly.' So saying, he went upstairs, with the uneasy stiffness of a sick man.

Halfway through lunch, Sophy, listening over the others' conversation, heard movement in the hallway. Starting up from the table, she hurried to investigate. A manservant was coming downstairs, carrying a letter.

'If that is from Mr Thomas, I wish to have it, thank you Prewett. I shall need,' she lied, 'to enclose something of my own.'

Taking the letter she hastily tried to hide it in her pocket.

'Mother,' said Tom, from the top of the stair. His face was stonier than ever.

246

Sophy looked up at him, too guilty to speak.

'A word with you.'

In Tom's study they stood facing each other.

'May I have my letter?' The reasonableness in his voice was terrible.

She handed it back. 'Tom – please – if you're never going to see or hear from Miss Bingham again – '

'If, mother? Our separation was decided for me before we'd even met.'

'Oh, Tom! In God's name, don't quibble at me!'

They glowered at each other in mutual desperation. Sophy drew a breath and went on, 'Since you've agreed to have no further contact with her – oh, please, don't write to her anything you'll regret! I'm sure she doesn't deserve it, and neither would you!' What she really meant was, please don't do anything for which, one day, you'll blame *me!*

'Look, mother.' Tom's eyes had taken fire and his breathing had harshened – he who all his life had been the mildest of creatures! 'If you want a separation, you can have one that's total. You – and father – and father's creditors – and all *her* people – *and* her' – brandishing his letter at Sophy as if threatening her with a clenched fist – 'You – and she – can all have exactly what you want, and then some more. Look in here,' tearing the letter open again, 'and see how successful you've been!' He thrust it at her with such violence that she instinctively turned her head away. All she glimpsed were the words 'Dear Madam'.

She faced him down, fired by apprehension and remorse. 'I said, I know you've been wronged. Your offer to Miss Bingham was treated shamefully. Do you think I, as your mother, don't feel offended at that? Knowing the facts as I do?' Tears of righteous anger stung Sophy's eyes. Truly it was intolerable, what she had been asked to do. 'I know you've been spurned for reasons that are wrong – and frivolous.' Charity had not hidden from Sophy her hope of marrying her daughter to Fitzpayne. 'But I – and your father – are not to blame. Good God, it's we, your family, who have been rejected – not you!'

His stare was unrelenting. Sophy felt her own resentment swell into something monstrous. What business had she with protecting Charity Michaelmas' good name at such a cost? She could not bear it.

'Damn you, Tom! You only say such things to me – and to this poor girl – because no one else is here to listen – because we're on hand! You don't really care whether we're to blame or not. So, you're suffering! What about me – made to do as I'm told because Charity Michaelmas thinks my son is not good enough! For – for her daughter!'

She trembled with uncertain resolve. If she offered Tom the truth, then would he see her as an ally?

He looked at her without moving. In a steady voice he said, 'Is that what she told you, today?'

She stared back at him. 'No,' she said in an uncertain tone.

His brow knotted with anger and surprise. 'When, in God's name? When did you know this?'

Sophy's frankness had misfired. But it was too late to retreat into dishonesty. In a shaken voice she admitted, 'Always.'

'And still you let her say that I'm not good enough? When her daughter is obviously illegitimate? Does she even know the father's name?'

'She does, dear Tom, and so do I.' Sophy gave a long sigh. Half of her was glad at letting out the truth, and half was fearful of what he might say. Then she told him all she knew about Georgiana's parentage.

He looked at her, incredulous, and then barked with laughter. 'What!' he exclaimed bitterly. 'You knew this, and you didn't protest?'

'It doesn't alter the financial facts, Tom.'

'But is the inheritance a fiction, along with the respectable birth? If the woman has had me deceived, couldn't she be playing you and father along on false pretences, too?'

'Not at all.'

'How do you know that?'

'Because – Dearest, if I'm frank with you, will you try to understand – ?'

'Just be frank with me because it's your duty, mother. I'm not a fool, and I've a right to the truth in any case.'

Sophy bit her lip and struggled not to look shamed. Watching his face, she described her own fragments of knowledge about the source of Charity's wealth.

'I know you have reason to resent the woman. But nothing of what she did was done from choice.' It was really herself, as Charity's tool, that she was defending. 'She was destitute when she arrived in London and couldn't find poor George.'

'So I suppose she became some rich old man's doxy.'

'Not at first. I glimpsed her once, in Piccadilly, just before Miss – Georgiana would have been born. She hadn't washed for a month, and she was seeking a living by trailing well-dressed women of the street. To make them bribe her to stay away.' At the time, the sight had filled Sophy with pity and horror. Maybe it wouldn't have, she thought, if she could have seen this far into the future.

Tom was hardly listening. The knowledge of these extra injustices was the final savour in the poisonous dish of his humiliations.

And there was one other injury, that cut too deep for him to have mentioned it – or even admitted it to himself. Until now. He turned away, as if seeking resolve, then back again. His voice was low and careful.

'Mother, you *are* to blame. I have tried not to say this – '

'I am not!' she exclaimed in a whisper.

'Yes, you are – '

'You do me wrong – '

'You are the one who is to blame – '

'No! How dare you say so!'

His voice rose. 'Believe me, I dare say more than that!'

'*You* have been forced in this matter? And I?' she shouted. 'What about me? What choice have I had?'

'Damn you, mother! You have been at fault in your dealings with me since my babyhood!'

They glared at each other, breathing hard. Sophy's face was a mask of anguish.

He went on, 'You were bound to choose Father's interests over mine, whatever was at stake. Because you've done so before. The first thing I can remember – almost my first memory – is of you sailing away from me. Leaving me, to be handed down into the care of strangers, for months on end. Just for the sake of being with Father for a matter of weeks. How could you have made such a choice? *I* needed you – I was an infant, left behind to be told you might never come back. He didn't need your company – not as I did. He was a grown man, full of his own business. Busy and invisible, just as he's been ever since.'

Sophy stared at him as if at an avenging ghost. His words, and the despairing look he gave her, seemed to spread paralysis out from her heart through her whole body. She opened her mouth to speak, though she had not the least idea what to say.

He motioned her to silence. There were tears in his eyes, and he spoke with an effort. 'Don't say you're sorry,' he whispered. 'Don't say anything.' With every breath, Tom felt as if his own heart were being clamped smaller. Too many passions bound him, tighter every moment. There was resentment of the shaken woman in front of him; and sorrow for himself in childhood, bewildered as a kitten thrust into a sack for drowning. Above all, as feared and longed for as a *coup de grâce* to a half-killed man, there was the relief of what he had just said.

He gave a sob, with a wrenching sound like the tearing of a limb. Tears ran down his cheeks.

Yet Sophy was wrong, if she thought grieving aloud would soften him. They stood, long enough for the shadows in the room to have moved, with no sound but his weeping. Her face was neutral with horror at what she had heard, as if shock had left her without the power to feel. Eventually, with forced calm, he gave her one more unforgiving look, and walked out without a word.

After Tom left, Sophy climbed the stairs to her bedroom. It took an effort, as though she were scaling a mountain where the air was thin. Instructing her maid that she was not to be disturbed, she locked the door and sat down at random by her dressing table. She stayed there, motionless, for a long time.

Was this the worst moment of her life? The handsome, fair-coloured woman in the mirror did not look distraught. She did not weep or cower or even sigh out loud. The hurt she felt was too great for that. Tom's words were like a fatal poison that seeps through the body for days before the victim begins to wonder how much is amiss.

Sophy had believed her husband's ruin was the worst thing she faced. She had tasted poverty for herself, after all – she knew its effects, in detail. Yet only now did she recognize the real risk to her happiness. Now that the love and respect of her firstborn was taken –

snatched away in a few violent moments – the pain of it was too great to be acknowledged then and there.

She forced herself to recall her return from America, all those anxious years ago. Sophy had spared nothing in making up to Tom for what she herself had seen as her desertion. People of all sorts had remarked that no child could have been raised with more loving care. He had been a quiet little boy, certainly, but he had always seemed patient and affectionate. There had been no hint of this, waiting in the future. His words had oppressed her so much that she sat now, for an hour, then another, as if at the quiet centre of a terrible storm. Sophy felt nothing, for the moment. But just beyond the limit of her immediate senses, a shrieking mob of passions pressed, waiting to invade her.

At the end of two hours and more, she was still empty of every emotion except growing hatred for Charity Michaelmas. Her fierce disdain became a purpose, but one which lacked immediate direction. How could that self-contained woman have committed such cruel folly for so long? Wasn't it enough to have escaped her terrible past, without keeping its memory alive, to oppress Sophy and her family, too? Her anger made her restless, so that for some time she walked up and down, pressing her hands together, or raising them behind her head, as she sought how to release this new, desperate energy.

Meanwhile, there were things to be done – surely there were. Letters waited to be written to several absent friends. Invitations must be issued for a large party next month. There was probably enough of the afternoon left to ring for the carriage and make some calls.

Unlocking the door stopped all such plans. The housekeeper appeared, curtseyed, and asked advice on arrangements for a dinner with twenty guests that was to be given two days hence. What was all this? thought

252

Sophy, gaping as stupidly at the woman as she had done at Tom earlier that day. How could she be asked to face any intellectual task as mighty as agreeing to this suggested menu? She could not imagine finding the initiative to go to bed that night, left alone get up next day. Gasping out an excuse, she hurried from the room.

She had to find Tom. He must know she would pay any price, if only he would say something to mend her despair.

He could not be found. His bedroom and study looked as if they had been looted. Shirts, stocks, waistcoats, top-hats, gloves, trousers, documents, hairbrushes, wooden boot-jacks and a coat wrenched inside out had been flung everywhere as if by a retreating flood. The desk drawers were hanging open, their contents stirred all about. One of them had been emptied on to the desktop and thrown on the floor. In a household run by fourteen noiseless, invisible servants such mess could not be more amazing than if a chimney-stack had crashed through all five floors.

A valise stood open on the bed, either half emptied or half packed up again. Had Tom been planning to travel somewhere? If so, he must have left without even pausing to ring for his manservant.

On the stairs she met Edward. He looked more serious than usual. 'What have you done, mother?'

'I? What – how do you mean?' exclaimed Sophy. The violent haste in which Tom had left filled her with misgiving.

'I asked Tom if you knew where he was going, looking like that. He said, of course not.'

'Like what? Tell me quickly – what's happened now?'

Edward reddened and gave an energetic shrug. If he was often careless about what he said, he was also over-ready to be embarrassed. 'Oh, mother – you know.

253

Like he did this morning.' He was still sorry for having teased his brother about Georgiana.

'But where is he?'

'Why, gone. I expect he's halfway into Surrey by now?'

'To Richmond?' Sophy looked astonished. After everything he had told her?

'He said Richmond first. *I* don't know why. Then, "Paris if necessary, and beyond" were his actual words. Mother, do you think the poor devil's rational?'

Sophy gave him a sharp look.

Mumbling, he added, 'He asked me to hand you this,' and disappeared.

It was Tom's last, cruel letter to Georgiana. Sophy felt a pinprick of relief at knowing it had not been sent. She skimmed it through, shuddering with surprise at its rashness and its cynical hate. The impulsive anger in Georgiana's letter had been a holy blessing by comparison.

And she herself had had a hand in all this.

Scrawled at the bottom was a message for herself. 'Mother, as you can see, I do not think this fit to send. Given what I know now, there are more things than this that must be said. And I cannot bear that they should not be said face to face. Till God knows when, adieu.'

With the letter in her hand, Sophy sank down against the wall of the grand staircase. She looked as cowed as if she were a street child caught trespassing there. Could it be that they were to be ruined after all?

She stayed where she was for several minutes, trying to think, once more frantic with thwarted energy. *Something* must be done – if only so that, whatever befell them all, it should not be her fault. One thing gave her the courage to face their possible bankruptcy: Tom's unforgiveness. What else mattered, if he hated her? And if he succeeded in forcing whatever insane confrontation he now had in mind, mightn't he then resent her even more?

Something bold must be done. It would not be enough to pursue her son and cling to him, whimpering and pleading. Whatever he was planning, Sophy herself must outdo it. It was too late to think of her husband as well.

At last, like a lock turning quietly, an idea took its place in her mind. Quickly all sorts of other possibilities tumbled after it.

No one else would ever forgive her. But in Tom's eyes she would stand redeemed. Now – finally – she knew what she had to do.

CHAPTER FIFTEEN

At the foot of the pass the carriage had to be left behind. From here the road over the mountains was only open to mules. It led up a barren hillside, far above the blasted upper limit of the forest, winding among fallen blocks of stone the size of a house. Within half a mile the five travellers felt their faces grow tight from the sharp August sun, while the cold, so high up, made their breath visible.

The real world, as one thought of it, looking down, grew blurred by distance. Deep below on the valley floor the sparse villages could be seen each as a speck of sunlight flashing from a bulbous spire where a church stood by a bright pebbly stream. Down there it was still hot, the cattle standing wherever they could find shade, in flat meadows fringed with marsh marigolds and blue cranesbill. Up here, streaks of snow lay to the north of every large boulder. It hurt one's chest to breathe.

The snowy peaks up at the rim of sight seemed only a stroll away through the crisp air. Yet however high the travellers toiled up the stony road, twisting through every point of the compass, the ring of summits never came any closer. Above the pass a golden eagle wheeled, so lazily that if you stared at it, the great bird looked motionless with the earth swinging beneath like a pendulum. The travellers felt their ears ache and their fingers sting from the cold.

From the first mile, Sophy had found herself falling asleep in the saddle, whether for seconds at a time or whole minutes, she didn't know. Even as they'd set out up the mountain after the last meal of the day, she'd been almost too tired to answer to her own name. At dusk, when the valley bottom had been dark for an hour and the peaks had gone from pink to icy blue, they stopped to pass the night, bedded on straw in a stone shelter near the Italian border. Sophy, wrapped in a travelling cloak purchased on the road, had fancied herself too exhausted for sleep, until she lay down. Around an empty hearth, she and the two servants she'd brought from London fell instantly unconscious.

Minutes later, so it seemed, they were awoken. It was almost dawn, and time to set out by lantern light beneath a heaven full of fading constellations. They lingered only long enough to breakfast, while the animals were watered, on brandy, goats' milk cheese and stale black bread. Then on again, where the main trackway into Italy passed chasms in which bottomless waterfalls stood suspended. At first the pale water was the only thing that could be seen in the darkness. The sound of each stream grew less as they climbed higher, and the lanterns carried on foot by their guides became faint. The shape of the sky, at times narrow above them, was now dimly visible.

At dawn they were walking across several acres of level ground littered with broken stone. There was no more water to be heard. Though the horizon was still only a short way ahead, the road began to go gently downhill. They had crossed over.

Sophy had had no intention of going in pursuit of Tom. If he were ahead of her now, her journey would be in vain. Meanwhile let him blunder off to Richmond, rehearsing words of hate for Georgiana and blind to the fact that he still loved her. The chances were that he would find only an empty house, and a rampart of silence put up against him by Charity's servants. Sophy herself had lost no time in posting direct to Dover. The weather in the Channel was turning foul, but she had been in time to embark on the last packet boat for France before the harbour was closed. Off Calais, high seas had kept their vessel bucketing at anchor outside the harbour bar for a full two changes of tide.

Would Georgiana really have been taken back to Paris, so soon after she had been seen to leave the French capital? Sophy had guessed not. In freak late-summer weather, amid black rains and slashing gales, she had ordered their driver to take the eastward road, through Rheims and the wide chalklands of Champagne. As early as the ancient Flemish town of Cambrai her gamble had been rewarded. Among the wealthy English taking the highway south at this time of year there was, the innkeeper had said, a party just as madame had described. Two carriages, six servants, two outriders. In the principal carriage, *une mademoiselle* – here the man had looked guarded, as people did when mentioning Euphemia politely. And in command, a beautiful milady with dark hair and pale face, accompanied by her ravishing younger sister. Alas, no, madame, he did not know their names.

It had been enough. Given some degree of likeness between Georgiana and her mother, and the still-ripening beauty of the peerless Charity, any bystander might mistake the relationship between the two women.

At Rheims itself Sophy had been told that the people she described were maybe fifteen hours ahead. By the fourth day of her journey, among the muddy oak forests and ruined vineyards of Burgundy, she had become convinced that at any change of horses she might find herself drawn up in the inn yard alongside

258

Charity's carriage. But by the Swiss border she had been forced to admit she had lost them. Charity, in her interview with Sophy and Fraser, had made no secret of her ultimate destination. But to get there she could have crossed the Alps by any one of several roads.

On the other hand, did it matter whether or not Sophy laboured over this huge barrier by the swiftest route? For Tom's sake she was desperate to arrive before he did. But, given her purpose in making this journey, she would have been happy to take the rest of her life to meet Georgiana and her mother. Sophy had only set out, after all, so that she could ruin herself.

Sunrise found them going down into a shallow bowl of brilliance, a mile above sea level. Below them lay an infinity of cloud – not a sea of white fog but a hazy brownish thickening of the atmosphere. The sky was soon blue enough to hurt. They rounded a bluff the size of a cathedral tower and went down among the first scrubby pines of a quiet forest, where few birds sang and mist distorted the sounds of rushing water.

By eight in the morning they had come down to the first clearings, where the pines began to give way to steep hillsides of sweet chestnuts. It was hot as well as still, with clouds of flies.

As they passed from a tiny shelf of field dotted with haycocks into more steep dim forest, Sophy felt the ground move. The next moment, she thought she had imagined it. A narrow tongue of wind, ruffling its way up the hillside, must have panicked the animals and made them shy about. The wood became very still again.

The leading animal stopped and brayed, planting both feet before him despite the curses of the guide. Another gust of wind could be heard coming up the mountainside, this time along a wide front of rising sound. The tree tops above them reeled, and the mules shied again, their hindquarters slewing on the steep trail. A tall chestnut sighed, leaned, and then slowly fell across the highway, not ten yards ahead. Its heavy foliage billowed upward as it thudded to the ground.

But there had been no wind. With a rush of surprise Sophy realized that the trees had not all bent one way, as they would in a breeze. They had leaned in every direction, like fur on a stretching cat. The earth *had* twitched beneath them.

One of the guides, grinning with surprise, turned round to her in the saddle and pointed at something. In a gully beside the highway a stream had changed colour, clouded with loosened earth.

'Might the road be closed, ahead?' Sophy called, in her correct drawing-room French.

The man made a gesture, as if to say, who can tell? They dismounted and led the mules, stooping beneath low branches and sliding about on a forest floor suddenly lit by shafts of new sun wherever a tree had lost its grip in the sodden ground. In this way, leaving the road from time to time, they lost an extra couple of hours.

It was nearly noon before they came down to the first houses, a hamlet of wooden chalets as tight-packed as any city street. Barefoot children played outside dark interiors where every corner smelt of the cattle stabled below. A warm meadow flowering with pink sainfoin and tall martagon lilies sloped down to a stream so noisy, it seemed impossible the people in the houses ever heard each other speak. Riding within ten yards of the foaming water, the travellers felt their skin pucker from the cold, then start to sweat again as they passed on. A thousand feet below, the livid green of the vineyards began, planted on stone-walled terraces that made the mountainside look like a great shaggy ziggurat. Half an hour beyond that, they came to the first village that was no longer alpine but part of Italy proper. Shallow red-tiled roofs were gathered around a tall square belfry. An empty piazza was shaded by pollard plane trees.

From yet another thousand feet down, at last the lake could be seen where Sophy's destination lay. A hot thin haze made the snowy peaks above it look insubstantial. The lake itself seemed to wind away down a valley that opened on to nothingness rather than the cities of the Italian plain. With no horizon visible, it just faded at its farthest limit into sky. On its shores, cypress-clad promontaries were edged by their own reflections. They appeared to overhang air rather than water. In the middle distance was the island on which stood the two-hundred-year-old villa owned by Charity. It floated like a wondrous planet made all of soft shadows, the colours of jade, malachite and onyx, amid an azure vacancy.

Late that afternoon, their animals stepping slowly through a heat you could see, Sophy and her party came off the packed dirt of the highway from the north, on to the cobbles of a village square by the lake. Her manservant, her maid and the two guides were put up at a vine-covered inn smelling of fish from the neighbouring quay. A boatman was sought — with difficulty, since most of the village was busy clearing away a derelict stone barn that had collapsed in the tremor, frightening somebody's goat and sending hundreds of lizards darting for shelter elsewhere. At length a man was found and a price agreed. Sophy, squinting behind her veil at the brilliance of the hot lakeside and the icy peaks behind, embarked for the perfumed gardens of the Isola Nuova, and battle.

While Sophy, her petticoats stiff with the dirt of three countries, was being rowed to the island, others were also making preparations.

261

Tom had hired a guide to take him across the Alps by a more easterly route. Since daybreak they had ridden down from winter, through late spring to high summer and the road to the head of the lake. In at least one place their way too was blocked by the tremor, where the retaining wall of a hillside vineyard had collapsed, releasing a torrent of rocks and wet earth.

On the Isola Nuova, disembodied voices echoed among the gardens. There, beneath orange trees and vines a small private dinner was to be given. Lanterns were being strung from the branches, and the fragrance of spit-roasted meat had been added to the scents of citrus, myrtle and late roses. The company was mostly English, with the token well-born Italian usually present at such occasions. As the guests lingered in the lengthening shadows of pleached lime walks, or strolled between shiny hedges of camellia fifteen feet high, the talk was mostly of other English in the area. From just over the nearest haze-covered hillside, at Cernobbio, scandal still reverberated around the names of the King's late wife Caroline, with her short skirts and rumoured foreign lovers, and of young Shelley, who had so embarrassed his critics by getting tragically killed and then by proving a genius. Another person deep in trouble seemed to be Harold Fitzpayne, who was shortly expected to take a house nearby, having travelled to London with his mother at the urgent request of Lady Fitzpayne's steward. The rumour was that his debts might shortly lead Lady Fitzpayne to sell the family's neglected place in Wiltshire. In some quarters it was whispered that Charity herself might be a potential buyer.

In the Villa Nuova itself, in a bedchamber bare of almost everything except a marble floor and splendid trompe l'oeil frescoes, Georgiana sat. Above her, a miracle of perspective showed a sunburst behind naked goddesses and careless cupids. Her maid was moving about with care, conscious of the floor giving off a faint crunching sound beneath her feet. After the earth had shuddered that morning, a fine dust had drifted down and coated every surface.

Georgiana, passive before her mirror, was trying to put the best face on her surrender. Stoical and tense, she had had her maid put her into her heaviest and most voluminous gown, in maroon silk trimmed with silver. The mirror reflected its colour dimly compared to the hues of the sky, which could be seen, through an open window, burning itself out from blue to rose and turquoise. Georgiana's hair was being strained back into an elaborate upright loop, to be dressed with white camellias. Though this style was *de rigueur* that year, not many women could wear it well. Several details of her appearance made her an unlikely latter-day princess – even an Americanised one – shut away in virtual captivity. The season's modes meant carrying no end of feminine clutter. There was a parasol – useless with that summer's hats, two feet across and trimmed with ostrich feathers – a fan, a reticule, a shawl, and for evening a nosegay of fresh flowers.

But just as Georgiana's strong, delicate profile made a triumph of wearing her hair in an Apollo knot, so her luminescent beauty could dignify almost any fashion. The light of early evening gleamed on her bare shoulders and stately neck, which rose above extravagant *gigot* sleeves a yard across. It fell from a pure sky turning silver at the western horizon. It glimmered from distant snowfields, from palace gardens along the far shore whose shadows changed colour every minute, and from a lake as smooth as molten gold.

Georgiana's thoughts were not on her surroundings, however fabled. She was dwelling on a scene of English

263

elms and grey mizzly horizons, beyond the house in Richmond where she and Tom did –

She was half glad of what had happened there. From now on, it would seem to take for ever, getting dressed for occasions like this. Oh, and how she hated that nightingale, out there in the big cedar. She found its song not yearning, but fierce and ravening. Since that moment in the house by the Thames-side meadows, terror and shame were the only things she'd been allowed to feel. And without her present mood of panic-stricken atonement, how else was she to go on making herself do as she was told?

Twenty miles to the east, below a range of hills so remote that the local dialect was still more Latin than Italian, the earth, having merely flinched, now prepared to shrug.

Sophy stepped ashore on the Isola Nuova, the New Island.

Once indeed, it had been new. At the turn of the seventeenth century it had been nothing but a few low rocks. There had been no cascading fountains, no grottoes with rustic stonework and dripping maiden-hair ferns, no secret gardens of potted lemon trees behind tall hedges of yew, no glimpses of shining water from arbours of clipped bay, no little outdoor rooms or spacious terraces planted with jasmine, pomegranates, magnolias or orange trees, no cool *bosco* full of the sound of invisible streams.

Driving along the shore one day in 1620, a Milanese nobleman had caught sight of the group of dry rocks and immediately guessed their possibilities. He himself had died before there was much more to the island than hundreds of tons of new soil, and the beginnings of a water-mill to work the fountains. But his son, then his grandson, had carried on the work. After half a century of effort, involving thousands of men and unimaginable expense, the island was as the old count had pictured it: a place of mystery, riding the waters like a barge of state, with tiers of terraces for decks, and trees for sails.

The main landing place was at the island's prow. A fan-shaped stone stair, lapped by the water, was flanked by two pavilions. Each was an eight-sided room within which flower-entwined openings alternated with mirrored walls.

As Sophy climbed the steps a pride of white peacocks hurried out of her way, trailing their stiff plumage with dignity. From inside the two airy pavilions the draperies of her soiled, elegant travelling dress were dimly mirrored, to and fro, to infinity.

Up at the head of a balustraded staircase rising in a double zig-zag, another summer house stood, above a fountain where Neptune drove a team of wild horses. With a roofline of pinnacles and prancing stone unicorns, it looked as whimsical as the pavilions by the shore. In fact it was meant for use, as a guest house. From within, its arcaded balcony framed the dreamlike silhouette of a nearby mountain, as though the gardens embraced the whole valley.

To one side, a cool arcade roofed with wisteria led to the main house. The outside of the Villa Nuova, stuccoed and drab, seemed too small to contain the sumptuous rooms inside. From the lofty entrance hall, Sophy glimpsed pillared doorways giving on to shuttered rooms with high cornices. The deep subtle colours of frescoes and marble pilasters could only be guessed at in the dimness.

A couple of rooms away a servant woman could be seen sweeping up around a statue toppled from its niche by the tremor. Under its newly broken nose a crack showed in the paving of the floor.

But where was everyone else? Sophy had found that

most boats in the neighbourhood had been taken, because of the entertainment being given there that evening. And out in the gardens, from several parts of the island, voices could be heard. But the villa itself held only the echo of her own footsteps.

The servant looked up and curtseyed. Conscious of her stilted, opera-goer's Italian, Sophy asked to see the mistress of the house.

'That can be contrived. If it's absolutely necessary.'

The hurried steps behind her had been those of Euphemia, coming indoors to chivvy Georgiana into joining their guests.

It had been some years since Sophy had last seen Kate's possessive sister-in-law. But she and Euphemia had no difficulty in recognizing each other. Euphemia was still agelessly plain, and Sophy's fine-boned fairness was in many ways more striking at thirty-nine than it had been in girlhood.

Despite their kinship, there was clearly no point in greeting Euphemia with a show of pleasure. From the set of her elbows and mouth, one might have thought the mountain pass at the head of the valley had yielded a yowling host of Goths rather than one travel-racked English gentlewoman.

Sophy said, 'I fear it is necessary, Miss Lee. If you might be so kind.'

'The kindness, Mrs Fraser, would not be on my part. In the circumstances, an interview from Mrs Michaelmas should be seen as a very great favour indeed.'

Euphemia led the way up a curving flight of the main staircase. With calculated rudeness she showed Sophy, not into the privacy of a room, but up to a landing with nowhere to sit.

'I take it yours is the only name I should give?'

It took Sophy, weary to the marrow of her bones, a moment to understand. Euphemia, it seemed, was

266

positively eager to accuse her of being leagued with Tom in some shameful deception.

Visibly paling with rage, Sophy turned and pretended to look out of the window. At that moment, ignoring Euphemia was the politest thing she could bring herself to do.

There was a rustle of petticoats behind her, and an exclamation, half-sigh, half-snarl, of impatience. *'Yes!'* said Euphemia.

Sophy turned and gave her a steady look. Her tired face was still blanched with anger. 'I beg your pardon?'

'Shall I give only *your* name?' Euphemia spoke carefully, as if to an exasperating child.

Meeting Euphemia's scowl with one of her own, Sophy exclaimed, 'I wouldn't care to say!'

It was what Euphemia had yearned to hear. She gave Sophy another foul look, meaning that *she* wasn't deceived by her, and scurried away, alight with purpose.

On her way to where Charity was greeting their guests in the garden, she went to see if Georgiana was still in her room. Seeing Euphemia open the door without knocking, the girl looked round from her mirror with mingled surprise and resentment.

Euphemia was not prepared to take any nonsense from her, either. In the face of this impudent new menace from the fortune-hunting Fraser household, she knew what she had to do. Without a word, she shut the door again on Georgiana. And locked it.

Two minutes later, as Euphemia hastened across the courtyard below, Sophy felt, rather than heard, something almost like thunder. A few seconds later, like a badly fastened rug, the floor was pulled from beneath her feet.

* * *

There should have been more signs, Tom thought. The sky should have been the colour of a bruise, and the waters of the lake should have reared up.

What had happened as he'd stood on the warmed stones of the lakeside village square, was that the evening, in every hue of rose and amethyst, had been as peaceful as a sigh of bliss. He had been looking across to the island. Nothing had suggested what came next.

The church bells began to ring. Or rather, they started jangling, while the tower suddenly trembled as if shaken in the fist of an invisible madman. The lake, which had been clear as the sky above, was blurred. Tom was no longer out of doors in the real world, but looking into a puddle in the hand of a palsied giant. Common sense told him what was happening. But like people in doorways all around, he stared idiotically about him, as if the explanation were somewhere just over his shoulder.

The noise grew. It consumed the senses as absolutely as a drug pumping into the blood. As the earth's roar swelled nearer, Tom felt his internal organs register the din, sooner than his ears. The soles of his feet were jarred, and his hands and scalp stung from the vibrations. He found himself slipping and slithering on the dusty ground. Looking up, on his hands and knees, he saw that while the sky was bright as new silver, the lake was furred over, as though beneath heavy rain. The boom of the rending earth rolled closer, then forked and multiplied. The mountains nearby had caught the sound and shrugged it this way and that. It rebounded up two scores of alpine valleys that climbed with no seeming end.

After the last echoes had died, there was silence; not a sparrow chirped. Then human noises began. A woman was crying out in despair, and a couple of boys, with unsteady voices, whooped with excitement. The

268

square was littered with rubble; Tom, thrilled and curious at what had just happened, had failed to notice that a stone coping twice his own weight had gouged a trench in the cobbles a yard away from his elbow. A distant mountainside smoked like a volcano where an avalanche had been shaken down on to flowering pastures. On the next lakeside promontary a hill had gone from bright green to dun; thirty acres of vineyard had fallen away.

Tom looked towards the island.

His racketing heart changed to a harsher beat.

Before the waters had moved, they had reflected a profile of rooftops and stately trees. Not so, however, once they cleared again. The massed cedars and chestnut trees had seemed to have been deeply gashed. Part of the villa's roof seemed to be no longer there. Notwithstanding the commotion in the village, from across the quarter-mile of water separating Tom from the island, other cries could be heard.

He felt no doubt or hesitation. Wrenching off his boots and hurling his coat aside, he ran into the water and struck out, strongly at first, for the island.

The cold was so great that after a few moments it was scarcely different from being scalded. As he cleaved through the water, Tom groaned aloud from shock. He had not stopped to think that the lake would be fed with meltwater, from glaciers untouched even by high summer. The ache in his ears seemed to fill his whole head. He could soon feel almost nothing beyond his elbows and knees. At one point his mouth and nose filled with dirt; he was swimming through a cloud of mud brought down in a stream whose course had just shifted.

Surely the river of death itself could not be harder to cross. Dozens of carp floated on the surface of the lake, their corpses belly-up. A sudden clapping noise made Tom yelp with astonishment, as the air above his head filled with broad wings. A black kite, falling like a rock from a hundred feet up, had snatched one of the carp. Others hovered, then dived, feasting on the dead fishes in mid-air as they flapped away.

The water seemed to grow colder. Soon it hurt Tom to breathe; he was gasping as if in a vacuum. He knew he must not pause, to tread water while he got his breath. To hesitate, risking cramp, was to sink at once, as certainly as if he'd been seized by some monstrous creature.

Had he failed, after all? Every fluid in his body seemed to have turned sluggish from the cold. Tom was no longer certain why he had made the journey here. Was it merely so that he could add fuel to his quarrel with Georgiana? The suspicion that he still loved her had speeded him on his way all the more recklessly. If his deadening limbs were about to falter, had he no tears for his own fate? It was not the fear of dying that made him want to weep, but frustration. There was no folly in what he had just undertaken – or none that he could see. Cost what it might, he had had to do this. Oh, but –

The island drew no closer.

Sophy was to have scant memory of what happened inside the Villa Nuova after an unseen force had cast her on to the floor. She found herself immediately blinded; the house had become a shuddering churn, in which billows of dust collided. Particles of alabaster, gilding, watercoloured plaster and soot from a fractured chimney swirled in a brown fog. Animal fear, not good sense, got her to her feet and hurtled her against the wall leading to the head of the staircase. Sophy fell rather than ran down most of the stairs, where a rivulet flowed, making the marble treads as slick as ice. The island's engineering achievements included not only its fountains and grand cascade, but a large cistern storing piped water on the roof of the villa itself. At least one broken conduit was spraying a mist of water through the ceiling of the hall.

The entrance doorway was just visible, as a rectangle through which fell a shaft of dulled light. Sophy's panic was such that, as she bolted through it, like a rabbit fleeing the last stand of corn in a harvest field, it was only from the heat of the evening that she realized that she was out of doors.

Racked by breaths like sobs, at length she straightened up and looked around. On this side of the villa the façade now had a forked crack. Several shutters hung awry from windows that smoked plumes of dust like openings to a furnace. From one part of the garden a confusion of voices could be heard. Sophy, leaking filth from every fold of her dress, made her way towards it.

In readiness for the evening's hospitality, Charity's guests and household servants had been assembling in a part of the grounds known as the 'green theatre'. It was an outdoor dining room, surrounded by a high wall of topiary with narrow openings on to the lake. Down most of its length ran a stone table supported by carved griffins. Beyond the head of the table, at the base of a broad flight of steps, the waters of a fountain played over the bodies of grim river gods and enigmatic satyrs. The steps rose to the theatre itself, a fantastical sculpted backdrop of pediments, balustrades, pinnacles, swags of flowers and exotic fruits, naked pagan figures, carved seashells, and honeycombed obelisks surmounted with stone plumes. The topmost statue, calm and uncaring, was that of the ancient Roman goddess of love. Against the warm evening sky Venus stood with one arm raised, either in greeting or as a warning, to claim the island for her own.

The goddess looked down on Charity, who wore

271

rose-coloured satin with balloon sleeves set low to show off her matchless bare shoulders. Under the serene gaze of the garden's statues, most of the guests and household servants were as agitated as barnyard fowls in a downpour.

Sophy had never seen Charity herself look flustered before. Much less as if she were on the verge of hysteria.

'Where?' she was saying. She had just risen to her feet, and was turning her face towards the rooftop of the house as if pleading with the sky. Close at hand stood Euphemia, looking hunted.

'Show me,' Charity exclaimed, thrusting past Euphemia. 'Or if you're wrong – ' Looks of bewilderment and dread surrounded her. She started to run, as fast as her frivolous shoes and heavy skirts would allow.

'What have you seen?' she called out, running towards where Sophy stood. Sophy did not realize immediately that Charity meant her.

'Where is she – what have you seen?' she cried out, seizing Sophy by the arm. Charity showed no sign of surprise at seeing Sophy there.

Sophy, looking as if she'd nearly been buried alive, could only stare aghast at the fear in Charity's face. Within her cloud of perfumed magnificence, Charity suddenly looked as shrivelled as the meanest beggar-woman on earth. Not saying another word, she stumbled wildly out of sight.

In Italian, Sophy heard someone say something about a young person in trouble. Irrationally, her first thought was of Tom; it was only then that she realized Georgiana was not to be seen. Running in the direction Charity had taken, she came upon another flight of steps at the water's edge. And stopped at what she saw.

Charity came towards her with a look in her eyes Sophy did not immediately understand. She took

Sophy in a tight embrace, turning her head to watch a group of people bending over something on the steps. There was a boat nearby.

In a firm voice Charity said, 'You must not think – '

'Ooh!' groaned Sophy, starting back in terror. A young man had been lifted out of the boat. His fair hair was darkened by the water that streamed from it; his unconscious face was almost transparently pale. From the way his limbs dangled along the ground as a couple of boatmen carried him ashore, there was no reason to believe he was still breathing.

Charity said fiercely, 'You are not to think the worst. I will not have you do that.' From within her arms Sophy merely clawed at the air, gaping soundlessly as if it were she who was drowning.

One of the boatmen rolled Tom over on to his face. There was a smacking sound as Tom's arm hit the pavement. A crowd of onlookers grew in silence as the man, without taking off his shoes, stood on Tom's back. He jumped, and water shot from Tom's mouth and nostrils. Twice more he jumped, while everyone expected to hear the crack of fractured ribs. Then the man stood aside, and at a word to his companions, three of them lifted Tom, feet uppermost. Tom's arms fell open; his legs, jack-knifed at the knees, dangled over the shoulders of one of his rescuers. Water went on hosing out of him.

No one wanted to look at Sophy. Supported by Charity, she was near to fainting. Her eyes were rolled up in their sockets and her mouth hung slack. Then Charity's embrace suddenly grew tighter. There was a movement through all the bystanders like a subterranean wind. One of the men who'd been handling Tom with such expert haste made some matter-of-fact comment, and another responded with a chuckle.

They lowered Tom to the ground and stood back. Sophy, nearly blind with dread, could still hear grunts

273

of urgent endeavour, and splashing noises on the wet pavement – but now they came from Tom alone. Lying full length and limp as a stale herring, he retched and retched, until the last dribble of meltwater had run from the corner of his mouth. All about him, people started talking elatedly. Only Charity, before she disappeared, was still haggard and intense.

Even now, however, no one cared to look at Sophy. In this country, as a mother whose son had perished, she would have been sacrosanct. She got down on her hands and knees to touch him, dumb with thankfulness.

After a minute or so he was able to stand, doubled up like an athlete who'd just lost a punishing race. Recovering further, he stared in confusion at Sophy and her dishevelled appearance.

'Oh, Tom!' She was almost inaudible through her tears. 'I wish you weren't such a damned fool. Take my arm, and let's find somewhere you can sit down.'

'Mother, for God's sake!' he said, trying to pull free. And fainted, to guffaws of merriment from the men who'd saved his life.

Tom was helped up to the villa, with Sophy hurrying anxiously at his side. Most of the garden was still a perfect scene of tranquil sky and fragrant shadows. A fallen chestnut had crushed a waterside grotto with pebble mosaics on wall and ceiling, sending loose stones rolling all about, and the little wood behind the grand cascade was turning marshy where a water pipe had fractured. The only serious damage was to the villa, where part of one wing had fallen in.

Sophy followed Tom up through the muddy indoor river overflowing the stairs. From the far end of the first-floor landing came a steady sound like the clunk of dropping masonry. A woman's voice was giving off

274

a series of shuddering yells; whether out of fear, anguish, or desperate effort, it was hard to say.

At the west end of the landing a ceiling painted as a sky full of rare and brilliant birds – pheasants, hoopoes, parakeets – had been broken into by real daylight, where the roof now ended in a mass of snapped timbers and ragged plaster. It let down a dust-filled shaft of light in which several men, reduced to silhouettes, were heaving broken masonry from one to another, to throw it down at randon a few yards from where Georgiana's door had been. None of them, guests or servants, had been dressed for this work; those who had not been due to dine were wearing uniforms thick with gold frogging.

Charity was standing at a window some yards away, staring at nothing. She was very pale, but no longer looked wild with fright. Watching her at a respectful distance was Hortense, her maid. Sophy cast the Frenchwoman a look of enquiry. Glancing first in Charity's direction, Hortense quickly indicated the scene of the rescue and shook her head in hasty reassurance.

'Mademoiselle is not injured, I think,' she murmured. 'But her maid has told us,' pointing out a tear-streaked young woman standing nearby, 'that the door had been locked against her.'

Georgiana's hysterical cries still rang out. Seeing Sophy's questioning look of dismay, Hortense added, 'But Mademoiselle has been very frightened, of course.' She added, without making it clear whom she meant, 'She is enraged, is she not?'

Sophy went towards Charity, who was looking hard by turns up at the sky, blooming with sunset, and down at her clasped hands. She wanted to give Charity her sympathy, even as Charity had just tried to comfort her. But the other woman, without looking round, checked Sophy abruptly. Sophy realized why. In

275

Charity, fear had turned to rage, at the danger to Georgiana. She had the self-control not to yell out loud. But she was nonetheless too angry to speak.

With a thrill of despair and admiration, Sophy saw that Charity also had the resolve, even now, to conceal any hint of maternal feeling. If the close-mouthed Hortense had guessed her secret, no one else could have.

Certainly Charity was as far as ever from being suspected by Euphemia, who was twitching about on the perimeter of the rescue with the look of a servant about to suffer ignominious dismissal. Her craven appearance was ill-matched with her formal status as principal hostess at the evening's planned entertainment. She wore an elaborate beret, a full two feet across and trimmed with bows. Her orange silk gown impeded everyone about her.

Instead of sharing the general relief, Euphemia looked even more hunted as Georgiana was at last gingerly helped over the hillock of debris that had trapped her behind the shelter of an opened wardrobe door. Other than Georgiana's hysterical gasps, the only sound was the continuous splashing of water from the broken cistern above her room. The girl herself was soaked, her hair plastered about her face and neck in streaks. Her sodden gown was almost heavy enough to pull her to her knees.

She seemed not to notice that Tom was among the men who'd struggled to free her. She went straight up to Euphemia, raised her fist until it was level with her shoulder, and smacked it hard into her chaperone's shocked face. Euphemia's nose instantly ran with blood, all over a hundred and fifty guineas' worth of lurid ruching, and Georgiana yelled with surprise at the hurt of the impact to her own knuckles.

Poor Tom, stepping forward with a crowd of emotions in his face, was not sure if he was seizing

276

Georgiana in his arms to comfort her or to hold her back. Anger fought within her, against shame and astonishment at her act of violence. She put her face in her hands. Overcome at the collision of her feelings, and at the knowledge that he was there, she put her head against his shoulder and sobbed with bottomless relief.

Through all this, Charity looked away, acknowledging nothing.

Mountains might budge, and forests turn their roots upward, in the time it takes a small cloud to cross the sun. But for everyone who survives such things untouched, there remains the everyday business of staying fed, watered and clothed.

Not that dinner had been meant as something homely, even with the dour Miss Lee for a hostess. Around the stone banqueting table and the steps of the sculptured theatre, hundreds of coloured lanterns competed with a many-hued twilight. They shone on services of crystal, silver and French porcelain worth the value of a well-appointed mansion. Many guests were from the expatriate circle who had so admired the lovely Miss Bingham upon her recent social debut in Paris. There was the wife of a London financier, whose husband's work had left her semi-widowed, and who travelled for something to do. Two immensely wealthy spinsters in their thirties, preferring to share a bed with each other rather than any man, were spending their millions abroad for privacy's sake. A famous poet was there with his mistress, an Italian lady so stately and so impressively titled that even behind their backs all mention of scandal was avoided. Young Alexander Anstye was also among the guests, combining pleasure with a judicious spot of heiress-hunting.

277

Already one or two people had rightly suspected him of having half an eye on Georgiana.

A new hour was set for dinner. Amid luxurious improvisation, the guests took their seats as sunset was being outfaced from the east by the glory of a full moonrise. A few fainthearts had sent their servants – where a boatman was to be found who had not absconded back to his village – to check on the state of their own property. But most saw the Act of God just passed as lending a welcome edge of excitement to an evening that would otherwise have been only routinely splendid. Even before any of the servants had stepped forward to set dinner in progress, eyes were bright and voices were loud with abnormal good cheer.

Dressed in borrowed evening clothes, Sophy waited to be shown to her place, amid feelings of unease. Charity, with perfect politeness, had skilfully avoided Sophy's attempts to engage her alone in conversation. Meanwhile the rituals of society carried on around them, unbroken as the movements of the planets.

Seeing Tom there, Sophy went to seize him by the cuff. She hoped that with him, too, she might speak privately.

'Mother – '

The stiffness of his manner made her forget her well-rehearsed words. They might as well both have been back in South Audley Street, at the moment of his leaving.

He tried to speak gently, without success. 'Mother, you can't change my mind. I'm sorry. You've made this journey for nothing, you know.' He hesitated, embarrassed. 'And besides, how can I respect your views, now?'

'I know all about that. Tom – '

'Excuse me, mother.' He detached Sophy's hand from his arm with a self-possession that was worse to her than any violence, and hurried after the butler,

278

presumably to offer him a bribe so that he could sit by Georgiana.

They took their places at table. Georgiana hastened out from being dressed again by Hortense. She looked shaken but no longer melancholy. With every word and look, she blushed, like an actress pitched into a play without knowing her lines.

Then Euphemia was found to be missing. In others, lateness usually left her beside herself. But she had just spent several unpleasant minutes with Charity.

At last she reappeared, looking ready to grovel to the company at large while sneering at many of the people who made it up. In Euphemia's absence, Charity had taken her place at the head of the table, before the fountain by the theatre steps. A vain woman would have appeared self-conscious with such a backdrop. Charity made it look as if it had been waiting the last two hundred years just for her.

For Sophy, it was the courtesy shown her that made her oppressed. How could she act on her reason for being there, when every moment found her deeper in Charity's debt, as her guest. No doubt this was what her hostess had in mind. A stiff napkin was shaken loose with a clap like a pheasant flushed from cover, and placed in her lap. Champagne was poured for her. She watched it dancing in her glass as if it were an evil potion meant to send her sense of justice to sleep for ever.

Tom was missing too, to reappear only when everyone else was seated. He glanced at the servant holding his chair, as if to say, I see you, but all this has nothing to do with me.

To Sophy he gave a quick look of pure unforgiveness. Without a flicker of change in his expression, he made as if to speak down the length of the table to Charity.

Because he was on his feet, everyone was looking at him. Charity was forced to meet his eyes.

'Miss Michaelmas,' he said, pointedly ignoring her fictitious marriage, 'why will you not speak with me in private?'

Sophy started to her feet, flustering the servant whose job was to anticipate her. 'Mrs Michaelmas, you must know why I'm here – '

'No, mother!' exclaimed Tom. 'You will not hinder me!'

'Tom – no! I shall say what I have to – I shall! – Tom – '

'How can you, mother – how dare you – ?'

'How dare *you*! How can you put words into my mouth – ?'

Resolutely he ignored her. 'Miss Michaelmas – ' he began.

'Georgiana.' Charity's voice was low, but breathed authority. One or two people, who had valiantly ignored Sophy and Tom, looked up.

Transparently uneasy, Georgiana gave a questioning look. 'Mrs Michaelmas?' Despite the girl's bewilderment, Sophy noticed, she had the same quick, firm voice as Charity.

'Your aunt has come to see you. I am so sorry that circumstances have prevented me from saying so until now.'

Sophy sat down as if pushed. Her face was all astonishment.

Georgiana, still uncertain, flushed nonetheless with delight. 'My Aunt Kate?'

'No – another blood relation of yours.' If Charity reckoned herself defeated at last, no one could have guessed it. Placidly she signalled to the butler to have the first course served. A dutiful murmur of conversation started up. Tom, still staring at Charity, felt obliged to sit down.

Georgiana said, 'I'm blood relation of Aunt Kate?'

280

She glanced in Tom's direction, her surprise tinged with pleasure. 'But why, madam – how?'

Charity summoned up all her whore's hardihood. Perhaps there were yet some secrets she might keep. 'Mrs Lee is related to you through your father.' Her tone hinted that in public at least, the subject might best end there.

'But how wonderful!' Georgiana threw another delighted look at Tom. He went on glowering at Charity, though no longer sure of his indignation. 'Then what relation was he, exactly, to my Aunt Kate?'

There was a tremor in her voice, as well as gladness. Georgiana was not by nature suspicious, but she was perceptive. What it was she suspected now, she had no idea. But somehow she doubted her godmother's good faith. Several people, noticing her tone, looked up at her.

Charity hesitated, even while looking calm as a Madonna. Sophy felt a twinge of sympathy. Around the table an atmosphere of expectation spread. A wren in a nearby fig tree ticked out a warning call.

Tom shared none of his mother's scruples. Setting his face towards Charity, he took Georgiana hard by the hand and said to her, rather loudly, 'Not was. He is. My mother's brother, Uncle George – ' He paused, reddening at having used such a childish description. 'I mean, my maternal uncle, Vice-Admiral Byford.'

There was a barely audible stir around the table. Some people were surprised; others let themselves enjoy a moment of sentimentality. It was one thing to be offended by talk of loose women and their shame, meaning children. But in the freedom of a setting combining Italy, natural disaster and good living, it was – one had to confess – piquant to hear tell of the youthful excesses, long ago and somewhere else, of a respectable English gentleman.

Sophy looked anxiously at Georgiana. The girl sat

very upright but with her head bent. She was determined to bear Tom's words with dignity, given that he'd blurted them so publicly.

Georgiana could not help leaning towards Euphemia, though, to mutter angrily, 'Why did you not tell me my "real" parents had also adopted me?'

Euphemia's recent interview with Charity had been so disagreeable that she was now a little afraid of saying the wrong thing. She looked at the girl, prickly with incomprehension.

Still gripping Georgiana's hand, Tom said in a low voice, 'No one could have told you that. There was no adoption.' He was trying desperately not to look embarrassed at what he had set in motion. Georgiana's furious, humiliated face was something he had not foreseen.

She lurched to her feet and wrenched herself free with a violence that made her totter. 'How could you!' She spoke in a whisper, yet it vibrated with a passion that could be heard in every nook in the garden. 'How could you dare! How dare you presume to defame my mother!' In Georgiana's imagination, the mother Charity had invented was still real – but now she was exposed as an adulteress.

Misunderstanding or not, Tom was too appalled to speak. Sophy interrupted hastily, before he or Georgiana could say more. 'But you must understand – there is no such woman. I mean – there are no such people as the parents whose memory you have been told to honour. Whether for better or worse, they were an invention.'

At the head of the table, Charity sat absolutely still. She was waiting now for events to unravel of their own accord. Her mild gaze rested on a cloud of moths around the nearest candles. Pale in the sharpening moonlight, she looked frail and exquisite. Some of the guests still laboured to hide their curiosity. Others stared at her openly. A few faint spirits, unable to go on looking urbanely interested rather than shocked, started to slip away.

Euphemia reached forward and seized Georgiana by the elbow. 'I think,' she said through set teeth, 'you would do well not to betray Mrs Michaelmas' generosity by pursuing this subject further.' She thought, in speaking thus, she had found a way to regain favour with Charity. 'If she has chosen to overlook the stain on your birth, at the least you might refrain from mentioning whatever degenerate woman bore you.'

Georgiana ignored her and looked steadily at Charity. The question, 'Who is my mother?' showed in her face so transparently, it needed no words.

Euphemia tried to insist on being heard. 'It is my duty, miss, to tell you so. Not everyone – '

'Your mother is here, Georgiana,' Sophy said quickly. 'I hope you will acknowledge her, with due respect – with love, if you can.'

The hope of being told the truth at last made all Georgiana's wariness melt away. 'Willingly!' She darted an enquiring look at Sophy, then all about her. Until all her uncertainties were banished, she scarcely dared to breathe.

Charity said nothing, framed by cavorting stone nymphs splashed with waters that the lamplight made translucent. Wearing diamonds and gracefulness in equal measure, she could not have looked less like the pinched repentant woman Georgiana evidently imagined. After all her years of plotting to prevent it, she had no fear of what Georgiana was about to hear. It was something else, now, that she dreaded.

Sophy went up to Charity, and bent to kiss her on the brow. Her feelings were not at all what she had expected. She had come ready for a fight, and felt only pity. Charity was cold to the touch, and unresponsive, as if in a trance.

To Georgiana, Sophy said, 'You must believe me when I say that you owe this lady all your love as a daughter. No mother could have tried harder to do her duty.'

A breeze mild as a sigh with a smile behind it stirred the trees beyond the garden. Georgiana's hopeful look vanished like a reflection in a ruffled pool. All about her, the rest of the guests were moving away in furtive dismay. She ignored them, motionless.

Her eyes rested on Charity, who suddenly looked stricken.

'No,' she told Sophy. 'You are wrong.' Georgiana's distress was obvious, but she was steeling herself to hide it.

She raised her arm like a duellist and pointed, to steady her resolve. 'This cannot be my mother. How can she be, when she – she, above everyone, has been so unready to show me any maternal feeling?'

Charity sat as if struck half dead by her daughter's unforgiveness. 'How indeed?' she murmured.

'Why should you not take me at my word?' Sophy pleaded. 'You are not an orphan. And you have never been unloved – not for an instant – by your mother.'

She was astonished at the urgency in her own voice. Sophy had come braced by anger and grief, ready to fight Charity as one might a swarm of demons. Now all she wanted was that Georgiana should not look at her mother with the same expression Tom had shown. 'Nothing your mother has done since you were born – not one thing – has been done for anything but love of you!'

'How can you say that!' Georgiana's scorn was unquenchable. Beside her, Tom looked amazed at the passions he'd aroused.

'How?' Georgiana insisted, turning to Charity. 'How have you ever shown love for me?'

Charity sighed – whether in hope or despair it was

284

hard to guess. 'If I told you everything I've done for your sake, then truly you would not forgive me.'

'It would make no difference anyway,' Georgiana told her. 'I've been told so many things at your behest. And every one of them was false! *How* have you ever made it clear that you loved me?'

'Oh, in so many ways! And each a thousand times over!'

'But how?'

Charity sighed, her voice quavering. 'Dear,' she said, 'by whoring.'

Georgiana, her lips parted, was too surprised to blush or look away. At length she muttered, 'That's – not evidence of loving anyone.'

'Dearest girl,' said Charity resignedly, 'my dear – if I may call you so, Georgiana – I have fucked more men than Messalina.' She stared at the two young people, daring them to protest. 'And every time for love!'

'That's not even proof,' Georgiana managed to say, 'that you love yourself.' She spoke faintly, intent on answering as one grown woman to another.

'No!' At the head of the laden, deserted table, Charity rose to her feet. Beyond the unsteady globe of lantern-light, twenty liveried servants stood like a double rank of heraldic statues, unresponsive. The English in Italy were notorious for trying to find or lose their true selves, and looking overexcited as a result. Encumbered by her satin shoes, she wrenched them off and flung them into the shadows. 'Every time, it was an act of love. For you!'

She had been ready from the beginning to give Georgiana every farthing she earned. Apart from sex, what else had she been free to offer anyone, in the course of her lonely life? Half pleading, half in anger, she exclaimed, 'Believe me!'

After so many falsehoods, Georgiana dared not. She shook her head, almost in tears.

Charity's voice became tremulous. 'I have done,' she murmured, 'such deeds for you!'

Georgiana stood her ground. She was thinking of her tryst with Tom, and Euphemia screeching at their nakedness. 'Oh, but if you really meant what you say – why, you would have treated us,' glancing at Tom, 'so differently!'

Charity too was remembering that scene and her own part in it. The thought of her hypocrisy was more wounding than any humiliation she had ever endured. 'You *will* believe me!' she insisted.

With her unshod feet and wild look, for the first time in years Charity was the ghost of herself at sixteen, when she'd still had to service her customers in the public street. Her lush hair, lacking perfect poise to keep it elaborately in place, was dishevelled. At last someone had the presence of mind to whisper to the butler. With a nod and a movement of his eyes he saw to it that all the servants were dismissed as though nothing was happening.

No woman would have gazed into the face of a lover as intently as Charity fastened her anguished eyes on Georgiana. Pulled both ways by hope and fear, the girl wept.

Charity struggled to speak. 'Oh, God!' she burst out. 'For you I have done everything. Everything that could be done, for you I have done – with this!' Placing her feet apart, she bent forward.

'No – mother – please!' whimpered Georgiana. It was not shame that shook her, but pity.

Charity ignored her. In a single movement she seized a double armful of her petticoats, straightened up and lifted them to flaunt her naked cunt and, with a look of surprise, fell slowly sideways to the ground. The stiff draperies of her gown lay heaped about her like the plumage of a slaughtered bird.

Fearfully, Sophy knelt to place a hand on Charity's

brow, and peer into the eyes of the poor distraught woman. They were rolled partway into her head. Charity's breathing was fast and shallow.

In the struggle to win over her daughter, Charity's will had fought in vain with her body. It made no difference how anxiously Sophy coaxed her, or Georgiana pleaded for forgiveness. Charity had swooned away, limbs rigid, to the point where almost nothing could reach her. When, some time later, she regained full consciousness, still she was unable to respond. Once again, she was paralysed.

CHAPTER SIXTEEN

Not all of Charity's island pleasure palace had cracked apart when the earth flexed itself the afternoon before. Amid precious old marquetry and gilding and new dust, Charity was put to bed. The few watchers who remained with her snatched sleep by turns on divans and unmade beds within call, or dozed by turns at her bedside.

One person who now had no sympathies with her was determined to stay, at least until first light. Euphemia would have the world end, rather than let herself be driven out into the night by the failings of others. Standing by one of the windows of Charity's darkened room, Sophy glimpsed a strange sight. Instead of lights being carried back from the garden theatre, along with the unused silver epergnes, standishes and sauce tureens, fresh candles were being taken out. So too was a glazed carp garnished à la Chambord, with truffles cut to look like olives, and a three-tiered *chaud-froid* of sixteen quails in aspic served on a moulded-breadcrumb plinth.

Originally, it was Euphemia who was to have presided over dinner. So now, proud of her refusal to be daunted by others' shortcomings, she was doing precisely that. Alone at the top of the stone banqueting table she sat, amid a blizzard of moths and waited on by three footmen. Others might be weak. They might even be fallen. But Miss Lee of Richmond, Virginia, had the strength of character to stand in for all of them.

As to 'that frail creature' as the ladies of local English society henceforth described Charity, she and her daughter were fit company only for that awkward woman and her son, who'd caused all the disruption in the first place. The other guests took some time to leave, swapping impromptu offers of supper as they waited beneath the flaring torches on the landing stage, and grumbling at the shortage of boatmen. It was not usually as inconvenient as this, being entertained on an island. At length, their servants each holding a lantern at ankle height to illumine the waterside steps, the last of them were gone. The villa's emptiness became ghostly.

Towards midnight Charity was recovered enough to look about her, though without speaking, like a passive wild animal in a trap. A doctor had been sent for, and bribed to attend her. By the time he presented himself at her bedside, in yesterday's cravat and stubbly dark jowls, Charity could sit up, with help from Sophy and Georgiana, and was able to talk. Mindful of the size of his generous fee, the doctor made a point of not yawning as the spoiled English lady, in a bed whose draperies vanished upward into the shadows, apologized for his visit. In elegant, only slightly accented Italian she explained that she had merely allowed herself to become agitated at being reunited with her daughter. She was so sorry, she said, that her friends and servants had misjudged the occasion. Their concern had been altogether too anxious and tender for what was essentially a fit of the vapours.

After the doctor had taken his leave, Sophy left Charity and Georgiana alone together. Wrapped in a fringed shawl, on an uncomfortable Egyptian-style couch the size of a barge, she thought she was too tired to sleep. But she was soon so deeply unconscious that, on being woken by movement nearby, she had no idea whether she had been asleep for minutes or hours. She took out her watch. Tears of fatigue squeezed from her eyes as she yawned. It was half past one.

'Oh, Mrs Fraser!' Georgiana stood before her, candle in hand. The flame and its halo made it hard to see her face clearly. But it was obvious from the girl's voice that she had tears in her eyes, and that she was smiling broadly.

She put down her candle and sat beside Sophy with a whoosh of stiff silk. 'Oh, Mrs Fraser,' she whispered again. In such heightened spirits Georgiana was finding it hard to keep her voice down. 'Aunt Sophy, I mean.'

Whatever the reason for her good cheer, it was impossible to resist. Sophy spoke more lightly than she'd felt a moment before, as she murmured, 'Tom thinks you won't marry him, now. He says he's been too much of a clodhopper.' Needlessly, she glanced along the landing to her son's room. While the women around him debated his future, Tom, still fully dressed, was unconscious. He had fallen asleep on the bed before he had even finished having his shoes taken off. 'He tells me that if you'll still have him, you deserve to be canonized.'

A look of solemnity flitted over Georgiana's bright face. She waved Sophy's words aside. 'I know. He told my mother the same.' She paused, then said, 'My mother asks if you will speak with her again — I mean, now. She means to leave here early in the morning.'

'Why — where will you be going?' Uncertain of how thing stood between Tom and Georgiana, Sophy could not hide her concern.

In the dimness it was hard to tell if Georgiana blushed. 'Only mother will be leaving, I believe. She plans to stay somewhere nearby. It's partly about that, I think, that she wishes to talk with you.'

The two women said goodnight and embraced. Georgiana briefly turned and watched as the bedroom door closed behind Sophy. Then, the flame of her candle fluttering like a pennant, she skittered away to bed almost at a run.

As soon as the waking household was making ready for Charity's departure, Sophy went to wake Tom.

She had to shake him hard before his eyes opened and unglazed. He spoke her name in a foggy voice, looking embarrassed. Somewhere between sleep and waking the sound of her clear contralto had evidently made him think she was Georgiana.

He had gone to sleep with his toes turned up and his arms thrown wide, as though flung down like that. With his long legs stretched before him he struggled to sit up and take stock. 'I hadn't meant to fall asleep,' he said with a frown of anxiety. 'Good God, it's not tomorrow, is it?'

'Only just; the sun's not up. But Miss Michaelmas' – Sophy too had dropped the pretence of Charity's widowhood – 'asked me to wake you when she was about to leave.'

Tom leaped from his bed. 'She can't. Neither of them can! They can't do that!'

Sophy had the guarded look of someone acting on instructions. 'Miss Michaelmas can – and intends to do so without another interview with you. In five minutes or so from now. But,' she added quickly, 'your cousin – Georgiana – will stay here.' For some reason, as she said this Sophy looked embarrassed.

Tom, looking for his shoes, straightened up and exclaimed, 'With you, mother?'

'What?'

'With you. As her chaperone?'

He meant, then she'll have me – we can marry! His look of rejoicing was so violent, Sophy took an involuntary step backward.

She found herself trying to avoid his question for the

moment. 'Miss Michaelmas apologizes for not staying to say goodbye. But I believe Georgiana has a message to pass on from her.' Sidling to the door, Sophy waited, anxious not to be questioned any further. Tom thrust on his shoes, ran his hands pointlessly over his ruffled hair, and followed her, tugging at his collar and cuffs. He looked soiled by sleep right down to the creases round his buttonholes.

Sophy led the way, in such haste that Tom, striding out at her elbow, was hard put to keep up. 'What's happening?' he said.

'That's for Miss Michaelmas to explain.' Sophy opened a side door into the garden. In the blue and grey light before sunrise everything was so still, the trees might have been made of rock. The first birds had spoken up, but the distant snowfields were still the same dull colour as the lake. Already it was warmer out of doors than in the house.

Sophy added, 'As I told you, she left a message.' They came to the steps that led to the *casino*. Glancing up at its arcade she steadied herself against the balustrade and with the other hand held her skirts clear of the stair. She paused, with a guarded look, as a footman passed them, carrying down an empty tray. In that ghostly, growing light, it might have been one of the stately naked figures along the *casino* façade who was suddenly walking in the garden.

Even someone as self-absorbed as Tom was at that moment could not ignore Sophy's manner. He caught her by the elbow. 'Mother! What *is* happening?'

'Ask your cousin.' She pointed up the steps as they climbed, though the *casino*'s terrace and arcade seemed deserted. At one end of the terrace, with a misty view down twenty miles of lake, a table had been set. There was scalding coffee in a silver tripod pot. A pierced silver basket held bread in a napkin, smoking hot. There was a dish of plover's eggs, and a steak and pigeon pie. A crisp pastry case shaped like an ornamental cottage held woodcock pâté. There were ortolans, spit-roasted, with truffles and ham; civet of bustard with wild chestnuts; galatine of pheasant; and a fresh pineapple tart with alpine strawberries. In a silver salver, pomegranates were still wet with dew. A dish of purple figs were oozing sweetness. There was a bottle of champagne dating back to the earliest year of his childhood that Tom could remember.

In the doorway under the arcade there was a swish of skirts. Georgiana appeared, modestly dressed in white muslin. Her dark cloud of hair was loose to her waist. She looked both unrestrained and demure. Her face was the brightest thing in sight.

Wordlessly she passed Tom a sealed letter. He gave her a fierce, anxious look, and turned away so that neither she nor his mother could see his face as he read. Was this something he should dread?

Sophy glanced at Georgiana. The girl, unconsciously twisting her hands, seemed rapt in examining a distant peak, whose snows were at that moment lightening from slate grey to the colour of a turtle dove's wing. Sophy knew that, like herself, Georgiana had been shown Charity's letter.

It said:

You must not think I am done with my apologies, even when you have finished reading this. But since your cousin has agreed to make her peace with me, I hope that one day, somehow, so too shall you. If, as I pray, you and she have not been wrested asunder by all that has been done wrong to each of you, I hope too that you will do me the favour of accepting some tokens of my contrition.

It is my dear wish, therefore, that the Isola Nuova and nearly all it holds may be my wedding present to you both; so too my daughter's inheritance.

By the rest of the Isola Nuova, I mean the casino, *which I greatly desire to be an engagement present to you both, as of this same morning.*

The casino *shall be, as I say, my present to you – but, again, with an exception.*

How best to say this?

To you yourself, in order to honour your betrothal as I should wish, I must give away the dearest thing I have had. Such a gift, as I write this, is not truly my own to give. But it is offered to you nonetheless – now – today – freely, with open hands and heart alike. For my own part, it is also given with my blessing – and my apology for all that has gone before.

Still I wonder, how else may I put this?

I mean, dear Tom, that if the casino *is a betrothal present to you both, then what it contains is for you alone. Understand me thus – and, better yet – forgive me.*

Yours in friendship, etc.

Tom turned around, to find himself alone with Sophy. With a look of frantic wonder he ducked past her and in through the doorway. Sophy, whose own face showed the makings of a nervous laugh, occupied herself with tracing the joins in the terrace paving with her toe.

From outside the door, only Tom was fully in view. Sophy saw him thrust the letter into Georgiana's grasp. He locked her hand in his own fist, with an urgent question. From where Sophy stood, his gesture looked more threatening than ardent.

'You?' he was saying.

Looking at him, Georgiana said yes. Not so much with a nod as with a perceptible quickening in her pulse and breathing.

They came back outside, to an unconvincing show

294

of ignorance from Sophy. Georgiana's smile was broad but unsteady as she said, 'Congratulate us, dear aunt!'

'Indeed you must, mother,' said Tom. For the moment his shock was even greater than his delight.

'Oh, yes, willingly!' Sophy heard herself say, as though the possibility had only just occurred to her. Really, it was ridiculous of her, at thirty-nine years of age, to be crimped with modesty over an act of mating. Even if it was to be between betrothed lovers rather than man and wife. After Tom had been conceived, on a downland summit above Cannings Fitzpayne village, the stains on her clothes from wet grass and old rabbit droppings had needed weeks of hard laundering.

She kissed Georgiana. 'And you will both dine at the hotel with your mother and me, as she suggests?'

'The day after tomorrow? Of course.' Both women found themselves speaking in an undertone – though Tom, gazing at Georgiana, was almost deaf to anything either of them might say.

On the pretext of being unable to wait for breakfast, Georgiana left Sophy and Tom together at the head of the steps.

'Tom.'

'Yes, mother?'

'I have to leave now.'

'Very well, mother.' His manner said, Oh, please, please, mother, go away this moment – fall through a crack in the earth – I don't wish you harm, only do anything, so long as we can both be alone without you or anyone else – don't wait; just vanish somehow, this second – please!

'I hope you too forgive me?'

'What?'

'For taking sides, together with your father. Against you.'

'Oh – yes, yes of course.' For the moment he had utterly forgotten what she meant.

'Well, goodbye. We look forward to seeing you both on Sunday next.'

'What? Oh – of course. Goodbye.'

As Sophy descended the steps without looking back, the boat carrying Charity away was already halfway across the lake. In the paling shadows reaching from the shore, the vessel's red-and-white awning seemed striped instead with greenish brown. Faint outlines of trees, rock and sky were massed above it. Around it the lake's surface was streaked with contrary currents, flat and still, as if the scene were painted on Chinese silk.

Sophy knew that she had blundered her way to success, in coming here. Not only would Tom be happy, but one day soon he would thank her for it. Maybe she hadn't deserved to succeed. But whether it was she, or hazard, that should take the credit, it was enough that the worst of her errors had been put right at last. Even as she was leaving the island, shortly afterwards, still she didn't choose to look up from the landing stair at the lovers on the terrace. She was as confident of the present, up there behind her, as she was of the foreseeable future.

Breakfast, for Tom and Georgiana, was no time for wordless mooning. For one thing, they were hungry; for another, there was too much to talk about. Not until the table, under its roof of vines, was the scene of a gastronomic massacre and the champagne bottle was empty in its bucket of melted ice, did they stop gulping, throwing out questions, and gabbling at each other.

Then, had Sophy looked back at the shore, she would just have seen the sweep of Georgiana's white dress as she rose and disappeared beneath the arcade.

What Euphemia saw, looking up at the head of the great staircase beneath the *casino*, was an extra statue.

On the terrace Tom was waiting for his cousin to prepare herself for him. By now the snowy summits to the east were white, shading to pink at the forests' upper fringe. Below where the facing peaks now cast a line of shadow, the blues of the valley were still mysterious and austere. Tom was daunted. He was triumphant. His eyes rested absently on a lofty waterfall two leagues away, as he stood up and took off his clothes without waiting to go inside. Up where the sun had just struck a wall of ice half a mile high, the water was a streak of dark against light, visible only where its spray cast a shadow on the glassy surface behind. Through a ravine between forests of pine and mountain ash and sweet chestnut it dropped, as far as a man might sprawl through emptiness for a quarter of a minute. Suddenly the brilliant torrent seemed to stop in mid-air; it had tumbled into another mountain's retreating shade.

Down near the lake the colours were still cool to the eye. The air felt as though it could warm one from the lungs outward. Tom walked to the edge of the terrace. Beneath his soles the paving had the temperature of fresh-baked bread. On a whim, he swung himself onto the broad top of the balustrade. Feet and arms wide for balance, he stood naked above the dizzying terraces that dropped down to the island's prow. A breeze gentled him, cooling his sweat. He felt every hair on his body stir like a brandished whip.

As Euphemia came into view below, following her luggage to the landing stair, it was by chance she looked up. She saw a man, pale gold down the side that faced the sunrise, spreadeagled as if lashed to the torturer's wheel. He saw her too, and held her stare.

Exultant, he guessed this was how a dying man might feel as his world fades from sight. Tom could not help himself. Overmastered by his own potency, he found the universe had grown small within himself somewhere. From every pore, from every opening in his body, his booming consciousness was about to blast free, leaving him at the heart of nothing. The charge from whatever-it-was, prickled and surged till it seemed he was formless. In his groin, in his armpits, in the hairs of his nape, in his cock, on his scalp, in the iridescent blindness behind his eyelids.

Euphemia stared. At her back the sun grew from a shout of colour behind a vague mountaintop. It heaved itself into sight, a disc of wavering brilliance as strong to the senses as the sounding of a gong. Tom felt, as he came, that he was fracturing the flank of the mountain. Then again as if he'd blown it away and its shape was a ghost on the retina. He couldn't believe he hadn't ruptured the sky beyond.

Still with the same look, Euphemia turned and walked away. Above a twenty-foot drop, Tom half fell, half sat, with a laugh as feeble as the yap of a new-born pup. He lay back shaking, one foot dangling in the void.

A warm garment shivered against his hand. He sat up on one elbow, instantly sober. Georgiana stood beside him in a nightgown of fine workmanship like a broken river. The sun gleamed on her bare throat and arms. Her eyes were not on him, but on the departing figure of Euphemia.

Georgiana was smiling – but how? He found her face as hard to read, for the moment, as that of the statue who stood with outstretched arm above the island's innermost garden. The goddess Venus. She to whom he was about to make an act of worship, upon the body of his betrothed. Georgiana took his hand and kissed

298

it. She waited, watching, with a gathering of unknown passions in her calm, eager face, until Euphemia's boat had cast off into the deep bright waters of the lake.

Then they went in.

POSTSCRIPT

Georgiana and Tom were married the following week. The ceremony was attended by Charity, Sophy, and a few of Charity's long-established family servants, in one of the secret gardens of the Isola Nuova. Later that autumn the young couple set out on a combined wedding tour and working expedition, to Pompeii and thence to Sicily, the islands of the Aegean Sea, and Anatolia, on the first stages of Tom's promising career in the young science of archaeology.

Sophy returned directly to London after the wedding, to bring her husband the news of her reconciliation with Charity, and of the removal of any threat to his firm's finances. Fraser's ship the *Albion*, once completed, was to be acknowledged for some years as unique. Her range throughout the world's oceans grew by stages, along with methods of fuelling such a new design: at first to the Baltic; then to Buenos Aires; and eventually carrying mails and passengers round the Cape of Good Hope to Zanzibar and Bombay, on a lucrative run that did much to pay for several of Fraser's later inventions.

In Richmond, Virginia, Kate was to have yet another child, in her forty-first year, before her cheerful family of four boys and two girls was completed. The eldest son, Henry, was soon to take over the running of part of his father's business. At about the same time Joseph himself entered Congress, to follow a career in the Federalist party as a practical-minded legislator and a popular if not always serious public speaker. The

300

family's partial removal to Washington was welcome to Kate as a means of avoiding Euphemia, who had returned home early in response to the decadence she had observed in the Old World. Euphemia in any case became a less frequent visitor to Kate and Joseph's house in Richmond, after she took up a public life of her own. As Secretary of the Association of Gentlewomen of Virginia for the Protection of Slavery, at last she was to find a role in which no one who counted could find fault with anything she did.

Charity travelled for some months more in Italy and the south of France. Returning to England, she completed a purchase she had had in mind for some time. It was a relief to the debt-ridden young Lord Fitzpayne to be able to raise ready money by the sale of his neglected country estate in Wiltshire. Before signing the deeds to Cannings Fitzpayne Hall, Charity took the opportunity of changing her surname to that of the old man, long since dead, whom few people but herself knew to have been her father. Thus equipped with yet another new identity, in the spring of 1829, twenty-two years after she had been dismissed from the Hall's kitchens, it was as Miss Fitzpayne that she returned to take possession of the place of her birth.